FATE

FATE

THE LOST DECADES OF UNCLE CHOW TUNG

IAN HAMILTON

SPIDERLINE

Published in Canada in 2019 and the USA in 2019 by House of Anansi Press Inc.
www.houseofanansi.com

House of Anansi Press is committed to protecting our natural environment.
As part of our efforts, the interior of this book is printed on paper that
contains 100% post-consumer recycled fibres, is acid-free, and is processed
chlorine-free.

23   22   21   20   19   1   2   3   4   5

Library and Archives Canada Cataloguing in Publication

Hamilton, Ian, 1946–, author
Fate / Ian Hamilton.

Issued in print and electronic formats.
ISBN 978-1-4870-0386-9 (softcover). —ISBN 978-1-4870-0387-6 (EPUB). —
ISBN 978-1-4870-0388-3 (Kindle)

I. Title.

PS8615.A4423F38 2018   C813'.6   C2017-905981-5
                              C2017-905982-3

Library of Congress Control Number: 2017953511

Book design: Alysia Shewchuk

 Canada Council
for the Arts
Conseil des Arts
du Canada
 ONTARIO ARTS COUNCIL
CONSEIL DES ARTS DE L'ONTARIO
an Ontario government agency
un organisme du gouvernement de l'Ontario

*We acknowledge for their financial support of our publishing program the Canada
Council for the Arts, the Ontario Arts Council, and the Government of Canada.*

Printed and bound in Canada

MIX
Paper from
responsible sources
FSC® C004071

For Kristine Wookey, who has been incredibly generous
with her time and advice, and whose judgment I trust.

TRIAD ORGANIZATION

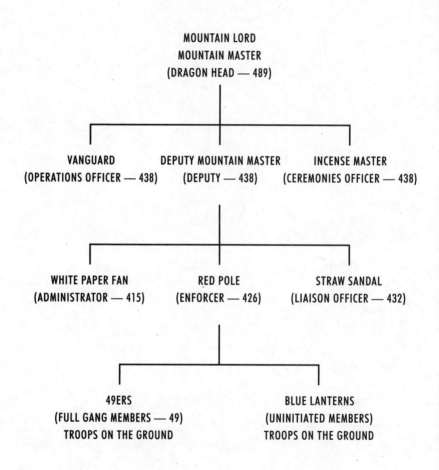

MOUNTAIN LORD
MOUNTAIN MASTER
(DRAGON HEAD — 489)

VANGUARD
(OPERATIONS OFFICER — 438)

DEPUTY MOUNTAIN MASTER
(DEPUTY — 438)

INCENSE MASTER
(CEREMONIES OFFICER — 438)

WHITE PAPER FAN
(ADMINISTRATOR — 415)

RED POLE
(ENFORCER — 426)

STRAW SANDAL
(LIAISON OFFICER — 432)

49ERS
(FULL GANG MEMBERS — 49)
TROOPS ON THE GROUND

BLUE LANTERNS
(UNINITIATED MEMBERS)
TROOPS ON THE GROUND

CHOW TUNG STOOD ON THE SHORELINE STARING across Shenzhen Bay at the flickering lights of Yuen Long four kilometres away. The water that lapped at his feet was black and gave off an odour that he couldn't identify, but it was strong enough to make him breathe through his mouth. It was two a.m. and there was a chill in the air.

Yuen Long was in the New Territories, a part of Hong Kong. Chow and ten companions were in a village on the outskirts of Shekou, in the People's Republic of China. They were preparing to swim the four kilometres that separated the two towns and two very different realities. *By the time the sun comes up, I'll either be dead or starting an entirely new life,* he thought.

"I'm scared," said Lin Gui-San, who was standing next to him. Her hand gripped his.

"We all are. It would be strange if we weren't," Chow said, squeezing her hand in return.

Chow, Gui-San, and five others were from the same village, Changzhai, near Wuhan in Hubei province, about nine hundred kilometres north of Shekou. The remaining four were from Dongguan, a city about eighty kilometres northwest of where they stood.

Chow was twenty-five and Gui-San twenty-four. They had met at the Changzhai village school eight years before, when Gui-San's father was sent there from a neighbouring town to become head teacher. There was an immediate attraction and they quickly bonded. Since then, their relationship had survived separations while they attended different universities and took whatever temporary jobs they could find. But they had been together for the entire past six months; their plan was to marry when they reached Hong Kong.

Their decision to flee China was fuelled by the madness of Mao Zedong's Great Leap Forward. Two years before, Mao had instituted his misguided program of communal and agrarian reform, resulting in the deaths of millions of Chinese from mass starvation. The period was already being referred to by the peasantry as "the years of slow death" and "the bitter years."

Gui-San and Chow were now the only living members of their families. When Gui-San's mother died, they no longer had a reason to remain in Changzhai. And so they made a commitment to each other to do whatever was necessary to get to Hong Kong.

"All we have now is each other. You and I are the beginning of a new family," Chow had said.

"And we'll start making it a larger family as soon as we get to the other side."

The task of getting to Hong Kong was too challenging for the two of them to do it alone, so they spent weeks gathering a group of like-minded people from the village, most of them young, all of them desperate. They recruited five: three men, Nui, Fa, and Tam, and two woman, Mei-Lin and Ai. Together the group rented a truck and driver found by Gui-San, and in early June they began a slow five-day journey to Shenzhen.

Chow had heard that the Chinese border town of Shenzhen provided the best options for people wanting to get to Hong Kong. He didn't have any specific information about crossing points, but when he reached Shenzhen, he found it full of people who were there with the same purpose and willing to share what they knew. The Changzhai group spent their first few days in the area learning all they could.

They learned of three main routes. One was on land, across Wutong Mountain; it involved getting over a five-metre-high barbed-wire fence and then past guard dogs and armed soldiers of the People's Liberation Army. The other two were by sea. To the east of Shenzhen was Mirs Bay, its coast only four kilometres from Hong Kong and its waters reportedly calm. But Mirs Bay was infested by sharks and heavily patrolled by the PLA, who shot so many swimmers every night that they'd been forced to hire thirty local crews to remove the bodies from the water each morning. The third option was Shenzhen Bay. It didn't have sharks and wasn't patrolled so vigilantly, but its water was polluted and putrid, and it had riptides and currents that could defeat even the strongest swimmers.

Many in the group were uncomfortable about swimming under normal circumstances, but as they listened to the stories about the ferocity of the guard dogs, the height of the barbed-wire fence, and the willingness of the PLA to shoot on sight, a water crossing became more and more appealing.

Choosing between Mirs Bay and Shenzhen Bay was easy once the group learned about the sharks.

But Shenzhen Bay remained intimidating. As Gui-San looked out onto its filthy, malodorous waters, she repeated, "I'm scared."

Jin Hai, the leader of the Dongguan group, heard her and moved closer. "We should be okay if that thing floats," he said, pointing to the wooden door that lay on the beach. Chow had purchased the door two days before, thinking it could function as a raft. Their group had carried it twenty kilometres from a campground near Shenzhen to the harbour near Shekou.

Jin Hai had met Chow the night before as they were each trying to determine the best spot from which to start their swim to Yuen Long. They had independently determined that the beach in the village was the closest point to Hong Kong they could reach without going into the much larger Shekou, where there was a greater risk of running into the PLA. Then they had talked about the dangers they faced in the crossing and how they might best cope with them. Chow had told Jin about the door he hoped to use as a raft. Jin had told him that he and his friends were strong swimmers. Then Jin said he believed that strength lay in numbers, and suggested they undertake the journey as one team. Chow liked the idea; he thought adding four strong swimmers to the group would improve their chances of getting safely across the bay.

"It floats. We tested it in a river and even had someone lying on it," Chow said in response to Jin's comment. "But it won't take more than one person at a time."

"What are those holes along the sides and bottom?"

"One of our group, Nui, is a carpenter. We borrowed an auger and he drilled those as handholds. Some of our people are nervous about swimming by themselves in open water. We figure two of them can hold on to the end of the door and kick, and two more can hold on to the sides."

Jin Hai walked closer to the door and examined the holes. "These are a great idea."

A woman who had been standing behind Jin stepped towards Gui-San. "Hello. My name is Mai. I'm from Dongguan."

"I'm Gui-San, from Changzhai, and the other women with our group are Mei-Lin and Ai."

Mai pointed at Gui-San's navy-blue Mao jacket and pants. "We're dressed the same, but I don't think these clothes will be much good in the water. What do you intend to wear?"

"We didn't bring swimsuits," Gui-San said. "The men are going in their underwear, and I guess we'll have to do the same."

"Good." Mai laughed. "Then I won't be alone."

"We'll wrap up our clothes, shoes, and a few small personal possessions in blankets and bundle them on the raft. There's room for another blanket if you want to do the same," Chow said.

"What do you mean by 'small personal possessions'?" Mai asked.

"I have a jade bracelet that belonged to my mother. Gui-San has a Zippo lighter that was her father's, and a small photo album," he said. "You shouldn't try to take anything much larger. We don't want to overload the door."

"No, of course not," Mai said. "And it is very kind of you to let us take some things with us. I was worried about my clothes."

"We are in this together, and none of us wants to walk into Hong Kong in our underwear."

"Shh, I think I hear something," Jin Hai said.

Everyone froze, afraid to move or speak. Chow heard a faint noise. "That's an engine," he said, and then to his left he saw beams of light flashing across the water. "It must be a patrol boat."

Jin turned. "There's a warehouse over there. We need to get behind it."

"What about the door?" Tam asked.

"Bring it with us," Chow said.

They scurried along the beach and then climbed a set of stairs to the warehouse. A wooden fence with some scattered rocks stood behind it. They put the door against the fence and then settled down to wait. The noise from the engine became louder, and to their left, part of the wharf was bathed in light. No one moved or spoke. The noise continued to increase. The light moved past the wharf, reached the warehouse, disappeared for a few seconds, and then reappeared on the other side. The boat then continued along a path that took it away from them, and gradually darkness and silence returned to the wharf.

"What should we do now?" Tam asked.

"Wait," said Chow. "We were told that patrol boats in this part of the bay travel between Shenzhen and Shekou every three hours. That boat should come back this way in about ten to fifteen minutes. Once it passes, we won't have to worry about it for at least another two hours, and by then we should be halfway to Hong Kong."

It may have been only fifteen minutes, but it seemed to Chow that an hour had passed before he heard the hum of the boat engine again and saw its lights flitting across the water until they reached the shoreline. Everyone was hunkered down, and he noticed that some people had their eyes closed. Even after the boat had gone past the warehouse and begun its journey back to Shenzhen, no one moved until the only sound coming from the water was that of waves rolling onto the shore.

Finally Chow stood. "We should get started."

The others slowly got to their feet and began to gather their things. Nui and Tam picked up the door and led the way back to the bay. When they reached it, they dropped the door at the water's edge. Ai was the first to join them. She spread her blanket on the ground and Gui-San quickly did the same. A few minutes later the blankets held the shirts, shoes, and clothes of the men from Changzhai and the most valued personal possessions of them all. Off to the side, the men from Dongguang were stripping and putting their clothes onto another blanket. The four women, still fully dressed, watched them, their discomfort obvious.

Finally Gui-San reached for the top button of her jacket. "What the hell," she said, and began to unbutton it. A few minutes later, four neatly folded blue jackets and pants were added to the blankets and the women were huddling together in their underwear. Gui-San shivered, crossed her arms over her chest, and said, "We should get going before we die of cold."

Tam tied the blankets together, carried them to the raft, and loaded them on.

"Who is going to be on the raft, who is going to push, and who's going to swim alongside?" Jin Hai asked, looking at the raft. Like the other men, he was trying not to stare at the scantily clad women.

Chow looked at his six companions and remembered their fears about the swim. "Ai will be on the raft. Mei-Lin and Gui-San will hold on to the end. Fa will use a side handle. Tam, Nui, and I will swim. That leaves room for someone from your group on one side."

"We'll start with Mai there," Jin said. "Wei, Bai, and I will swim."

"We can change positions as needed," Chow said to everyone. "But you have to speak up if you need a rest or are in some difficulty."

People nodded but no one spoke. Jin reached down, grabbed the end of the raft, and pushed it into the water. Ai clambered on top. Mei-Lin, Gui-San, Fa, and Mai reached for their handholds. They waded into the bay.

The first thing Chow noticed was the temperature — the water was even colder than he'd found it at the shoreline. The second was how slimy the bottom was beneath his feet. And the third was that the odour from the water was nauseating. He heard someone gag and fought back the same reaction.

"I hope it doesn't stink as much when we get further into the bay," Jin Hai said.

"I hope the water gets warmer," Chow said.

"I don't think it will, but we should be able to get used to the temperature. I'm not sure I can ever get used to this smell."

Chow walked until the water was above his waist. He was moving alongside the door, fearful, despite the test in the river, that it wouldn't be as buoyant as he'd predicted. But even with Ai on the door, it floated high on the water. His spirits rose.

Gui-San walked next to him, one hand gripping the raft.

"It's time to swim," he said.

She reached out with her free hand. "I want a kiss."

He leaned over and kissed her gently on the lips, then wrapped his arms around her and squeezed.

"Stay close to me," she said.

"I'll try."

"Promise me."

"I promise," he said, and kissed her again.

As the group sorted themselves into position around the raft, the tide suddenly strengthened, knocking some of them back on their heels.

"We should expect more of this," said Jin Hai. "But we'll have to swim through it."

With that, they all slid into the water.

The first half-hour was more difficult than Chow had anticipated. He did start to acclimatize to the water's temperature, but the stench remained unabated and the raft and swimmers kept bumping into unknown objects. The current seemed to run directly against them. Somehow, despite these challenges, they were making decent progress; when he looked back, he could see the lights of Shekou slowly receding in the distance.

Chow swam in open water on the left side of the raft. Gui-San was on his right, one hand holding the raft, while she kicked like mad. He couldn't see how everyone else was doing, but no one was asking for help, so that was a good thing. The only person who spoke was Ai, who twice said, "I should take my turn in the water."

"And I could use a rest," Nui responded after Ai said it a third time.

As Ai moved to the edge of the raft and prepared to get into the water, Chow asked, "Who else needs a break?"

The raft came to a halt and they talked among themselves as they clung to its edges. When they began to swim again, three of their group had changed positions. The raft began to move noticeably faster. Chow wasn't sure if that was caused by a change in the current or if the new swimming configuration was generating more power.

They moved deeper into the bay. With the moon hidden by clouds and the lights from Shekou and Yuen Long no more than faint pinholes on the horizon, it became darker. The wind died down a little, the water became less choppy, and the grunts from the swimmers and the sound of arms and legs thrashing in the water became more distinct.

Chow lost track of time. From his position, he could only see the swimmers on his immediate right and Nui sitting on the raft, and he had no sense of where they were in relation to land. After what seemed like an hour but was certainly less, his legs began to tire. He stopped swimming for a few seconds, turned, and floated on his back. When he started up again, he felt revived, only to have the tiredness creep back after a few minutes.

Gui-San had moved from the end of the door to the left side. With her head lowered and her face almost immersed in the stinking water, she never stopped kicking. Chow was impressed by her energy but said nothing, not wanting to distract her.

"I think we should take a rest," Jin Hai shouted.

"Yes," Chow replied, more than pleased with the suggestion.

The raft came to a gradual stop, and as it did, Chow could hear the others breathing heavily.

"Thank God we have this door," Tam said. "I don't think I could have made it without it."

"Do you want to change places with me?" Nui asked.

"Yes, I'd like that."

"Does anyone else want to rotate?" Chow asked.

When no one answered, Jin Hai said, "Then let's get started again. We're doing well, really well, everyone."

As the raft began to move again, it occurred to Chow that they were now so far into the bay that there was no turning back. When he'd considered the swim, even up to the moment they got into the water in the village near Shekou, he hadn't discounted the possibility that they might have to. Now there was only one direction they could go, and that was towards the lights of Yuen Long. The thought was liberating, and he felt a rush of adrenalin surge through his tired limbs.

Chow wasn't a natural swimmer. His strokes were rather mechanical but he could repeat them, and as long as he didn't think too much about what he was doing, he was confident he could keep up with the raft. He tried thinking about a host of other things, but it was his thoughts about Gui-San that were the most distracting — specifically Gui-San and him in bed, his hands on her breasts and hers on his groin. It might be misery that had brought them to Shenzhen, he thought, but they were going to make something wonderful from it.

"Ahh!" The scream came from the other side of the raft.

"What happened?" Chow shouted.

"I just swam into a dead body," Bai yelled.

The group stopped swimming. They gathered around the

raft, holding on to the sides as they bobbed in the water. Ai and Mai began to cry. Bai was by himself on the right, except for the corpse floating next to him. Jin Hai and Wei swam over to him. A minute later, the three men rejoined the raft.

"It's the body of a young man," Wei said. "It's not bloated and it hasn't been chewed or gnawed, so I'd guess he died very recently. He might even have tried to make the crossing earlier tonight."

"He may have been alone," Jin Hai said. "There is strength in our numbers."

"And we have the door," Tam said.

As Tam spoke, the door suddenly rose higher than their heads.

"The wind is getting stronger, and that means rougher water," Jin said. "I figure we're about halfway there. I'm still feeling strong and you all look good, so rough water or not, we're going to make it if we keep working together."

Chow had moved next to Gui-San while Jin Hai was talking. "How are you doing?" he asked.

"Okay. As good as can be expected under the circumstances."

"Jin is right about our strength lying in numbers."

"I really want to believe that."

Chow looked towards Yuen Long. "Those lights keep getting bigger and brighter. Soon they'll be right on top of us."

"I wish we hadn't found that body. It's one thing to imagine not making it to Hong Kong, but it's another to see the naked reality of what will happen if we don't," Gui-San said.

Leaving the floating body behind, they swam for the next fifteen minutes with an intensity that Chow knew was spurred by their collective fear and a desire to get as far away from it as possible. Regardless of their motives, they made good progress. The lights from Yuen Long seemed to grow ever brighter, pulling them like a magnet.

Then they began to slow. Their efforts didn't lag, but the wind continued to increase and was blowing directly against them. As it moved across the bay it churned the water, and they soon found themselves confronting waves that washed over them, knocking them back.

"We aren't getting anywhere," Tam shouted.

"The wind is up and we seem to have run into a current. We have to fight through it. If we don't, we'll be stuck in the same place until the conditions change, and who knows how long that will take," Chow said.

"Maybe we should rotate positions," Jin Hai said.

"I'm tired," Mai said. "Can I take a turn on the raft?"

"Sure," Chow replied. "It's time for a change anyway."

It took several minutes to get everyone rearranged. While they were repositioning, wave after wave slammed into the raft and seemed to push them back towards Shekou. Chow knew they were probably just staying in place, but the perception was different. He moved next to Gui-San, who was gripping one of the side handholds. "We need to make a big push," he said.

"I'll do what I can."

Chow nodded, lowered his head, and began to swim. He'd been reluctant to put his face in the filthy water when they'd started, but it was tiring holding his head high, so he'd given in, although he tried to keep his mouth clear of the water when he breathed. He wasn't always successful, and several times he found himself gagging and spitting.

The wind fluctuated, so there were moments when the

waves subsided. Whenever that happened, the group seemed to sense the opportunity and their swimming picked up in intensity. It was the opposite when the wind whistled and the waves battered them: they would back off until the water became calmer. Chow wasn't sure that was the most efficient use of their energy, but he wasn't about to stop and discuss it. He guessed they'd been swimming for about an hour in those conditions when Tam shouted, "I need to rest."

Chow stopped, raised his head, and looked towards Yuen Long. The lights seemed closer — they'd made progress. He smiled.

As they gathered around the raft, Chow saw Jin Hai twisting his head from side to side. "Is something wrong?" he asked.

"I can't see Wei."

Chow did a quick head count. There were ten people holding on to the raft. He looked back in the direction of Shekou. He could see maybe twenty or thirty metres before everything became completely black. There was no sign of Wei.

"He was just behind me and off to the side, but I can't remember the last time I saw him," Jin said.

"We'll wait for a while. He'll show up," said Chow.

Fifteen minutes later they restarted their slow journey to Yuen Long, their group smaller by one.

As if in recognition of their increased vulnerability, the wind grew even stronger, creating waves big enough to lift the front end of the raft out of the water. The first time it happened, Ai, clinging to the door like mad, screamed. Somehow she held on and managed to prevent their bundles from sliding into the bay. They swam on, fighting their way through the cascading water.

Chow could now see shapes framing the lights from Yuen Long, and he knew they were getting close. He was exhausted. His legs felt as if they were pulling up cement boots, and his arms were stroking at half the pace they had been generating an hour before. When he glanced around him, he saw that most of the others were also struggling. He thought about calling for another rest period, but Yuen Long seemed so near, and he didn't know if he could start up again if he stopped.

Gui-San was still on his left, holding on to the raft. He eased towards her. Her face was pale and gaunt and her lips were unnaturally red. "Are you okay?" he shouted, and then regretted it immediately as a wave hit him. His mouth filled with water and, without thinking, he swallowed it.

"How much longer?" she asked.

"I really don't know. Maybe half an hour."

"I can last longer than that," she said.

Chow swam as close to her as he could without bumping her. Every minute now seemed like five as they continued to fight the waves and inch closer to shore. After another ten or fifteen minutes, however, the lights didn't seem to be that much closer. For the first time since he'd left Shekou, Chow felt real despair and began to doubt they would make it.

"A break — I need a break," someone yelled.

Nui appeared to be struggling to stay in contact with the raft.

"Let's stop," Chow shouted.

The raft came to a halt. Like bees drawn to nectar, they all quickly gathered at its sides, holding on and resting their foreheads on their hands.

"We're almost there. All we need is one more strong effort," Jin Hai said.

Chow started to say something, but a pain in his stomach made him catch his breath. He closed his eyes and tried to will it away, but what had started low in this gut was climbing higher, and contracting as it went. He groaned.

"What's the matter?" Gui-San asked.

"My stomach. At the last stop I swallowed a ton of that shitty water."

"Throw it up."

His body convulsed and he gagged. "I'm trying," he said.

Chow drew a deep breath and immediately felt lightheaded. Then he convulsed again and almost let go of the door. His arms felt sapped of all the strength left in them. The discomfort was so disorienting that he hardly knew where he was. He gagged again but found no relief.

The others watched him, their interest blunted by their own exhaustion and sense of self-preservation. "We need to get moving," Jin Hai said.

"I can't swim in this condition," Chow said.

"Then climb onto the raft."

"Yes, get on," Ai said. "I'll manage on one of the sides."

"That's fine, but I'd like to put our two strongest swimmers at the end of the raft for the final push. We need to get through these waves as quickly as we can," Jin said. "Is everyone okay with that?"

No one objected, and their watery game of musical chairs began again. When it was finished, Bai and Mei-Lin were at the end of the raft while Tam and Ai hung on to the sides. The others swam in open water, Gui-San and Mai side by side.

It took an enormous effort and a final shove from Bai to

get Chow onto the raft. He crawled to the far end, tucked the bundles under his body, and held on. The door rocked back and forth on the waves and his nausea intensified. He tried to ignore it, but he was dry-heaving every fifteen seconds, and he knew it wouldn't end until he vomited.

The group began kicking and the raft lurched forward. Chow tried looking straight ahead at the lights of Yuen Long, only to have them disappear as waves continued to crash over the raft. He retched, leaned over the edge, and threw up. A long stream of bile spewed from his mouth and he felt some relief as the pressure on his stomach eased. Then he thought about the people behind the raft who might have to swim through his vomit. "Sorry," he said, and then threw up again.

This continued for the next few minutes, the pressure easing and then building until more bile was released. When that finally stopped, and after a few minutes more of dry heaving, Chow dropped his head onto the raft. He was completely drained, devoid of all energy. This wasn't how he had envisioned arriving in Hong Kong. He hoped everyone would understand his predicament. Even if they did, it didn't lessen his sense of shame for letting them down.

Chow buried his face in the bundles and extended his arms so he could grip the edge of the door as it pitched wildly in the water. The nausea and stomach cramps had subsided, but his head continued to pound, his mouth felt like sandpaper, and he barely had the strength to hang on.

"Fifteen minutes more — I swear that's all it will take," Jin Hai shouted.

Chow heard him but the words barely registered. He couldn't lift his head and he seemed to have lost his sense of time and place. All he could think about was holding on and not letting the bundles slip into the water.

A few minutes later the water was suddenly calm. Chow turned his head and stared directly into the sun as it edged over the horizon. He thought he could feel someone standing next to him, and he wondered if he was hallucinating. He saw hands pushing the raft towards shore, and looked up. The upper halves of Tam and Jin Hai's bodies were visible, rising above him as they walked along the bottom of the bay.

He stayed on the raft as it was dragged onto the beach. Voices that had been lost in the waves and wind began to penetrate his consciousness.

Tam knelt down beside him. "We made it," he said.

Ai was behind Tam, her arms wrapped around him. She was crying into his back, her shoulders heaving.

"I didn't think I was ever going to see land again. It terrified me," Chow said.

"You were sick. You weren't thinking straight."

"I kept thinking that I hadn't done enough with my life, and how could it end like this. Then I thought about Gui-San and all of you, and I thought, 'No, this can't be our last night. We deserve a future.'"

Ai's crying grew louder. Chow noticed that Tam wouldn't look directly at him.

"What's happened?" he asked.

Tam paused before answering. "There's no sign of Gui-San or Mai."

1

June 1969
Fanling, New Territories, Hong Kong

CHOW TUNG STARED AT HIMSELF IN THE MIRROR. IT WAS four-thirty p.m. on a Tuesday, and it was almost time for him to leave his apartment and walk to a restaurant near central Fanling. There he was to attend an initiation ceremony that would secure the futures of two young men as full-fledged members of the Heaven and Earth Society — triads, as they were more commonly known.

He was dressed, as usual, in a black suit and a white shirt buttoned to the collar. Chow had several black suits and many white shirts in his closet. Not having to decide what to wear every day made his life easier, and the garments conveyed to others that he was not a frivolous man. The last thing anyone would call Chow — the White Paper Fan of the Fanling triads — was frivolous.

His phone rang. Chow had been so absorbed in his thoughts about what lay ahead that it startled him. He hesitated before answering but gave in to its persistence.

"*Wei,*" he said.

"Uncle, it's Xu. When are you leaving?"

"Ten minutes," he said to his assistant. "Why?"

"Fong just called after speaking with Yu. He seems prepared to support your idea of opening a night market, if you are prepared to give him assurance that you will keep the massage parlours running as they are now." Fong was the assistant to Yu, the Straw Sandal, and he, Xu, and Chow were the youngest and most progressive officials in the gang.

"I haven't proposed changing anything that relates to the operation of Yu's massage parlours."

"I know."

"How much clearer can I make it that we would eliminate protection payments only from the merchants who rent space from us in the night market?"

"You have made it very clear, but there is concern that you secretly want to get rid of all the old ways of doing business."

"Just because I want to expand into some new areas doesn't mean I don't value the old ways."

"Fong and I understand where you want to go, and why you want to go there, but not everyone does."

Chow sighed. "Please thank Fong for the advice about Yu, and my thanks to you for passing it along."

"Uncle, you know we are both with you."

"I know, and I'm grateful for your support."

"But I have to say we're disappointed with how Gao is handling things. He has the authority to make the decision about the night market on his own. Putting it to a vote at the executive meeting tomorrow feels like he's offloading his responsibility."

"What I'm proposing is not a minor change. It will have a broad impact on our business. He wants to make sure that everyone understands the full picture," Chow said. "He thinks that having a discussion will spread around the accountability. If it goes badly, he wants everyone to share in the blame. But I'm realistic enough to know that won't happen. These are my ideas we're discussing, and if we adopt them and they don't work as planned, I'm the one who'll pay the price."

"And Gao knows that. He's being cowardly. He should act like a proper Mountain Master and make the decision himself."

"Having the meeting is the smart thing to do, so I can't fault him."

Xu hesitated, sensing that he'd already said enough on the subject. "I won't be at the initiation ceremony but I'll be at the dinner that follows it. Maybe we can talk more then."

"I'll see you at the dinner," Chow said, and ended the call.

If an outsider had overheard the conversation between Chow and Xu, they might have found it odd that Xu referred to Chow as "Uncle," since the two men were not related. Xu was using the word as a sign of respect, something common in Chinese culture when a younger person speaks to an older man. In this case, however, the oddity was that both men were in their thirties. Odder still was that gang members much older than Chow also called him Uncle.

It had started five years before, when, after five years of working on the streets, Chow was promoted to the position of assistant White Paper Fan. The White Paper Fan was responsible for keeping the books, managing the gang's money, and devising legal and business strategies. In keeping with the new position, Chow had got rid of his jeans and casual shirts and started wearing a black suit and white dress shirt. It became his signature look, and the clothes reflected his persona as a dependable, serious, perhaps even sombre man. It didn't take long for his former street colleagues to notice his new style. They teased him that he was dressing like an old man and jokingly began referring to him as Uncle. It stuck as a nickname, and when the old White Paper Fan died and Chow was promoted, his peers started to call him that as well. Now it was even how he thought of himself.

His reputation, though, wasn't limited to being thought of as dependable and serious. He had proven while working on the streets that he could be thoughtful and calm in almost any situation, but if circumstances demanded it, he wasn't afraid of confrontation. Even though he stood only five foot five and weighed 130 pounds, Uncle wouldn't back down from anyone if he thought he was right. It was a reputation he valued and guarded, but he never let it go to his head. He knew that the truth about himself was different from the image, and he wasn't a man who embraced illusion.

Chow looked at his watch. It was time to go. He reached into his jacket pocket and took out a pack of Marlboro cigarettes. He lit one as he left his one-bedroom apartment and made his way down three flights of stairs to the street. It was a fifteen-minute walk to the restaurant, which was two doors down from the gang's offices, above a women's clothing store on Luen Wo Road. Fanling was in the northeastern part of the New Territories, closer to mainland China than to Hong Kong Island, which was thirty-five kilometres away. Although the gang was identified with Fanling, its actual turf extended beyond the town to the traditional marketplaces of Luen Wo Hui and Shek Wu Hui. Another gang controlled Fanling's sister town, Sheung Shui, with about 150 members, but both groups paled in comparison to the other territorial gangs in places like Tai Po, Sha Tin, Tai Wai, Yuen Long, Tuen Mun, Sai Kung, and Kam Tin, and they were like minnows compared to the gangs in Hong Kong and Kowloon.

The full name of the Fanling Mountain Master was Gao Lok. He was the leader, sometimes also called the Dragon Head, of the Fanling triad. Once in power, a Mountain Master held his position for life, unless he chose to step down or was involuntarily retired. Gao was the only Mountain Master Chow had ever known. He was in his fifties, like everyone in the executive group except for Uncle, and his management style was to tend to traditional businesses in traditional ways within the strict confines of the gang's turf. This approach maintained the status quo and kept the Fanling triad small enough not to attract the attention of larger gangs eager to expand.

In recent years, though, Chow had proposed a number of changes to the way they ran their gambling businesses; these had generated a lot more money for the gang and made it more difficult to stay below the radar. Now he was proposing changes that would affect their protection business, and Gao was getting enough resistance from other members of the executive that he was reluctant to make the decision by himself — as was his right.

As he walked to the ceremony, Chow mentally reviewed the pitch he was going to make to the committee the following day. He didn't need prepared notes, although he had written some and had them typed, copied, and sent to every member of the executive committee. He had gone over the proposal and the numbers attached to it so many times that they were ingrained in his mind, but he knew that his delivery was going to be as important as the content. Aside from whatever objections they had to his proposal, Chow sensed that some of his older colleagues were resentful of his quick ascent, and he worried that any display of overconfidence or enthusiasm on his part would rub them the wrong way. He had to remain low-key, calm, and measured, he reminded himself. *Listen to their questions without interruption, and then answer them directly and respectfully.*

There would be seven people at the meeting. In addition to Gao and Uncle, there would be Ma Shen, the Deputy Mountain Master and Gao's oldest friend and confidant; Ren Tengfei, the Vanguard, or operations officer; Yu, the Straw Sandal, who was responsible for communications within the gang and liaising with other gangs; Wang, the Red Pole, who ran the men on the street and was the gang's lead enforcer; and Pang, the Incense Master, who officiated over triad rituals, including initiations.

Although he hadn't yet committed, Chow thought Gao was leaning towards supporting him. If Fong was to be believed, so was Yu. Uncle could usually count on support from Wang, under whom he'd served as a forty-niner and developed a trust and friendship. On the other side, Ma seemed to dislike him and opposed just about anything he suggested. Ren bounced back and forth, his support normally tied to his own self-interest rather than the best interests of the gang. Pang aligned himself with Ma more often than not, but he had shown a willingness to agree with proposals that would increase the gang's income. Although Gao wouldn't put Chow's proposal to an actual vote, Uncle had no doubt that the Mountain Master would take everyone's opinions into account, so it was important to win over as many of them as he could.

He arrived at the restaurant ten minutes early and saw Wang standing outside the door. Wang was an imposing man just over six feet tall, with a thick, muscular body. As usual, he was wearing blue jeans and a black T-shirt. His naked arms were heavily tattooed and his lean face was scarred on the right side and above his left eye; the scars were his professional badges of honour. Wang was in his fifties but had the body of a younger man, and a temperament that hadn't matured much over the years. He was intelligent but not particularly thoughtful, preferring action to contemplation.

"Hey, Uncle," he shouted. "You ready to take in two new members?"

"I'm always ready, especially when they are good men."

"Well, these two are maybe a bit too eager, but they know how to follow orders and they are respectful. In fact, they remind me a bit of you when you were a Blue Lantern."

"If you say so."

"What the hell does that mean? It isn't like you to be so agreeable."

Chow took out his cigarettes, offered one to Wang, and then lit them both. "I'm a bit distracted by the meeting tomorrow. I've been assuming that I have your support," he said carefully. "Am I wrong?"

Wang smiled. "You should know by now, Uncle, that you always have my support. But thanks for asking and not taking me completely for granted."

"You know I'd never do that," Chow said.

Wang took a deep drag on the cigarette, threw it onto the ground, and stubbed it out with his white running shoe. "We should get going," he said.

The Emerald Phoenix wasn't a restaurant that Chow often frequented. It seated more than two hundred customers and was often too noisy for his taste. But late on this June afternoon, when it should have been busy, there wasn't a customer in sight. The gang had booked it for the initiation ceremony and the celebratory dinner that would follow.

"There's our boys," Wang said as he and Chow walked through the front door.

Two young men stood off to one side, each of them holding a strip of bamboo. Chow knew that the strips bore their invitations to the ceremony.

Wang waved at them. "See you soon," he said.

The restaurant was divided in two by a line of tall screens. On the near side it was all tables and chairs, but past the screens, Pang and his assistant had spent most of the day creating a traditional triad lodge. The lodge had no fixed, permanent address. It was built whenever there was an initiation and could be anywhere, even in a basement or alleyway. Wang and Chow walked around the screens to find Pang, the Incense and Ceremonies Master, and Ren, the Vanguard, standing in front of three archways, the first of which was made with crossed swords. Pang and Ren would lead the initiations.

"Is the entire executive here now?" Gao asked.

"Yu isn't here yet," Pang said.

"We'll give him another five minutes."

As the men waited, Chow examined the lodge and

marvelled at the history it represented. The Heaven and Earth Society — the Hung Society — had been founded in the 1760s. As their symbol they'd adopted a triangle with the character *hung*, representing the union of heaven, earth, and man. The word *triad* hadn't come into use until 1949, when the Hong Kong police, perverting the meaning of the symbol, used it to refer to the society's members. Now it was common enough for society members to do the same.

Originally the Hung Society had been one of several secret fraternal societies that emerged in the mid-eighteenth century with the goal of overthrowing the Qing Empire and restoring the Ming Dynasty. They were rebels, regarded as traitors by those who supported the Qing. Because of that, early society members were forced to develop secret forms of communication, and they created an initiation ceremony that impressed upon the brothers the need for absolute loyalty and bravery. The two-hundred-year-old basic elements of that ceremony would be practised in just a few minutes, inside the lodge at the Emerald Phoenix.

The secret societies eventually overthrew the Qing Empire, but in the process the Hung members became rebels without a cause and were forced to rethink their reason for existing. Some groups became martial arts associations, others turned into labour unions and trade organizations, and some turned to crime. But, as Chow knew, not everyone who was involved in crime was a willing participant, and some members had been branded as criminals simply because they belonged to a secret society that several governments had made illegal.

Strangely, despite its Chinese roots, the Hung Society no longer had a presence in mainland China. Mao Zedong had set out to eradicate it after he took power in 1949, and the

People's Liberation Army made a good job of it. Thousands
of Hung members were forced to resettle in Hong Kong,
Taiwan, Singapore, Manila, and several cities in the United
States. Getting pushed out of China wasn't necessarily a bad
thing, Chow thought, since it had helped expand the society's business reach into much more profitable markets. Still,
he believed that one day they would return there.

"Yu is here," Pang said sharply, bringing Chow back to the
present. "I'll get the men."

Chow watched Pang walk around the screen and heard
him greet the young men, instructing them to remove their
shoes, socks, and shirts. When Pang returned, the two men
followed with bare feet and bare chests.

Ren stepped forward and pointed to the first arch. "This
is the Mountain of Knives," he said. "Do not take one step
through it unless you are loyal."

Both men walked under the arch without hesitation.

Ren joined them and asked their names, birthdates,
hometowns, and how long they had been Red Lanterns, or
trainees. Their answers were repeated by Ren but were not
written down.

Pang came to stand alongside. "The second arch is called
the Loyalty and Righteousness Hall. The sign on it declares
that before this gate all men are equal," he said.

The initiates nodded and once more walked through. Ren
met them and held out his hand. The men reached into their
pockets and took out red envelopes that contained their initiation fees.

The third gate was called the Heaven and Earth Circle,
and on its archway was a sign that read "through the heaven
and earth circle are born the hung heroes." The men walked

under the archway, hesitated, and then stepped through a bamboo hoop that Pang held in front of them. The hoop represented the start of their rebirth into the Hung Society. It had been the most emotional part of Chow's initiation.

The next two hours were anticlimactic as Pang and Ren took turns recounting various events in the society's history and then led the men to a triad altar at the end of the hall, where they recited poetry. At his initiation the poetry had surprised Chow, but he later learned that many books of triad poetry had been secreted away and carefully guarded for as long as the society had existed.

When the poetry reading ended, the two men were guided to the right of the altar, where Pang stood holding a basin of water. After the men washed their faces and removed their clothes, Ren stepped forward carrying white robes and straw sandals.

"Your old life has been washed away," Ren said to them. "You are now prepared for rebirth as a triad."

The men returned to the front of the altar. Pang handed them sheaves of paper. "You will now swear the Thirty-Six Oaths," he said.

As the men read the oaths, Ren poured what Chow knew was cock's blood into a bowl. He then added wine. Pang joined him with two strips of yellow paper. The paper was lit and held over the bowl, its ashes falling into the blood and wine. Ren stirred the mixture with a knife. When the last oath was sworn, Ren presented the men with the bowl. Each drank deeply from it, and then they jointly held it for a few seconds before throwing it to the ground, where it smashed. The broken bowl was a symbol of what would happen to anyone who betrayed his brothers. It was the last part of the rite.

"You are now initiated," Ren said. "You are full-fledged members of our society."

Wang laughed. "And now we can go into the restaurant to eat like pigs and get drunk."

2

CHOW TUNG WAS NOT A MAN WHO LIKED PARTIES, BUT in the Emerald Phoenix among his peers and the people he thought of as his family, he felt a depth of camaraderie that threatened to overwhelm him. Fortunately he was sitting between Xu and Fong, and their conversation rarely went beyond casual bantering that made him smile.

Xu and Fong were his closest friends. They had joined the Fanling triads within three months of each other, served as Blue Lanterns together, and were initiated as entry-level forty-niners at the same time. Chow was a few years older, and from the outset Xu and Fong had treated him like their big brother. Ten years later, the three men shared a level of respect and trust that didn't have to be discussed. But despite the depth of their friendship, the men could not have been more different in the way they lived their lives.

Xu had come to Hong Kong from Shanghai as a boy, with his mother and triad father, in 1949. He was a homebody, and he liked nothing better than spending time with his wife and newborn son, to whom Chow was godfather. Quiet, observant, and clever, Xu was the man who Chow turned to when he needed strategic advice. But despite an apparently mild disposition and his unimposing height and build, Xu was also a good man to have by your side in a fight. Whenever there was a threat, he never hesitated to fully commit himself to take it on.

Fong, from Fanling, was far more outgoing, fun-loving, and irreverent. Tall, lean, and with unfashionably long hair that hung to his shoulders, he was attractive to women but fickle in the way he treated them. Girlfriends came and went almost as regularly as the systems he devised to beat the gaming tables in Macau. Gambling was his weakness. He freely admitted that he was addicted but never gave a thought to stopping. To help protect him, Chow had him barred from the off-track betting shops, mah-jong parlours, and mini casinos operated by the gang in Fanling, but he couldn't prevent him from getting on the jetfoil to Macau. Fong, though, was a diligent assistant Straw Sandal, and he had the ideal personality to handle the amount of communication it involved. Everyone in the gang knew him and liked him. He was the person Chow turned to when he needed to know what the men were thinking.

Chow was far more solitary than his friends. He lived in a sparsely furnished one-bedroom apartment above a restaurant near the centre of town. He had never had a girlfriend that Fong or Xu knew of. His life was regimented to the point that even his social activities — dinner at Xu's home every second Friday, trips to Happy Valley every Wednesday night and Sunday afternoon during the horse-racing season — were almost scripted. Nearly all his friends were triads, some of them much older men who saw in him qualities that needed to be cultivated.

The empty bowls that had held shark-fin soup were removed from the tables and replaced with platters of sautéed crab, Peking duck with pancakes, whole fish steamed in soy sauce, sizzling sliced steak, and gailan. Fong was explaining to Xu a new system he'd developed for roulette that he was convinced was going to work.

"This is the third or fourth system that I can remember you talking about," Xu said. "You seem to mention them only once and then they're never heard of again. I wonder why that is. Is it fair to guess that they all failed?"

"Tell you what, come to Macau with me this weekend and I'll show you," Fong said. "I'll even pay for the jetfoil and buy you dinner."

"You'd have to buy me dinner before you got to the tables, because after you're finished you won't have enough money left to buy instant noodles."

"Are you saying you would come with me?" Fong said, ignoring the gibe.

"No, I'm not."

"What, you have to ask your wife for permission?"

"Enough, you two," Chow said. "Here comes Wang with our newest members."

The Red Pole had a large bottle of brandy in his right hand and a small glass in his left. He had been taking the young initiates from table to table for toasts. Each of them held a slightly larger glass and already seemed quite drunk. Their glasses were empty, but as soon as they reached Chow's table, Wang filled both of their glasses to the brim, pouring just a few drops into his own.

"Raise your glasses, please," Wang said. "Let's welcome these fine young men into our society."

The eight men at the round table stood up. Most of them, including Chow and Xu, were drinking San Miguel beer. Fong was indulging in Maotai *baijiu*, a lethal liquor made from fermented sorghum.

"*Ganbei!*" Wang shouted, and downed the contents of his glass.

The men at the table followed suit and then watched with amusement as the young men struggled to empty their glasses. "I doubt they'll make it to the last table," Xu said as he watched them stagger away.

"We did," Chow said.

"I know, but it put me off liquor for ages," Xu said.

"The more you eat, the more you can drink," Fong said, flicking his chopsticks towards the gleaming golden slices of duck skin.

The three friends ate almost uninterruptedly for half an hour, savouring the food that the gang had paid a small fortune for. When they finally set down their chopsticks, Chow said, "What a fine meal."

"About to be ruined, I think," Fong said. "Ren is coming in this direction, and he looks rather determined. I suspect he wants to talk about night markets."

"That could be a good thing," said Xu.

"Not the way he operates. He'll be looking for weaknesses in Uncle's position and he'll be hoping that a couple of beers will have clouded his judgement."

"Fat chance," Xu said.

"Still, the man is the Vanguard and needs to be respected," Fong said.

"Of course," Chow said, rising to his feet to greet his colleague.

"I hope you are enjoying the evening," Ren said when he reached the table. "There is nothing I like more than initiating new members into our society."

"I thought that you and Pang handled the ceremony beautifully," Chow said.

"Uncle, you are always so silver-tongued."

"Do you doubt my sincerity?"

"Never," Ren said with a laugh. "You are nothing if not sincere."

Chow shrugged. "Are you visiting because you want to talk?"

"Yes, but I would prefer it if our conversation was just between the two of us."

"Do you want to step outside?"

"No, that's not necessary. It will be fine if Xu and Fong give us a little more room here at the table."

"We're moving," Xu said, standing and poking Fong in the arm.

Ren took Xu's seat and smiled at Chow. He was a large man, more broad than tall, with a full-fleshed face and a mass of thick, grey-streaked hair. "I want to talk to you about tomorrow's meeting," he said.

"Did you read my notes?" Chow asked.

"I'm not much of a reader. I'd rather you explained it."

Chow lowered his head as he gathered himself. "It is quite basic. Right now we are collecting protection money — what some of our brothers refer to as 'insurance money' — from most of the merchants in town. In these tough economic times, some of the merchants are becoming unhappy, and many of them are going to the Hong Kong police with complaints. It isn't a healthy situation."

"And what are you proposing as an alternative?"

"There is no night market in Fanling. I am suggesting we create one. I've already discussed the idea with some local politicians, and they say they'll support us. They would close off two or three streets in the middle of town every night. We would set up stalls that we would then lease to the merchants. They wouldn't have to pay insurance, but we hope they would also buy goods from us."

"Hope?"

"The goods are knock-offs, and they'd get them at a discount. I've talked to our brothers in Kowloon, where they have a huge night market. They don't mind sharing their sources of supply."

"So the local merchants would buy the knock-offs from us?"

"That is the plan. If they do, we'll make money twice over — from the leases and from the purchases," he said. "Which should make us happy as we make them happier. I mean, who needs merchants running to the police with complaints?"

"I thought you had the police under control."

"No one ever truly has the police under control," Chow said, lowering his voice, dismayed that Ren would broach such a sensitive subject in public. "There are limits to everything. The police have been adding men to the New Territories northern region and they've been making themselves more of a presence on the street. That's given some of the merchants the confidence to tell us they won't pay. Wang has been able to get most of them to come around, but it isn't always easy, and sometimes it can be messy. I don't see that situation improving on its own."

Ren stuck a toothpick between his teeth and turned his head to one side. "I like what you did with the off-track betting sites, casinos, and mah-jong parlours."

"You didn't at first."

"True. I thought that eliminating bookmaking would cut our income. I didn't realize how much the bookies were stealing."

"All I did was centralize and organize the process. The bettors like the comfort of our shops and knowing that they will get paid immediately if they win. We simply made it difficult for freelance bookies to steal from them — and us."

"What about those extra cops you mentioned? You don't think they'll start interfering with our gambling operations?"

"I do not," Chow said, more forcibly than he intended, and then flashed a quick smile at Ren. "What the police dislike and feel compelled to address is chaos, unhappy citizens, and disrespect for the rules of a civilized society. Our gambling business is victimless; in fact, you could almost call it a community service. We run it fairly and above board. The citizens are happy with it, so the police have no reason to get involved."

"Except for the fact that we're breaking several laws."

"Laws that the police are quite content to ignore as long as things remain calm and orderly."

"I have always assumed — though Gao won't discuss it — that we're also paying the cops to turn a blind eye."

"That isn't the case," Chow said, again sharply but this time without a smile. "I know it is common practice among other gangs to pay the police, but we don't, and it should never be suggested that we do."

"Then how do you keep them off our backs?"

"That's a question you'll have to ask Gao," Chow said.

"No, I won't bother, and I don't really care anyway — the results speak for themselves. The cops basically leave us alone and that's good enough. But let me come back to your night-market idea," Ren said. "I've always understood how the betting shops can be profitable, but I'm not as certain that this market can replace insurance money."

"It won't just replace it; it will add more money to our bottom line," Chow said.

"You seem certain about that."

"I am. And I'm equally certain that having those merchants as partners in the night market will eliminate a lot of their complaints and give the cops less reason to harass us."

Ren nodded, sipped at his beer, and then stood up. "I like your confidence, Uncle. I still have to think some more about this, but for now you should assume I'll support you."

"Thank you."

Xu and Fong returned to their seats as Ren walked back to his table.

"Was that as positive as it appeared to be?" Xu asked.

"I think so. But with Ren I'm never quite one hundred percent sure," Chow said.

"Well, I can tell you that I'm sure Ma is crapping all over us right now," Fong said. He nodded in the direction of a table where the Deputy Mountain Master was speaking intently to Gao. "He keeps looking at us as he's talking."

"Don't leap to conclusions," Chow said.

"It doesn't take much of a leap to figure out what position he's selling."

"We'll know soon enough," Chow said abruptly. "Gao is coming this way."

They watched as the Mountain Master weaved around several tables and wayward chairs, stopping a few times to acknowledge greetings from brothers. He was over six feet tall and as broad as Wang, with a shaved head and tattooed arms. The stories of how vicious he'd been as a Red Pole were legendary, but those days were gone. He'd put on a lot of weight, and as his body had softened, so had his personality. Gao preferred to lead by consensus rather than dictating. At times Chow found his management style onerous, but given that more often than not he ended up with what he wanted, it was a criticism he didn't voice.

"Boss, how are you feeling?" Chow said when Gao reached their table.

"It was a good day and that was a good meal," Gao said. "Are you prepared for tomorrow?"

"I'm ready."

Gao moved closer and lowered his voice, but not so much that Xu and Fong couldn't hear. "I'm thinking that it might be a good idea for us to talk before the meeting. I'm going to Sha Tin tonight. Wu is going to pick me up in the morning and drive me to the office. Why don't you come with him. We can talk in the car."

"That's fine with me."

"He'll get me at eight-thirty, so he should meet you in Fanling around eight. Where will you be?"

"Jia's Congee Restaurant."

"I'll tell him."

"And I'll see you in the morning," Chow said.

The Mountain Master was leaving by the restaurant's front door before anyone spoke, and then it was Xu who said, "What's in Sha Tin? I thought he still lived in Fanling."

"His new girlfriend is in Sha Tin," Fong said.

"Does his wife know?" Xu asked.

"If she does, she probably doesn't care," Fong said. "By my count that's his fifth or sixth girlfriend since I joined the gang, and the wife is still hanging around."

"I don't understand why, when a man has a good wife, he needs a girlfriend," Xu said.

"You are still young, and more to the point, so is your wife," Fong said. "You'll get the itch yourself one day."

"I don't think we should be discussing the boss's personal life so freely," Chow said.

"Or mine," Xu said.

"Or Xu's," Chow said with a smile.

(3)

IT WAS CLOSE TO TEN WHEN CHOW LEFT THE EMERALD
Phoenix to walk back to his apartment. After only a few
hundred metres, he stopped to light a cigarette. He leaned
against a wall, took a couple of deep puffs, and replayed in
his head the conversations with Ren and Gao. He thought it
had gone well with Ren, but he couldn't stop wondering what
Ma had said to Gao, and if it was the reason why Gao wanted
to talk to him before the meeting. Regardless of what Chow
thought of Ma, Gao trusted him. They had both been born
and raised in Fanling and had been friends since they were
boys. The underlying strength of their relationship surfaced
periodically, and Chow had seen it undo proposals even from
Wang. Was it his turn to be undone?

I'm overthinking this, he told himself. *I've made a good
case, and unless I'm totally misreading everyone, I have the
support I need. Now it's out of my hands. Gao will make a
decision and there's nothing more I can do to influence it, so
I should stop worrying about it.*

He started to walk again, stopping at a small newsstand to buy the racing form for the next night's card at

the Happy Valley racetrack. He tucked it under his arm and continued on his way home. As he passed the restaurant on the ground floor, he caught a whiff of garlic and ginger coming through the open door. He hesitated, but it had been several hours since he'd eaten, and the aromas had rekindled his appetite. He went inside and bought noodles with beef and XO sauce.

He'd been living above the restaurant for eight years and hadn't changed a thing since the day he moved in. Its single bedroom held a double bed and dresser. The living room contained a large leather reclining chair near a window that looked out onto the street. Flanking the chair were two small portable metal tables and one metal folding chair. One table was bare; on the other sat a large glass ashtray and several pens. The bathroom had a sink, toilet, and shower stall. The kitchen had a stove — which Chow had turned on less than five times in eight years — and a small fridge that held beer, bread, butter, and a jar of marmalade. He put the noodle container on the empty table and the racing form on the other, and sat down to eat.

Chow took the lid off the container and smiled. There weren't many foods he enjoyed more than the dish in front of him. His chopsticks plucked a sliver of glistening beef from the bed of noodles. It was so tender he barely had to chew. He took another bite of beef and then attacked the noodles. He ate quickly, almost with urgency, as if he was afraid someone would take the food from him. Eating so fast wasn't a good habit, he knew, but he couldn't seem to break it. He suspected it was a subconscious carryover from the time in his life when getting enough food to stay alive was all he could think about. Xu had once observed that for someone who seemed as calm as Uncle was on the surface, the way he ate hinted at some hidden inner turmoil. Whatever the underlying motivation, he finished off the entire container in less than ten minutes.

Chow went to the kitchen, took a San Miguel beer from the fridge, and returned to the living room. He eased into the leather chair, reached for the racing form and a pen, and felt a rush of anticipation as he opened the paper's pages.

The Hong Kong horse-racing season lasted ten months, from September to June. Races were held twice a week, on Wednesday nights and Sunday afternoons, at the Happy Valley Racecourse on Hong Kong Island. The track had become his escape. From the moment he walked through its gates, he thought of nothing beyond its confines.

It was Fong who had introduced him to Happy Valley and given him a rudimentary education in the intricacies of the racing form. The first time he went, he'd won, but that first-time luck and the money that came with it meant far less to him than the exhilaration he'd felt watching the horses race down the home stretch, accompanied by the screams and exhortations of fifty thousand frenzied bettors. It was a place, he quickly discovered, where you could be part of the crowd but still completely alone. It was a place where he could turn loose all the emotions he kept in check during the rest of the week.

Chow did not consider his forays to Happy Valley as gambling. In fact, he intensely disliked most games of chance and felt badly for people who lost money they couldn't afford, in the legal casinos of Macau and even the illegal ones like those operated by the gang in Fanling. All casino games were rigged, not because anyone was cheating but simply through the mathematical certainty that the house odds would always prevail if a gambler played long enough.

Horse racing was different. The odds were not preordained. Each race had a plot and a cast that was singular and unique. The bettor was free to make his own judgement about how a race might unfold, based on his analysis of the information he had at hand. And there was no better source of information than the racing form. The form was available to everyone, and within its pages and rows of numbers there were histories to be gleaned about the horses, jockeys, trainers, and owners. When those details were combined with the race distance, track preferences, recent training workouts, past race performances, race conditions, and the weight a horse had to carry, an educated person could make an informed decision about how any race would unfold, and about which bet offered the best return.

Horse racing had become Chow's sole hobby. It provided an emotional release, it challenged him intellectually, and occasionally it provided him with a deep sense of satisfaction, almost superiority, when some nugget of information he'd unearthed in the racing form led him to choose a winning horse that the mass betting public had overlooked. It was also a timeless exercise, something that could be trusted and counted on. There had been racing at Happy Valley since 1846, and there would always be a next race.

The previous Sunday had been a good day for him financially, but now Uncle put those memories aside as he began to examine Wednesday's card. Almost at once he was lost in the minute details of past performances, race fractions, and closing last furlongs. His pen crossed out, circled, and under-lined the numbers that eliminated or enhanced a horse's chances in his mind.

He finished his San Miguel, got another, and opened a fresh pack of Marlboros. Fuelled by the racing form, ciga-rettes, and beer, the night sped by. Several times he checked the time and thought about going to bed, but he put it off until his eyes closed and — as on many other Tuesday nights — he fell asleep in his chair.

Chow woke at five a.m. after about four hours' sleep, which was fairly normal for him. If he had a choice he wouldn't sleep at all, for his nightly dreams were so disturbing that he dreaded closing his eyes. But he couldn't go without sleep entirely; his body and mind had apparently agreed that he could survive on four hours a night.

He slid from the chair and went into the kitchen. He put a large teaspoon of Nescafé instant coffee into a cup and then filled it with hot water from a Thermos on the counter. It would be his only coffee of the day. He enjoyed it, but he found that when he drank too much, it put him on edge. Tea would be his beverage of choice for the rest of the day. It might have as much caffeine but, for whatever reason, it didn't have the same effect as coffee.

He carried the coffee back to the chair and sat down. He took a couple of sips and then reached for the racing form. Reading the form was never a one-time project, and many times he was still going over it when there were only a few minutes before the race started.

At quarter to six he put the paper aside and walked to the bathroom. He shaved, brushed his teeth, and showered. Twenty minutes later, he left the apartment wearing a fresh white shirt and a clean black suit, the racing form tucked under his arm.

The weather was mild for June. It wouldn't be much longer before the typical Hong Kong summer, with its oppressive heat and humidity, descended on them. Chow hated that kind of weather but stubbornly refused to give in to it; he wore his suit on even the hottest of days. Despite the early hour, he wasn't alone on the street. Two elderly female street cleaners were already sweeping debris from the sidewalk, and a news agent was organizing his papers on top of wooden crates. Chow bought a copy of the *Oriental Daily News* from him. The paper had been launched just a few months before; he liked its news coverage, and the paper employed a race handicapper who was quite astute.

He continued down the street for another four blocks towards a twenty-four-hour congee restaurant. It had opened five years before, and Chow ate there every morning. He had been greeted on virtually every one of them by the same server, Jia, a short, stout woman with a perpetual grin. She and her husband owned the restaurant; he worked in the kitchen while she ran the front. Chow had never been in the restaurant, night or day, when one of them wasn't there. As he walked in, Jia waved at him and pointed to a booth near the back with a "reserved" sign on it. Even at that hour of the morning the sign was necessary, because the restaurant was almost always full.

Chow had no sooner sat down than Jia placed a pot of tea in front of him. "Good morning, Uncle. What are you having today?"

By itself congee epitomized blandness, but he never ate it plain. The boiled rice porridge could be improved by adding ingredients such as dried pork belly, sausage, salted duck eggs, scallions, black pickled cucumber, tofu, or various sauces. Chow also typically ordered youtiao, sticks of fried bread that he used for dipping.

"Youtiao, pickled cucumber, and scallions."

"I'll add some sausage as well," she said.

He smiled. "One day we will agree on what I should have on my congee."

"I like all my customers, but you are the only one I worry about," she said. "You're too skinny. You need meat as well as vegetables."

"Then put in the sausage and bring me two salted duck eggs."

"Great choices."

Chow opened his newspaper when she left and turned to the racing page. He scanned the handicapper's comments on each race and made a mental note of his picks. They had chosen the same potential winner for three of the ten races. He sighed. Normally this handicapper's picks were heavily bet on, and Chow didn't like betting on favourites or short odds. He would have to rework those three races and see if he could find another horse to back.

The congee and accompaniments arrived and he turned his attention to breakfast. As soon as he was finished, Jia came back to the table. "Can I get you more of anything?"

"No food, but I'll have more tea."

As she turned to go, he saw a young man step inside the restaurant and look in his direction. It was Wu, a Blue Lantern who reported to Wang but was assigned to Gao as his driver. "Wu," Chow said loudly. "Are you looking for me?"

Wu nodded and hurried towards him. "Good morning,

Uncle. I've been waiting outside. It is already past eight and I was beginning to think I'd come to the wrong place."

Chow checked his watch. "I lost track of time. I'll be with you in a minute." He took a Hong Kong hundred-dollar note from his pocket, put it on the table, picked up his racing form and pen, and then slid from the booth. "Let's go."

When they reached the grey Mercedes idling on the street, Wu stepped in front of Chow and opened the back door for him. Chow had been prepared to sit in the front, but he quietly appreciated the show of respect. He climbed into the car and promptly reopened his racing form.

Sha Tin was about twenty kilometres southeast of Fanling, on the way to Kowloon. Traffic was light, Wu drove quickly, and the car reached Sha Tin at 8:25. He came to a stop across the street from a twenty-storey apartment building.

"I have to let the boss know we're here," Wu said, getting out of the car. He ran across the street and entered the building's lobby. Chow could see him speaking into the intercom. When he was finished, he stepped back and gave Chow a thumbs-up.

Chow put his racing form to one side and started to gather himself for another conversation about the viability of the night market. He understood that he was asking his colleagues to give up a sure thing — their protection racket — in exchange for income that was only hypothetical. He'd faced the same argument when he proposed getting rid of the bookies and opening off-track betting shops. But Chow had prevailed, and within a few months the gang's income from those shops was triple what the bookies had brought in previously. One reason for that growth was that the safe, comfortable environment of the shops attracted new customers from surrounding towns. Chow hoped the night market would likewise attract people from beyond Fanling, but he hadn't built that into his projections. *Maybe I should have*, he thought.

He looked towards the apartment building and saw Gao walking across the lobby. He was wearing the same clothes he'd worn the night before and looked like he hadn't had much sleep. Wu went to the lobby door and opened it for his boss. Gao exited and Wu followed, careful to stay several respectful steps behind.

Chow climbed out of the car to greet Gao. The Mountain Master stepped off the sidewalk and started to cross the street, walking with his head down. Just then Chow heard a noise and looked to his left. A white panel van was pulling away from the curb in a hurry. The van's speed increased as it headed straight for him.

"Look out!" Chow shouted.

Gao raised his head in Chow's direction, then looked quickly in the direction of the van barrelling towards him. He took several rapid steps backwards. Chow saw the van swerve slightly and thought the driver had seen Gao and was trying to avoid him. He was wrong. Chow heard a dull thud, the sound of breaking glass, and Wu screaming. Gao's retreat had changed the angle of impact just enough so the van didn't hit him head-on, but it had hit him all the same, the right fender smashing into his side. Gao's body was airborne for a few seconds before crashing headfirst onto the pavement.

Chow stood transfixed. He looked in the direction of the van, expecting it to stop. As it disappeared around the corner, the realization of what had just happened hit him. He ran towards Gao. Wu was already there, his body shaking as he stood over their boss.

"We need an ambulance," Chow said. "There's a payphone on the corner. Call for one, and make sure they know it's a real emergency."

"Is he dead?" Wu asked.

Chow knelt down by Gao, took his wrist, and felt for a pulse. "He's alive, but he won't be for much longer unless you get an ambulance here now."

"I didn't see the van until it was too late," Wu said.

"Forget about the van. We need an ambulance. Now get going!"

Wu nodded and started to run towards the phone booth.

Chow looked down at Gao and felt ill. The van had struck him on the right side of his body. His right arm, exposed by a short-sleeved shirt, was twisted out of shape, and Chow could see a sliver of bone protruding through the flesh. He was wearing jeans, so Chow couldn't immediately see what damage had been done to his legs and hips, but there wasn't much doubt that his head had taken a beating when it hit the pavement. There was blood seeping from his left ear, his nose was distorted and bloody, and his face was scraped and streaked with even more blood. Chow took off his suit jacket, gently raised Gao's head, and slipped the jacket underneath.

Gao was unconscious. Chow felt for his pulse again; it was weak, but it was there.

"Is he alive?" a voice asked.

Chow looked up and saw an elderly man standing about ten metres away. Behind him, other people were coming out of the building and gathering on the sidewalk.

"He is, and we're calling for an ambulance. I think it's best if you stay back, and ask everyone else to do the same."

"This is the third accident on this street this year, and it looks like it could be the worst," the man said. "There's a warehouse at the end of the street, and trucks and vans are always coming and going. Those drivers don't care about pedestrians."

"How did you know he was struck by a truck or van? Did you see the accident?"

"Yes. I was standing by my window having a cigarette. My wife can't stand the smoke, so I blow it out the window," he said. "The driver must not have seen him, because he didn't slow down."

"How could he not have seen him? My friend was in the middle of the road."

"How would I know? That's a question for the police."

"But you saw what I saw, correct? A white panel van going full speed?"

"I saw a white panel van."

"Did you notice any names or markings?"

"It seemed to be just a plain white panel van."

"Did you see the licence plate?"

"No. Did you?"

Chow shook his head. "Has anyone in the building called the police yet?"

"I wouldn't know. But I wouldn't be surprised, they're such a nosy bunch."

Chow looked in the direction of the phone booth and saw Wu running back towards him. "Well?" he said when the Blue Lantern reached him.

"They'll be here in about five minutes."

"He's been badly hurt. He's going to need a lot of help," Chow said.

Wu was still shaking and his face was pale. "I should have warned him," he said.

"This isn't your fault," Chow said. "He's a grown man who should know how to cross a road safely."

The elderly man had gone back into the building, but the other people began to inch closer to get a better look.

"Stay back!" Chow shouted at them, and then looked at Wu. "Keep those people away from here. Tell them to get back in their building or at least stay on the sidewalk. This isn't a freak show."

While Wu wrangled the onlookers back towards the sidewalk, Chow considered what his first responsibility would be after the ambulance arrived. Phone calls would have to be made. People needed to be told. He weighed his options and ended up with one name — Wang. He was the fixer, the man who had everyone's phone number. He'd know better than anyone who to tell and when to tell them.

A siren sounded and Chow saw an ambulance at the head of the street. As it came to a stop in front of him, another siren sounded. A police car was starting down the street towards them.

What a disaster, Chow thought.

CHOW AND WANG SAT IN THE WAITING ROOM OF OUR Lady of Maryknoll Hospital in Sha Tin. The only other occupants were a woman and the small child she was holding in her arms. Wang had arrived in a taxi half an hour after getting a phone call from Chow. Now, two hours later, they were still waiting for a medical update on Gao.

"What could be taking so long?" Wang asked.

"He had a lot of injuries. I'm sure it isn't a case of just one thing needing fixing," Chow said.

Wang looked at his watch. "Our meeting is supposed to begin in a few hours. I didn't want to start making phone calls until I know how he is, but I don't think I can wait much longer."

"How about calling his wife?"

"I thought it was best if Ma phoned her. Their families have been close for years; he was the best man at their wedding."

"I know his son, Chi. We were Blue Lanterns together for a few months, before he decided the life wasn't for him and moved to Hong Kong and an office job," Chow said. "He,

Xu, and I have kept in touch and see one another a couple of times a year."

"I remember him — he was a good guy. Would you mind calling him? He might be an even better choice to talk to the wife."

"I don't mind, but I'd still like to wait until I have something definite to say."

The door leading into the emergency department opened and a nurse appeared. The two men looked at her expectantly, but she ignored them and motioned for the woman with the baby to follow her.

As the door closed behind them, Wang lit his tenth cigarette since arriving. "What can be taking so goddamn long?" he repeated.

As if on cue, the door swung open again and a man in a white jacket with a stethoscope around his neck walked through. Chow took one look at his face and anticipated the worst.

"Mr. Chow?" the man said.

Chow stood. "Yes, that's me,"

"I'm Doctor Chiang. I've been treating Mr. Gao."

"How is he?"

"We did everything we could," Chiang said, not looking directly at them. "He had multiple broken bones and internal injuries, but the main problem was the damage to his brain. We were waiting for a neurosurgeon to operate, but I'm sorry to tell you that Mr. Gao wasn't able to hold out."

"He's dead?" Wang said, disbelief registering on his face.

"Yes, that's what I meant."

"Fuck, fuck, fuck," Wang said.

Now the doctor did look at them.

"Excuse my friend. This is a terrible shock," Chow said.

"I understand, and I'm sorry I had to be the one to give you such bad news."

"When news is this bad, there isn't any right way to give it. I'm sure this is difficult for you as well," Chow said.

"Thank you for understanding that. We are in the business of saving lives, and we take it badly when we're unsuccessful," Chiang said. "Now, unfortunately, we all have to move on, and that includes the matter of notifying the next of kin. We've been so busy treating Mr. Gao that we haven't had a chance to contact his family."

"If you don't mind, we'll look after that," Chow said.

"That will be fine, but we'll need to know who they are and how they want us to handle the body."

"Of course," Chow said. "I'll call Mr. Gao's son, Chi. I imagine he'll make arrangements with a funeral home."

The doctor nodded. "The police also have an interest in Mr. Gao's case. They asked us to notify them if there were any dramatic changes. I'll do that as soon as I go back inside."

"Thank you for doing that, and for all of your efforts," Chow said.

The doctor started to leave, then stopped and turned back to them. "If it makes it any easier, I don't think the neurosurgeon would have made much difference. There was just too much damage."

As the door closed behind Chiang, Chow sighed. "I'll call Chi."

"I'll let Ma and Ren know. They can contact the others."

"There are payphones on the wall by the door. We shouldn't waste any more time. But make sure they know we're trying to have Chi call his mother."

"I will. They'll probably be relieved that they don't have to break the news to her," Wang said. "One more thing, Uncle. I'm sure I'll be asked if Gao's death was accidental or not."

"I really don't know," Chow said. "I didn't see the van when I arrived with Wu, so it could have come from a warehouse like the neighbour suggested. And the driver could just have been inattentive."

"The neighbour told you there have been similar accidents on the street?"

"He did, but I have trouble believing the driver didn't see Gao. And if he did see him, why didn't he slow down?"

"But you said the van swerved."

"Yes, but I don't know if it was trying to avoid Gao or hit him. One thing I'm certain of is that he maintained his speed."

Wang shook his head. "We don't need any confusion about this. Ma thinks in black-and-white terms. If there's any doubt about what happened, he'll run around like a chicken with its head cut off. I want to be able to tell him that it was an accident or it wasn't."

"I'd like to give you a more definite answer, but it isn't that easy," Chow said.

"I'll tell you what I'm thinking," Wang said slowly. "If it wasn't an accident and was in fact deliberate, then the killer most likely would be someone from another gang. There have been rumours that some of the other gangs have been thinking about moving in on us. All the money you've been making for us with those betting shops and casinos has made us attractive."

"Are you taking those rumours seriously?"

"Seriously enough that I made some calls," Wang said.

"The result was that I found nothing to worry me, but now Gao is dead. It would be stupid of me not to start worrying again."

"But running someone down with a van is hardly what you would expect from a triad. If another gang wanted Gao dead, they would have shot him or used something more traditional."

"Like a machete?"

"Yes. And there's one more point. How would they have known he was spending the night with his girlfriend in Sha Tin rather than with his wife at home in Fanling? Someone would have had to leak that information, and the only people I can think of who knew were a handful of our own gang members at the dinner last night," Chow said, and then paused. "I have real trouble believing that one of our people could be that disloyal, that much of a rat."

"I agree, that's not too likely," Wang said. "So it seems to me that you and I are in agreement that if he was killed deliberately, it probably wasn't by a triad."

"I think we are."

"That means that some civilian was responsible."

"I guess it does."

"What are the odds of that happening?"

"Not great. Not great at all," Chow said.

"Again we agree. So where does that leave us?"

"It leaves us with you telling Ma that we think it was an accident, or at the very worst a hit-and-run by some bad driver."

Wang nodded. "It would be beneficial to all of us if the police thought along the same lines. Could you call your contact?"

"I'll call him, but I can't promise he'll go along with us if the local cops think differently."

"Still, it doesn't hurt to ask."

CHOW AND WANG WALKED OVER TO THE BANK OF phones. Chow put five cents into one that was as far away from Wang's as he could get. He dialed Xu's office number. When there was no answer, he phoned his home.

"*Wei*," Xu's wife answered, hesitantly.

"It's Uncle. I'm sorry for calling the apartment, but I need to speak with Xu."

"Just a minute."

"Hey, what's up?" Xu said seconds later.

"I need Gao Chi's work number; I don't have it with me," Chow said. "And before you ask, I'm in Sha Tin, at Our Lady of Maryknoll Hospital, with Wang. Chi's father was brought here this morning after getting hit by a van. He died about ten minutes ago."

Xu didn't reply right away. Chow figured he was connecting the dots. Then Xu blurted, "The Mountain Master is dead?"

"He is. And do me a favour — don't ask for any details. Right now, all I want is Chi's number. When things calm down, I'll tell you what happened."

"But —"

"But nothing. Just give me Chi's phone number."

Xu hesitated, then rattled off a phone number, which Chow wrote down on his racing form.

"Thanks. I'll call you later. In the meantime, keep this to yourself." Chow hung up and looked at Wang. The Red Pole's back was to him, but his shoulders were heaving in all directions as he relayed the news to someone on the line.

Chow took several deep breaths and then called Chi's Hong Kong number.

The phone rang five times before it was answered with a brisk "This is Chi."

"And this is Chow from Fanling."

"Uncle, this is unexpected."

"Unfortunately it is also going to be unwelcome."

The line went silent.

"It is bad news," Chow continued.

"How bad?" Chi asked hesitantly.

"It couldn't be much worse. Your father is dead."

"God . . ."

"It was a traffic accident," Chow said, putting the best spin on it he could. "He was struck by a hit-and-run driver. He died a short while ago at Our Lady of Maryknoll Hospital in Sha Tin."

There was another long pause and then Chi asked, "Does my mother know?"

"Not yet. We thought it might be best if you were the one to tell her."

"I understand."

"But if you don't —"

"No," Chi said quickly. "I'll tell her."

"Good."

"When was the accident?"

"A few hours ago," Chow said.

"What was he doing in Sha Tin?"

"He was leaving his girlfriend's apartment. He was crossing the road when he was struck."

"That's the new girlfriend. My mother knew about her, so that won't come as a shock, but his death is really going to rattle her. The girlfriends made her angry but she kept quiet, figuring they didn't matter as long as he always came home. She loved him that much."

"I'm sorry."

"How did it happen? Was it really a hit-and-run?"

"Yes."

"So the driver took off?"

"He did. The police are looking into it."

"A lot of good that will do."

"I have no opinion about that."

"Oh fuck," Chi said. "What am I supposed to do now?"

"I think you should call your mother, and then I suggest you call the hospital to make arrangements to get his body transferred to a funeral home."

"Will the police release the body?"

"I don't see why not. There's no indication it was anything but an accident."

"Except for the fact that my father had a job that often ends with someone getting killed."

"Even so, running over someone with a van isn't triad style," Chow said.

"I guess not. In a way that's comforting," Chi said. "I would hate to think this was deliberate."

"I can understand that."

Chi sighed. "Look, thanks for calling, Uncle. I need to get out of here and head for Fanling. I can't tell my mother about this over the phone."

"If there is anything I can do to help, please let me know."

"I will."

"Will there be a public funeral?"

"I expect so. And at least a day or two of official mourning. My mother will respect the usual traditions."

"Could you call me as soon as you have arranged something? Your father was highly respected. You should expect a large turnout."

Chow put down the phone, glanced at Wang, and saw that he was still talking to someone. He put another coin in the slot and dialled a number he knew by heart and had never written down anywhere.

"Hello," Zhang answered.

"It's me," Chow said. "I'm in Sha Tin at Our Lady of Maryknoll Hospital. Have you heard about Gao?"

"No."

"He was run down by a van earlier this morning in Sha Tin. He's dead."

"Are the local police involved?"

"Yes, they're on it, but they may not know exactly who Gao is."

"They'll find out soon enough."

"I assume they will. But the thing is, I don't think they should read too much into it. It looks like it was an accident, and we haven't been told anything that suggests otherwise."

"If you did know something, would you tell me?"

"Maybe."

"I always appreciate your honesty, Uncle." Zhang laughed. "What is it you want me to do?"

"Have the case classified as an accident, a hit-and-run. Limit the investigation to the van and the driver. I'm sure you'll find him fast enough."

"Are you sure that none of your brothers was involved in this?"

"As sure as we can be."

"If that changes, I want you to promise to tell me, because it could have an impact on us all."

"I'll tell you."

"Okay," Zhang said. "I'll talk to my people, and if they're leaning towards a hit-and-run, I'll tell them to go with it. There's nothing to be gained by creating a lot of publicity around Gao's death."

"Thank you."

"Keep me posted," Zhang said.

Chow ended the conversation just as Wang was ending his. "Let's talk for a minute," Chow said. "I spoke to Chi. He's heading for Fanling to tell his mother in person. He expects there will be a public funeral, and he'll call me once he has the details."

"I'm glad he's telling her and not us," Wang said.

"Who did you speak to?"

"Ma."

"No one else?"

"He's Mountain Master now, or at least Acting Mountain Master. He's going to tell Ren, Yu, and the others. And he'll contact as many Mountain Masters in Hong Kong, Kowloon, and the Territories as he can," Wang said. "At four this afternoon he wants the executive committee to meet at the Golden Pagoda restaurant. He says he'll book a private room."

"Why so fast?"

"He probably wants us to confirm him as Mountain Master."

"Shit," Chow said.

"Yeah, I know. This may not work out too well for you and your night-market plans."

"You don't sound so enthusiastic either."

Wang shook his head. "The only reason he is Deputy Mountain Master is because he was Gao's best friend and Gao always looked after him. He isn't even close to being as smart or tough as Gao. I can picture the other Mountain Masters running right over him."

"Then why does he automatically get the job? Gao has been Mountain Master since I joined the gang. I don't know how he got the position, but as I remember our rules, Mountain Masters are elected."

"The rules say Mountain Masters *should* be elected, not that they *must* be elected. It has become more common — almost standard — simply to confirm the deputy. That's how Gao got the position, and Tong before him."

"Is there anything to prevent an election?"

"No. All the executive would have to do is agree to hold one."

"And how hard would it be to organize?"

"It would be easy enough. Each gang member has one vote by secret ballot. There are only about 150 of us, so we wouldn't need more than a day," Wang said.

"Then why don't we ask them to do that?"

"This is really quick thinking on your part. Our boss is

dead. We need to take some time to mourn him before we start talking about replacing him," Wang said.

"I'm as upset about this as you are, but like it or not, he is gone, and replacing him is what every member of the executive committee is going to be thinking about. All I want is for them to consider an election."

"What makes you think they'd ever go along with that idea?"

"Maybe some of them have the same doubts about Ma's ability, and maybe one or two think they might make a better Mountain Master than him."

"I imagine a couple of them think that way," Wang admitted.

"Who?"

"Pang probably, and Ren for sure."

"I don't know if Pang would be any better than Ma," Chow said. "I've never found him to be very thoughtful, and he's certainly not progressive."

"By that you mean that neither of them tends to agree with you?"

"You could put it that way if you chose."

"I do choose, but I can't deny that Ren is a notch or two above them in terms of being progressive," Wang said.

"So what do you think?"

"About what?"

"Electing Ren as Mountain Master."

"Uncle, don't try to drag me into this. I've spent my life avoiding gang politics."

"I'm asking for your opinion, that's all. If Ma isn't qualified for the job and if an election is an option, then why not have one?"

"Deciding to have an election is one thing, but having one with more candidates than just Ma is another. What if no one else chooses to stand?"

"Do people have to declare? Why couldn't we have a blank ballot and let the brothers write in any name they choose?"

Wang nodded. "Actually, now I think about it, a blank ballot is the way it would be done. But you can't expect the guys to vote for someone they aren't sure wants the job. Some kind of commitment would have to be made."

"I'll talk to Ren."

"Be careful," Wang said quickly. "You don't want Ma to think you are being disloyal."

"How can following our rules and regulations be considered disloyal?"

"Let me at least tell you how it could be counterproductive where you are concerned," Wang said. "Suppose you talk to Ren and he declines to run, then reports your conversation to Ma. Ma is grateful to Ren and becomes pissed off at you. He also probably appoints Ren as his deputy, and in that position Ren will have to be pissed off with you as well."

"I guess there is that risk," Chow said.

"You guess? If you go to Ren and he decides not to take up your suggestion, I guarantee that you'll end up alienating both him and Ma."

"I see that danger, but if I don't do anything, it seems that Ma will become Mountain Master and everything I've been working on will go up in flames."

"You are so fucking stubborn," Wang said.

"No, I just don't think I should avoid doing the right thing because it is difficult or will piss someone off."

"What is it with you? Why do you always act like that?"

Chow turned and looked at him. "Of all people, I thought you'd understand how I feel."

"Why would I?"

"You are originally from Guangzhou, right? As I remember, you escaped across the border twenty years ago."

"Twenty-two years ago."

"And you're not married, you have no family, and as far as I know, you don't have any interests outside of being Red Pole."

"What's your point?"

"I'm in exactly the same situation. We're the only two members of the executive and two of the very few people in the gang who aren't from Hong Kong or the Territories. When I left China, I left behind a dead family and everyone I loved. This gang took me in, and when I took the Thirty-Six Oaths, it became my family. It is all I have left in this world that I care about. It is only natural that I want to protect it."

"*After having entered the Hung gates, I must treat my sworn brothers, their parents, and relatives as my own kin. I shall suffer death by five thunderbolts if I do not keep this oath,*" Wang said. "It's the first oath that all of us took, but not everyone takes it so literally."

"I do."

CHOW AND WANG REMAINED AT THE HOSPITAL FOR another hour. They met with the doctor again, and then with a hospital administrator. Chow told them about Chi and said they could expect to hear from him sometime soon.

Two policemen arrived. Chow went over to them the moment they entered the building. He said he was a friend of the family and had informed them about the death. He added that the family was anxious to claim Gao's body and have it moved to a funeral home.

"I don't know if they can do that," one of the policemen said. "I'll have to make a call."

While he did so, Chow chatted with his partner and learned that they didn't know about Gao's triad association. If Gao had died in Fanling the connection would have been immediate, but the distance and the localized nature of gangs and police divisions had kept Gao's name secured to his turf.

After making his call, the other policeman returned. "I spoke to Headquarters; they've just classified it as an accident," he said. "The family can claim the body after the hospital has finished the paperwork. That may take a few hours, but I'll let the hospital know it's okay to release the body after everything is done."

"Thanks," Chow said, and then cast a glance towards Wang, who had gone back to the bank of telephones. He waved at him, motioning that maybe it was time for them to leave. Wang ended his call and joined Chow.

"The cops have classified it as an accident. The family can claim the body," Chow said. "We can go."

They left the hospital. Wu was standing by the car about fifty metres down the road. He looked questioningly at them as they approached.

"The boss is dead," Wang said. "Drive us back to Fanling."

Wu's face collapsed. For a second Chow thought he was going to show even more emotion, but he gathered himself together and reached for the back door.

"Who were you talking to on the phone?" Chow asked as the car pulled away from the curb.

"Fan, and then the Red Poles in Sha Tin and Tai Wai."

Fan was Wang's deputy, so it made sense for Wang to brief him, but Chow was puzzled that Wang had spoken to the other Red Poles.

"We still can't assume this actually was an accident. I told Fan to get as many of our men on the street as possible, and for everyone to be on high alert," Wang said. "The guys in Sha Tin and Tai Wai are old friends. We've shared many confidences over the years. I wanted to know what they'd heard about Gao."

"And?"

"They've heard nothing, not a word. They didn't know he was dead until I told them. They were surprised, maybe even a bit shocked. Then I asked them point-blank if there had been any rumours about someone gunning for Gao. They both said they hadn't heard his name mentioned in any way, good or bad, in months."

"Which leads you to conclude . . ."

"That I should still keep Fan and my men on high alert."

"In case . . ."

"Killing Gao is the first step for another gang trying to take over."

"When I asked you about the likelihood of that earlier, you dismissed the idea."

"Not entirely. Being paranoid comes naturally to a Red Pole."

"Fair enough," Chow said.

Wang looked out of the car window. "Where do you want Wu to drop you off in Fanling?"

"I'll go to the office and talk to Ren if he's there. If he isn't, I'll try to get hold of him before four."

"You're not giving up on the idea of an election?"

"No."

Wang sighed. "I admire your persistence. And when I made that remark about how seriously you take the Thirty-Six Oaths, I didn't mean any disrespect."

"I didn't think you did."

"In fact, I remember your initiation. Ren was already Vanguard then."

"Yes, and Pang was Incense Master. The two of them presided over the ceremony."

"That was a long day."

"A long ritual anyway — it took four hours. Tian Longwei had briefed me on some of our history and the ceremony, but there were still things that surprised and awed me."

"Tian was your mentor?"

"Yes, he was the older cousin of one of the men, Tam, who I escaped with from China. The plan had been for Tam and me to work with Tian. We didn't know he was triad until we started. He ran some gambling operations and did some loan-sharking. Tam had trouble fitting in, so he left for Hong Kong and a regular job doing construction or something. I stayed."

"And flourished."

"I was good with numbers."

"There is no reason to be modest around me," Wang said. "You are the best White Paper Fan I have ever known."

Chow started to reply but saw Wu glance at him in the rear-view mirror. He decided that silence was the best policy.

Several minutes later the car entered Tai Po, a town that stood almost halfway between Sha Tin and Fanling and butted up against the southern boundary of Fanling. One of the biggest and most aggressive gangs in the Territories called Tai Po home. Gao had negotiated several agreements with them over the years that had kept them at bay. *Is Ma capable of maintaining that kind of relationship?* Chow wondered as they drove past the town sign.

The car slowed as it left the main road and began to crawl through narrower streets towards Fanling and their offices on Luen Wo Road. Chow checked the time and saw that it was almost one o'clock. Ren normally got to the office around noon, so he expected to find him there.

Wu dropped him off near the office door. As Chow climbed out, Wang said, "Be careful, huh?"

"As careful as I can be under the circumstances," Chow said. "See you at four."

He started to climb the stairs and was halfway up when he heard a buzz of conversation. When he opened the door, he saw that all the office staff and several other people were gathered around Xu's desk.

"Pang just told us about Gao," Xu said, making it clear to Chow that he hadn't relayed their own conversation. "We're in shock. Pang said you were at the hospital with Wang. Is there anything else we should know?"

"It is a terrible thing," Chow said, "but if there is any comfort in this, it is that the police have classified Gao's death as an accident. The driver fled the scene, but I'm sure they'll catch him, and when they do, he will turn out to be a drunk civilian."

"Does the boss's family know?" one of the clerks asked.

"Yes, I spoke with his son, Chi, and he's with his mother now. They will be able to claim the body sometime today and start to make funeral arrangements. We will pass along all the details as soon as we have them."

"What happens now?" the clerk said.

"It's business as usual. Gao wouldn't want it any other way, so why don't we all get back to work," Chow said, and then looked around the office. Most of the private office doors were closed, but lights were on in Pang's and Ren's. He walked over to Ren's and knocked.

"Who's there?" Ren asked.

"It's Chow."

"Uncle, come in."

Ren sat at a desk that was empty except for a large plate of chicken fried rice and a mug of coffee. "What a horrible morning," he said, remaining seated. "It's hard to believe."

Chow took a chair across from him. "I just told the men that the cops have classified it as an accident."

"That's good to hear, I guess, though it won't make any fucking difference to Gao. Just goes to prove that you can't take anything for granted," Ren said. "Ma spoke to the son after you did, and he's at the wife's house with him now. We might know about the funeral arrangements by later today."

"Gao was widely respected. I'm sure there'll be a big turnout."

"Again, what does that matter to him now?" Ren said, then looked at his rice. "Do you want something to eat? I have enough of this for both of us."

"I'm not hungry."

Ren eyed him. "How tall are you?"

"Five foot five."

"And how much do you weigh?"

"About a hundred and thirty pounds."

"I'm only four inches taller but I have twice your weight. You could eat for a month straight and still look like a chopstick next to me."

"I eat a lot, but I burn it off."

"All you do is push paper. How does that burn off energy?"

"I worry a lot."

"We've all noticed how much you worry. Some people don't believe it's all that necessary."

"Planning is an important part of my job," Chow said. "I can't plan without thinking, and I can't think without worrying, particularly given the line of work we're in."

Ren shovelled rice into his mouth as his eyes — small slits beneath broad, thick brows — focused on Chow. "I guess Gao's accident is going to throw a wrench into your latest plans."

"It's a bit too soon to tell."

"If you say so," Ren said with a smile that suggested otherwise. "I'll admit this, though — you've done a hell of a job."

"Thanks."

"I remember when He Wenyan wanted you to become his assistant White Paper Fan. Everyone, including Gao, thought it was too soon to give you that kind of responsibility, but he fought like hell to get you. His judgement was right. When he died, you didn't miss a beat."

"He trained me well."

"I don't know about that, but he did trust you, and for that matter, so did Gao."

"Gao trusted me to do my job."

"Nothing more than that? He didn't share confidences?"

"He treated me as the numbers man, not a confidant."

"And how do you think Ma is going to treat you?"

"Assuming that Ma becomes Mountain Master . . ."

Ren lifted his head from his plate to look at him. "He is the next in line. The job is his by right."

"Well, if he does take the position, I would expect him to be less progressive and more traditional than Gao, so I won't expect very much, if any, support," Chow said. "I also wouldn't expect him to be able to communicate as well with the other gangs, and that would not be a positive thing for us."

"Never mind dealing with the other gangs. I think Ma would do okay. Maybe not as good as Gao, but okay," Ren said, waving a hand. "When it comes to being less progressive, I'm guessing you mean that he won't support your idea that we stop taking protection money and instead move into night markets."

"That's just a continuation of his opposition to most new

ideas," Chow said. "He was just as opposed to my suggestions about our gambling operations."

"I know the numbers. So does Ma, and if you ask him now, he'll probably say he liked your plan but was just testing it."

"I've tried to get him to look at the numbers for the night-market business. He says he doesn't want to waste his time, that I can make numbers do whatever I want."

"I'm sure you can."

"But why would I? Do you think that six months from now I want Ma, you, and the rest of the executive pissed off at me because I manipulated numbers to get what I wanted? How would that be good for my future, not to mention my health?"

Ren turned his back on Chow and looked out to the street. "So, what is it you want from me?" he asked. "If you want me to convince Ma to go along with the night markets, I think that is something I could bring myself to try."

"I'm pleased that you would consider doing it, but that's not why I'm talking to you like this."

Ren swung his chair around so he was facing Chow again. "Uncle, I don't like to play games. You are here for a reason. Be blunt. Tell me what the hell you're trying to say."

"Okay," Chow said, and leaned forward. "I think you should be our next Mountain Master."

Ren blinked, stared at him, and then said, "How did you come up with that fucking idea?"

"I started thinking about it at the hospital when I knew Gao was dead, and the idea firmed up on the car ride back from Sha Tin."

"You were with Wang, right?"

"I was."

"Did you tell him what you were thinking?"

"I did."

"And what did he say?"

"He said he didn't want to get involved in gang politics, and that if I pushed this idea I could end up making enemies of both you and Ma."

"Yet here you are pushing your idea."

"Only because, in good conscience, I don't believe I have any other choice. I don't think Ma is smart enough or tough enough to be Mountain Master. These are difficult and challenging times. We can't afford to take such a large step backwards in terms of leadership."

"You keep forgetting the fact that the position is Ma's by right."

"No, it isn't," Chow said. "Our rules call for an election. One man, one vote, and his choice written on a blank secret ballot."

"Yes, those are the rules, but there hasn't been an election in years."

"That doesn't mean there shouldn't be one now, and that we shouldn't have the right to vote for whomever we choose."

Ren shook his head. "Listen, Uncle, even if I shared some of your opinions about Ma — and I'm not saying I do — I would be reluctant to get into that kind of contest. It could divide the gang. It could make an enemy of Ma."

"You don't have to get into anything officially. All you'd have to do is not deny your interest," Chow said. "Leave the politicking to us. We'd lobby like hell for you, and I don't think it would be that hard. You are respected, and many members would be happy to vote for you if they knew you were willing to serve."

"Who is this 'us' that would be doing the politicking?"

"Fong, Xu, and me. And I think you could count on Wang sending some support your way," Chow said.

"Xu is your assistant, but Fong works with the Straw Sandal."

"Fong is first and foremost my friend. He's loyal to me."

Ren ran a thick index finger down the side of his nose. "As much as I don't like to admit it, you've given me something to think about."

"If Ma has called the four-o'clock meeting for us to confirm him as Mountain Master, we don't have much more time for thinking."

"What if I told you now that I'm not interested in becoming Mountain Master?"

"I'd be disappointed, but I would still make the argument at the meeting that an election should be called."

"What if I told you I was interested and I ended up winning?" Ren said. "What would you want in return?"

"My night markets, Pang named Vanguard in your place, and Fong promoted to Straw Sandal."

"You rattled that off very quickly."

"I've been sitting here thinking about it."

"How did you know I was going to ask?"

"It would have been irresponsible of me not to be prepared for that possibility."

"*Irresponsible* is not a word I've heard used to describe you."

Chow stood up. "Will you let me know what you decide?"

"If the subject of an election is raised at the meeting, you'll find out then, at the same time as everyone else."

(7)

CHOW LEFT THE OFFICE AT THREE-THIRTY TO WALK BY himself to the Golden Pagoda. After meeting with Ren, he had gone into his office to be alone with his thoughts.

Xu had knocked and stuck his head around the door. "Sorry, Xu, I don't have time to chat," Chow told him. "There's an executive meeting at four and I have to get ready for it." This consisted of mentally preparing his arguments in favour of an election and assessing how each of his colleagues would react to them. When he finished, he felt no more certain about the outcome than when he'd started.

He was a few hundred metres from the restaurant when he heard a familiar voice call out. Chow turned and saw Wang walking in his direction.

"I'll go the rest of the way with you," Wang said.

"Any developments since I saw you last?" Chow said.

"No. How about with you? Did you talk to Ren?"

"I did."

"How did he react?"

"He didn't ask me to leave his office. I guess you could say he's still thinking it over."

"Or he's already gone to Ma and dropped a load of shit on you."

"Even if he did, I don't care."

When they were near the restaurant, Wang stepped to one side. "You go in first. I don't want people getting the wrong idea about us."

Chow thought that was ridiculous but nodded. He stepped inside the restaurant and mentioned Ma's name to the host.

"Your group is in our private dining room," the man said, lowering his head respectfully.

Chow followed him to the rear of the restaurant, where they encountered a closed black wooden door painted with a golden pagoda. The host knocked and opened the door. Ma, Ren, Pang, and Yu looked up from a round table.

"We're drinking beer, but if you want anything stronger, just order it," Ma said. "I thought, given the circumstances, that we should keep this as casual as possible. Gao would have preferred it this way. As you all know, he wasn't a man for formalities."

"San Miguel will do just fine," Chow said to the host, and then sat down beside Pang.

"When do you want us to start serving food?" the host asked.

"As soon as our last colleague arrives," Ma said, and turned to the others. "Since this is the beginning of a period of mourning for Gao's family, and as we all consider ourselves part of that family and they a part of ours, I've ordered rice, vegetables, and *lo han jai*. I hope no one minds going without meat."

"I'm sure that's fine with everyone," Wang said, appearing in the doorway.

"And what will sir have to drink?" the host said.

"Beer — San Miguel."

Wang walked to the table and took the seat next to Yu. "This has been quite a shock," he said.

"How are things on the streets?" Yu asked.

"Quiet, but I have as many men as I could get out there."

"I thought the police ruled it an accident," Ren said.

"I know, but we can't be too careful."

"Exactly right," Ma said. "But before we start talking about that kind of business, I want to say that I spoke with Gao's son, Chi, about half an hour ago. The family has decided to use the Hop Sing Funeral Home in Fanling. The service and burial will take place this Saturday. Friday will be a day of mourning and visitations."

"That's very fast," Pang said.

"It seems that Gao planned for this eventuality. The family is doing what he wanted."

The door opened again and two servers entered, carrying trays of beer and food.

"Just leave everything on the table," Ma said.

When the servers left, everyone reached for a beer.

Ma raised his bottle. "To the memory of Gao, a good friend and Mountain Master." The others repeated his toast and drank.

"I know we're devastated by the suddenness of this loss. Gao should have been with us for many more years," Ma said. "But he's gone, and he would have expected us to support each other. I want to say that I've been very pleased by the support I received this morning, particularly from the Mountain Masters in Hong Kong and the Territories."

"Those are big shoes you have to fill," Yu said. "But I'm sure you're up to it."

"Thanks," Ma said. "Now, most of the Mountain Masters made it clear that they'll be coming to the funeral, and we should assume that they will each be sending a band. It will be one hell of a procession when the body is taken from the funeral home to the cemetery, and I don't want us to be outdone. I want to book three bands to represent us."

"It seems strange to be talking about funeral bands," Yu said.

"Perhaps, but this is our new reality."

"Speaking of new, when will you officially become our new Mountain Master?" Pang asked.

"I've been thinking about that, and I've decided I should wait until after the funeral before formally taking the job," Ma said. "It doesn't seem right to do it before Gao is at rest."

The table went silent. Chow noticed that both Ren and Wang were looking down at their plates.

"What do you mean by 'taking the job'?" Chow asked.

"I meant *assume*, of course," Ma said.

"As I remember our rules, the Mountain Master is supposed to be chosen by election. The brothers have the right to vote for their new leader."

"Technically, Uncle, you are correct," Yu said. "But it has become standard — almost a tradition — for the Deputy to step right into the job."

"And why should we bother with all that election nonsense?" Pang said. "There was no vote held when Gao became Mountain Master. He was the Deputy and rightfully rose into the position. Why should this be any different?"

Silence descended again. After an awkward moment,

Chow said, "It has been more than ten years since Gao took over. We have new members who think differently about how things should be done, and I'm one of them. I escaped China and those fucking Communists and was blessed to become part of this family. When you accepted me, one of the things I cherished most was the rights I was given. And one of those is my right to vote for who should be my Mountain Master. I can understand why some of you think it isn't necessary and may be a waste of time, but I promise you, it would be a mistake to ignore what some of the younger members think is an essential right."

"Are you suggesting that Ma shouldn't become Mountain Master?" Pang said.

"Of course not. I can't imagine that having an election will change anything," Chow said. "All I'm trying to say is that we shouldn't take the younger members for granted. Holding an election can only strengthen their commitment to the society and to Ma."

"Uncle does make a point worthy of consideration," Ren said.

Chow saw Wang glance at Ren and thought he detected a slight smile.

"If there was an election, how would it be conducted?" Wang asked. "Pang, you are the ceremonies officer. Does this fall under your jurisdiction?"

"It does, and it isn't complicated. Our rules require a secret ballot. We currently have 162 initiated members and they all have the right to vote," Pang said. "There would be 162 slips of paper numbered between 1 and 162 but otherwise left blank. Each member would register with me or my assistant. If he is on our membership list, he writes his choice for Mountain Master on a slip and then puts the slip into a sealed box. The slips are counted at the end, and the man with the most votes becomes Mountain Master."

"Sounds simple enough," Wang said.

"Simple and virtually foolproof."

"How long would the voting take?" Chow asked.

"There's no set rule, but I think one day — a twelve-hour period — would be reasonable," Pang said.

"Aside from you and your assistant, who else is permitted to supervise the vote?"

"Every initiated member has the right to watch the votes being cast and counted."

"Uncle, are you insinuating that someone might try to cheat?" Yu said.

"I'm just trying to understand the procedure, since I've never experienced it."

Pang shook his head. "What I don't get is why you think you need to experience it in the first place."

"Uncle has made his opinions and his reasons for them quite clear. We should all take a little time to think," Ma said, and pointed at the food. "Lunch is here. Let's eat. We'll talk again when we're finished."

They ate quietly, each man deliberately focusing on his food. Chow imagined that the others, like him, were thinking about how the conversation might develop when they stopped eating. Ma's reaction had been more moderate than he'd expected, but maybe he was using Pang to establish his claim. Ren's intervention had been encouraging without indicating any firm position. Similarly, Wang's questions about the nuts and bolts of the election process were hardly a promise of support. Still, it seemed to him that an election was more of a possibility than he'd thought when the meeting began.

They emptied the plates of food and several more beers were consumed. When the chopsticks were finally laid down, Ma looked around the table. "Okay, you've had some time to think. What does everyone have to say on the subject of an election?"

"I don't see any need," Pang said quickly.

"I don't either," Yu said. "All it would do is delay Ma's appointment and cause short-term confusion."

"I have to say that I agree with Pang that an election probably isn't necessary," Ren said, and then looked across the table at Chow. "On the other hand, I can't dismiss Uncle's argument that it would be a good way to bring our family more tightly together and give our new Mountain Master the strongest possible mandate to lead us into the future."

"Is that a yes or a no?" Pang asked.

Ren shrugged. "It isn't black or white in my mind, but if I'm forced to make a choice, I'd opt for having an election."

"I'm like Ren," Wang said. "I don't feel strongly about it one way or the other, but I don't see how having one could cause any harm. And it might, as Uncle suggests, be a good thing for everyone."

"You know where I stand," Chow said.

"This puts me in a bit of a difficult situation," Ma said, and then paused. "Truthfully, I don't think an election is necessary or that good an idea. But if I support that view, it might look like I'm afraid to have one, and that wouldn't be good either. In fact, it might seem that I'm appointing myself Mountain Master."

"No one would think that," Pang said. "The men would support you."

"I'd like to think that would be the case, but some might not," Ma said.

"What about my point?" Yu said. "Delaying your appointment would only cause confusion. We need things to be settled as quickly as possible. The gang needs to have certainty about its leadership."

"Excuse me, Pang, but just how long would it take to organize and hold an election?" Wang asked. "From what you outlined earlier, it seems it could be done in quick order."

"It could," Pang said.

"We don't want to do anything that will distract from Gao's period of mourning or funeral," Ma said.

"If the funeral is on Saturday, could we have a vote as soon as Sunday?" Wang asked.

"I guess so," Pang said.

"If that's the case, I don't think Yu's point about a delay has much value. What's wrong with waiting three or four days?" Wang said. "Ma said he won't take on the job permanently until after the funeral anyway, so that timing doesn't change. All that changes is that instead of getting appointed on Sunday, he gets elected on Sunday."

Ma sipped his beer and then carefully placed the bottle on the table. "Okay, I've decided. We will have a vote. I don't want it, but I understand the reasons why some of you do. But let's have it on Monday. Sunday is our biggest business day of the week. I don't want to disrupt it."

"That makes sense," Wang said.

Ma turned to Pang. "Where would you hold the vote?"

"We could use our offices. There's lots of space and it will give us privacy," Pang said. "The voting hours could be between ten a.m. and ten p.m."

"Any objections?" Ma said. When no one spoke, he continued. "Then that's settled. Pang, you'll need to inform every initiated member about the date, times, and procedure."

"Yes, boss. I'll put the word out first thing tomorrow morning."

"Great. So, with that out of the way, let's make a point of using the next few days to concentrate on honouring Gao. If Chi sticks to the family's schedule, the wake will be on Friday, followed by the funeral on Saturday and then a funeral dinner that night. We should attend all those events, and I'd like to see as many of our men out as possible," Ma said. "Now, unless there's something urgent one of you wishes to raise, this meeting is over."

All the men except Ma rose from the table and began to leave. Before the door closed behind them, Ma said, "Wang, could you stay for a few minutes? There's something I'd like to discuss with you."

The other four continued through the restaurant and onto the street. Yu and Pang started walking in the direction of the office while Chow and Ren lingered behind.

"Ma was more decisive and a bit smarter than I thought he would be," Ren said when Yu and Pang were out of earshot. "The only reason for that meeting was to get a quick endorsement as Mountain Master. All that stuff about Gao and the funeral could have waited until the family finalized the details. I have to give him credit — when he saw which way the tide was running, he was quick enough and shrewd enough to react to it."

"He didn't get what he wanted, thanks to you and Wang."

"You started it. You put forward a solid case and you hit all the right notes."

"Thank you. Now we need to get to work gathering votes for you."

"I supported having an election," Ren said. "But I don't remember agreeing to let my name stand."

"Is that a joke?"

"Only partially," Ren said, and smiled. "Obviously I can't stop men from voting for me, and if enough of them do and I win, it would be ungrateful of me not to accept the job. But don't expect me to start campaigning or cutting deals for votes. I'll talk to a few friends who I trust, but otherwise I'll be keeping my head down."

"As I told you in the office, we'll handle the campaigning," Chow said.

"Low-key, right? I don't want you to be too aggressive. I don't want Ma to think I'm pitting myself against him," Ren said. "We're all going to have to get along when this is over, and nothing sours working relationships more than women, money, or politics."

"I understand."

"Of course, what I said about not cutting deals doesn't apply to you. If I win, you'll get your night markets, Xu will become Straw Sandal, and I'll be open to every other idea you have, as long as I think it will make us money."

"Thank you."

Ren nodded and looked at the restaurant. "I wonder why Ma asked Wang to stay behind."

"I'm going to ask him when he comes out," Chow said.

"Let me know if it's anything important."

"Sure," Chow said.

"I'll leave you now. You can reach me at home if you need me."

The men went in separate directions. Chow stopped outside a shoe store about twenty metres from the restaurant and waited for Wang. Ten minutes later, the Red Pole emerged. Chow shouted his name and watched as Wang walked casually towards him. "What did Ma want?" he said as soon as Wang was close enough to hear.

"He isn't a particularly happy man," Wang said with a thin smile. "You put a spike in his plans."

"What did he say?"

"He's too subtle to say anything negative about you or the fact that we're having an election he doesn't want. He just asked me if you might have some ulterior motive for promoting the idea of an election. I told him you don't."

"Thanks."

"But then he asked how I could be so sure," Wang said. "I told him that we spent years on the street together and that a man's character gets exposed there. When it comes to your character, I said you're a straight-shooter who is absolutely loyal to the gang."

"That's what I'd like to think everyone believes."

"Not everyone knows you as well as I do, and that includes Ma. When I said you're absolutely loyal to the gang, he asked me if you're loyal to him."

"He's not Mountain Master yet."

"In his mind he thinks he is."

8

ON A NORMAL WEDNESDAY, CHOW WOULD HAVE SPENT
the afternoon in his office poring over the racing form and
then leave for Happy Valley around five. But events had over-
taken that schedule. When he left Wang, he headed for the
office in the hope of talking to Xu and Fong. Xu was there,
but there was no sign of Fong.

Chow approached Xu. "Do you know where Fong is?"

"He got drunk last night, and after you left the restaurant
he and a couple of forty-niners went to Macau. He's on his
way back now and he'll be here any minute."

"Does he know about Gao?"

"Yeah, that's why he's returning so soon. Yu managed to
reach him and gave him the news."

"Is he coming back to the office?"

"That's the plan."

"Then please don't leave until he gets here. I need to speak
to you both, and I'd rather do it when we're all together,"
Chow said, and then walked into his office before Xu could
ask any questions.

He closed the office door behind him, took out his pack

of Marlboros, and lit a cigarette. When he lived in China, he'd smoked Zhonghua cigarettes, a brand that was famous and readily available because it was Mao's favourite. He'd switched brands as soon as he arrived in Fanling, trying Player's and Capstans before settling on Marlboros. He smoked more than a pack a day, and though he understood that he was addicted and that it wasn't good for his health, he just didn't care. He remembered the days in Changzhai when he'd had to ration a pack of Zonghuas to two smokes a day because that was all he could afford. He'd also collected butts off the street in Wuhan, scraping out the few meagre shreds of tobacco left in them in the hope that he'd finally get enough to be able to roll a whole cigarette. Now he could indulge his habit, and doing so as much as he did was just another way to blow smoke at the Communists.

Chow leaned back, his head pressed into the back of the chair, and replayed in his mind the meeting and its aftermath. They were going to have an election, so he had done what he'd set out to do, but truthfully it didn't give him any real sense of satisfaction. He had most likely alienated Ma, and Ren hadn't displayed as much enthusiasm as he would have liked. *Still,* he thought, *what else could I have done? Ma would have killed the night-market idea, and any other idea that ran contrary to the way things have always been done. He likes the tried and true, the easy way.*

Chow tried to think of a single positive thing that Ma had accomplished as Deputy Mountain Master, and couldn't. From a negative viewpoint, aside from trying to block Chow's initiatives, he had contributed to worsening relations with the residents of Fanling by continually trying to expand the number of people and businesses who paid protection money. Chow liked to think there could be a healthy inter-dependence between the citizens and the gang. Ma acted as if he was a lord and they were his peasants. Chow knew how people who were treated like peasants thought and acted; he wasn't that far removed from having been one himself. They could be dangerous if pushed too far — desperate people do desperate things. He was living proof of that.

In some ways Ren's basic attitudes weren't that much more refined, but at least he had shown an ability to listen and to adapt. He had been a strong supporter of the changes Chow wanted to make with their gambling operations, and when those changes were approved, Ren, as Vanguard, had made sure they were implemented in a competent and thor-ough way. *With Ren*, Chow thought, *you don't get a knee-jerk reaction. You actually get some thoughtfulness. Although, if truth be told, it's usually directed towards his own self-interest. And self-interest is what he has displayed during our talks and meeting.* Chow didn't see that as necessarily a bad thing, because if that self-interest was tied to the health of the gang, the gang's future and his own would be inseparable.

"I'm overthinking this," Chow muttered as he put out his cigarette and reached for another. As he did, his phone rang.

"*Wei.*"

"This is Ma."

"Yes?" Chow said, trying to remember the last time Ma had called him.

"Gao Chi just called me. Everything has been confirmed. The funeral will be on Saturday at noon at the Hop Sing Funeral Home. The wake will be on Friday from noon to five. I need you to do something for me."

"Sure. What is it?"

"Normally I would have asked Pang, since he's the ceremonies master, but he's going to be busy organizing the election and I don't want to dump everything on him," Ma said. "I'd like you to order flowers for the wake and I'd appreciate it if you could book three funeral bands. The flowers should be there by Friday morning. Of course, we don't need the bands until Saturday."

Chow was about to say that Pang had an assistant who could look after such matters, but he bit his tongue. This was undoubtedly Ma's way of putting him in his place. "I'll be pleased to look after those things," he said. "Do you have any particular flowers in mind?"

"Whatever Hop Sing thinks is suitable."

"I'll call them as soon as we're off the phone."

Ma paused. "Uncle, I also want to tell you that even though you and I have disagreed about gang business in the past, it was never personal. I have a lot of respect for you. I'm just more of a traditionalist."

"I understand," Chow said, wondering what had prompted that remark.

"And you shouldn't have any worries about holding on to your position. I want you to continue in that job."

"That's good to know."

"Great. Now, make sure you book three bands," Ma said. "I don't want to be embarrassed in front of the other Mountain Masters."

Chow stared at the phone as Ma hung up on him. *What the hell was that about?* he thought. *How many assumptions has Ma made about what I'm thinking? And was that his idea of an attempt to win me over?* He put the phone back on its cradle, but before he could find the number for the Hop Sing Funeral Home, there was a knock at his door.

"Come in," he said.

Fong and Xu entered and sat down in chairs across from the desk.

"How was Macau?" Chow asked Fong.

Fong grimaced.

"How much did you lose this time?"

"Five thousand."

"Do you need a loan?"

"No, I'm okay."

"How did Yu get hold of you?"

"He knew where I was. I have to say, I've never heard him quite so shook up."

"It was a shock to us all," Chow said.

"So now what happens?"

"Gao will be buried on Saturday. There will be a wake on Friday at the Hop Sing Funeral Home, and then the service is on Saturday. Ma has been busy inviting all the Mountain Masters he can reach. I've been put in charge of buying flowers and hiring three funeral bands," Chow said.

"Shouldn't that be Pang's job?" Xu asked.

"According to Ma, Pang is too busy organizing an election for the next Mountain Master."

"Election?" Fong said, surprised.

"You haven't spoken to Yu since you got back from Macau?"

"No, I came straight here."

"How about you, Xu? Have you heard anything about the election?" Chow asked.

"No."

"Well, we're having one this coming Monday. Each initiated member has a right to vote for his Mountain Master, and the executive committee decided that everyone would be given that opportunity."

"I thought Ma would be appointed. Isn't that how it normally works?" Fong said.

"That has become the tradition, but it isn't set down in the rules," Chow said. "I managed to persuade the committee to hold an election."

"Ma went along with that?"

"Reluctantly, and only after Wan and Ren supported me," Chow said. "Your boss backed Ma."

"The two of them are tight," Fong said. "They must be pissed off with you."

"Ma certainly is. He thought the job was his by right."

"The thought of Ma as Mountain Master doesn't fill me with optimism," Xu said. "He's been opposed to everything we've tried to do, and I've never found him to be that capable."

"That's why I wanted the election."

"But even if there is an election, what's to prevent him from winning?" Fong asked.

"Not what. Who," Chow said. "We need to rally behind another candidate. Are the two of you willing to work with me on this?"

"Uncle, are you going to run —"

"Not a chance," Chow said quickly. "I'm too junior, and my mainland background is a huge negative. No, I was thinking of Ren. In fact, I've done more than think. I've pitched him on the idea and he's on board."

"He is competent, he's senior, and he's from Tai Po, which

is local enough. And he has supported a lot of our initiatives," Xu said.

"And if we can get him elected, he's promised to keep supporting them," Chow said.

"I can understand why we'd want to do this, but even if people think Ma is incompetent, not everyone will be prepared to support Ren," Fong said. "Ma is from Fanling and has the loyalty of the local brothers. I know the two of you, with your mainland roots, might think of Tai Po as local, but they sure as hell don't, and there are some who actually think he's too close to the Tai Po gang."

"Then when we're promoting him, we should avoid mentioning Tai Po," Chow said.

"Uncle, do we really want to go down this road?" Fong asked.

"It's too late for me to back away from it now. I made a commitment to Ren, and whether you're with me or not, I have to go through with this," Chow said. "I know Ren isn't perfect, but it seems to me this isn't a choice between better and best. It's more like choosing who we think will do the least damage to the gang and give us some hope for future growth."

Fong looked at Xu and shrugged. "What do you want us to do?" he said to Chow.

"Pang will let everyone know about the election tomorrow. Until he does, I don't think we should do anything. But once it's declared, I want you to round up as many votes for Ren as possible."

"Round up how? And from whom?" Xu said.

"Ren wants us to be cautious. He'd rather not have Ma know that he's contesting the position," Chow said. "So I suggest we talk to the guys who work with us and the guys you consider friends. We should keep it low-key, maybe suggesting that Ren is the better man for the job, rather than push him at people. I also wouldn't be openly critical of Ma."

"Sounds a bit too subtle for some of our guys," Fong said.

"That may be the case, but that's how Ren wants it. He doesn't want to start a war with Ma."

"He'd rather sneak up on him."

"Yes, I guess you could put it that way. You could also say that he doesn't want to generate any animosity that would make it hard, moving forward, for the two of them to work together."

"That does make some sense," Xu said. "I think I can operate within those guidelines."

"Me too," Fong said.

"Good. Now, how many men do you think you can talk to in the next few days?"

"Maybe twenty to thirty," Fong said.

"Same here," said Xu.

"Make sure you compare names. We don't need both of you talking to the same guy. My own list will probably just consist of Wang and Tian Longwei. If I can get them on board, they might bring some of their men with them."

"How many votes do we need?" Xu asked.

"There are 162 eligible voters, so we need eighty-two to get a majority."

"Well, who knows, we might just be able to come up with that many," Xu said.

"Let's hope for all our sakes that we can," Chow said.

Fong yawned and stretched. "I'm tired. It's a good thing you don't want me to start until tomorrow."

"Go home and sleep," Chow said with a smile. "And Xu,

you can take off too. I have to order some flowers and find three funeral bands before I leave for Happy Valley."

"You're still going to the races?" Xu said.

"I am, unless for some reason they've closed the track. And the only time I'm aware they did that was during the Japanese occupation in World War Two. I'll miss the first few races but I'll get there for most of the card," Chow said. "Let's talk again first thing tomorrow morning."

When Fong and Xu had left his office, Chow immediately called the operator and asked to be put through to the Hop Sing Funeral Home. A woman answered his call. "My name is Chow. I'm an associate of Mr. Gao. He died this morning and I've been told that his family has made arrangements for the body to be delivered to your funeral home."

"This is Mrs. Hop, and your information is correct. It should be here within the next few hours."

"Have they finalized the dates and times for the wake and funeral?"

"The wake will be held on Friday between noon and five. The funeral will be on Saturday at noon. The family is concerned that the event on Saturday could be very crowded. They are asking that as many people as possible pay their respects on Friday."

"I will pass on that message to my colleagues."

"Is there anything else I can do for you?"

"Yes. What florist do you recommend?"

"White Lily is in Fanling. They do a lot of funerals."

Chow made a note of the name. "And we want to hire some funeral bands and thought you might be able to make a recommendation."

"How many names do you want?"

"At least three."

"How many do you intend to hire?"

"Three."

"That's a lot."

"He was an important man with a lot of friends."

"I know how important he was — he and my husband were acquaintances," she said. "Give me a minute and I'll see what I can find for you."

One minute turned into several and Chow was starting to get impatient when she came back on the line. But the wait was worth it; she gave him the names and phone numbers of five bands.

Chow knew nothing about funeral bands, but after half an hour on the phone asking questions, he was starting to feel like an expert as he negotiated the numbers of players and banners each of them would provide. After talking to the last one, he reviewed his notes, compared numbers and costs, and phoned three of them back to confirm their attendance on Saturday.

The White Lily flower shop was his next call. It went quickly, because the second he mentioned the name Gao, the florist began talking about how important it was to have a spectacular floral presentation.

"Do whatever you think is appropriate, and then do a bit extra," Chow said. "I don't want to hear a single criticism of the flowers in terms of either quality or quantity."

"We'll make you happy," the florist said.

Chow ended the call and then wondered if he should phone Ma to tell him everything was organized. He looked at the marked-up racing form sitting on his desk. *Fuck him,* he thought. He had done everything he'd promised. There was still time to get to Happy Valley.

9

HAPPY VALLEY RACECOURSE WAS ON HONG KONG Island, and the only way to get onto the island was by ferry. Chow normally took a taxi to Kowloon, the Star Ferry across Victoria Harbour to the island, and then another cab to the track.

It was almost eight o'clock when his taxi came to a halt on Wong Nai Chung Road. He climbed out and made his way into the grounds. Chow paid for a reserved seat on the second floor of the massive seven-storey grandstand. He had just missed the third race, but as he eyed the results, he smiled. His selection hadn't finished in the money, so he figured he was already ahead. He took his seat, looked at his notes on the fourth race, and quickly banished, however temporarily, any thoughts of the day's events in Sha Tin and Fanling.

One of Chow's criteria for evaluating a horse was its trainer. He didn't believe that any trainer could take a mediocre horse and turn it into a stakes winner, but a trainer who always had his horses ready to run and never put them in races where they were outmatched was someone whose horses Chow liked to bet on. In the current season, which was nearing its end, Jerry Ng was a certainty to be named trainer of the year. Ng had a horse in the fourth race, and although its statistics weren't as good as some of its competition, Chow saw that the horse hadn't run in a month and was sure to be fresh. He had made it his pick the night before and saw no reason to change his mind now. He went to the betting window and placed HK$1,000 on it to win and place.

The horses left the paddock and formed for the post parade. There was a buzz in the air, a sense of anticipation that only increased as post time drew nearer. Chow examined Ng's horse and thought it looked magnificent. His confidence swelled and he thought about going back to place an additional bet, but he knew the lines would be long enough that he might get shut out. He decided to stay in his seat.

The 1,200-metre race began. Ng's horse got off to a decent start and the jockey positioned him near the middle of the fourteen-horse field. Chow watched the race unfold with increasing intensity, his attention totally locked on his horse. At the halfway point the jockey eased his mount to the outside of the pack. Chow smiled as he saw the horse almost gliding, with a clear path to the finish whenever the jockey decided to turn it loose.

"Don't wait too long," Chow shouted, his voice lost among the thousands of others giving advice to their jockeys.

Several horses at the front began to fade as Ng's horse picked up its pace and moved into fifth position, then fourth. The jockeys on the leading horses began looking sideways as they gauged the competition. The pace quickened again as the riders urged their horses forward down the final two hundred metres of the home stretch. As they sped by his position in the grandstand, Chow saw that his horse was going full out; the distance between it and the front-runners was shrinking with every stride. With about fifty metres to go, four horses were side by side, separated by no more than a neck's length. Chow yelled his horse's number over and over. As if in answer, it seemed to find another gear and inched forward. It won by a lunging head.

Chow screamed, "Yes, yes, yes!" Then, almost as an afterthought, he looked at the odds board. His horse had gone off at six to one. His win and place tickets were worth HK$12,000.

He waited until the result was official and the first wave of bettors had rushed the pay window before going to cash in his tickets. He was tenth in line at the window and studying the form for the next race when he heard his name being called. He looked to the left and saw Sammy Wing standing in another line.

Wing was about Chow's age and had already made his mark with the triad gang in Wanchai, a district of Hong Kong. He was the assistant to the Vanguard, and it was assumed he would inherit the position when the incumbent, already in his seventies, retired or died. The Wanchai triad was at least four times larger than the gang in Fanling, and it generated substantially more revenue, mainly through drugs and prostitution.

"Hey, Sammy, did you back the winner?" Chow asked.

"I did, Uncle. Did you?"

"Yes."

"Hang around after you cash in. I want to talk to you."

A few minutes later, Chow stuffed his winnings into his jacket pocket. Wing was leaning against a pillar waiting for him. The two men shook hands. Although Wing was only a few inches taller than Chow, he was plump and looked twice as big.

"We were all stunned and sorry to hear about Gao. Condolences."

"Thanks. There's a wake on Friday and the funeral is on Saturday."

"You can count on some of us being there. Chin, our Mountain Master, might make it too," Wing said. "I saw him earlier today; the death shocked him. Gao was younger than many of the other bosses."

"You never know when death is going to come to any of us."

"No, you don't." Wing lowered his voice. "Who is going to replace Gao?"

"Ma is the Deputy."

"I know, but that doesn't answer my question."

"It's the only answer I have."

"If it is Ma, you should tell him to be careful."

"Why?"

Wing shrugged. "There are rumblings."

"What do you mean by 'rumblings'?"

"I'm not sure how much I should say."

"Then why are you saying anything?"

"We young guys have to stick together. If we both stay healthy, we could be working in this business together for a long time."

"I agree, Sammy. So, in the spirit of sticking together, why don't you stop dancing and tell me what it is you're trying to say."

Wing moved closer, his smoky breath engulfing Chow. "When Ma spoke to Chin this morning, he told him Gao's death was an accident. Chin doesn't believe it, and neither do some of the other Mountain Masters on Hong Kong Island."

Chow felt a sudden chill. "Ma told us he talked to Chin and some others, but he didn't mention that they have doubts about its being an accident."

"That's because they didn't tell him what they really thought."

"Why the hell not?"

"This is where it gets tricky," Wing said, reaching for Chow's elbow to pull him so close his lips were almost touching Chow's ear. "First, you need to swear to me that you will never name me or mention my gang as the source of this information."

"You have my word," Chow said, his discomfort growing.

"We have been told that one of the gangs in the Territories is going to make a play for Fanling," Wing whispered. "Getting rid of Gao was the first step in their plan. He was really respected — he had a lot of ties to a lot of gangs and was owed a lot of favours. If they'd gone after your gang while he was still alive, they knew he could call for help and probably get it. Ma doesn't have those ties, and no one owes him anything."

"Which gang is coming after us?"

"I can't tell you that," Wing said.

"Why not?"

"Because we're not a hundred percent sure. We have a good source and we believe him, but even good sources can be wrong. And when they are, things can really blow back in your face."

"But you have enough faith in this source to repeat his story to me?"

"We do."

"Then tell me who he is. My word will be good."

"Uncle, I'd like to but I can't. My boss was very specific about that. He has no business in the Territories, and telling you who it is would be like taking sides — which he won't do, because that would only create enemies in a place where he has none. He thinks the Territories should sort out their own problems. He has enough to deal with in Hong Kong."

"If that's the case, why are you telling me this in the first place?"

"My boss hates it when gangs go to war with each other. All it does is attract the cops' attention, and even though the fighting may be in the sticks, we still get a ton of heat in Hong Kong. He doesn't want that kind of trouble from something that's got nothing to do with him or our business," Wing said. "But he figures that if Ma knows something is on the boil, he'll at least have a chance to talk to the other gang leaders in the Territories. Maybe Ma can find out who wants to come after you guys and work out some kind of deal to forestall it."

"So why doesn't Chin call Ma and tell him what you told me?"

"You aren't listening to me," Wing said. "My boss doesn't want to be involved in anything that's going on in the Territories, even one phone call. I mean, think about it. If he called Ma, what would Ma do?"

"He would probably reach out to the nearby Mountain Masters," Chow said.

"Exactly, and he'd also most likely throw around Chin's name and drag him into it," Wing said. "Ma doesn't have a reputation for being subtle or discreet."

Chow took a step back. "Sammy, it's just occurred to me that you came here tonight specifically to tell me this."

"You are a man with known habits. Wednesday night is Happy Valley night. Even though Gao died this morning, I thought I might find you here."

"There are fifty thousand people at this track. I'm like a needle in a haystack."

"There are ten other men from the gang looking for you on the grounds. One of us would have located you," Wing said. "And if you weren't here or I hadn't found you, I would have contacted you some other way."

"I'm glad you did, though the reason doesn't thrill me."

"So now what?" Wing asked.

"I don't know," Chow said. "I really need to think this through."

"Whatever you decide to do, just remember that the names Chin, Wing, and Wanchai must never cross your lips."

"I gave you my word," Chow snapped.

"Sorry. I shouldn't have said that," Wing said. "You know I wouldn't have been sent to talk to you at all if you weren't trusted and respected."

"*Momentai*," Chow said.

"In fact, you are so respected that if things turn to shit in Fanling, my boss wants you to know there's a home for you in Wanchai."

"I won't let things turn to shit, but thank him for the offer anyway, and for sending you here tonight," Chow said. "Is there anything else we need to discuss?"

Wing shook his head and then looked at Chow's racing form. "You could tell me who you fancy in the next race."

Chow opened the pages. "I like number eight, China Doll," he said, and then reached into his jacket pocket and took out the wad of bills. "Here, put two thousand on it to win for me."

"You're not staying?"

"You know I'm not. I've got to get my ass back to Fanling. I just hope that by the time I get there I'll have some idea of what to do."

10

CHOW TOOK A TAXI TO THE HONG KONG ISLAND STAR Ferry terminal and rode to Kowloon, where he caught another taxi for the trip back to Fanling. He guessed he'd get back to his apartment by ten, so it wouldn't be too late to contact some of his colleagues. But before doing anything, he had to sort out who to call and what to tell them.

If Gao were still alive, he wouldn't have had to think about any of that. He could have repeated the entire conversation with Sammy Wing without mentioning Sammy, Chin, or Wanchai. Gao would have understood the reason for keeping those names out of the discussion and wouldn't have pressed him. Instead, he would have taken the information they'd been given and thought long and hard about its accuracy, then longer and harder about how to act on it.

But Gao wasn't there for him to talk to. And if Sammy was correct, his death had created doubts about the gang's leadership that others were eager to test and exploit. So who should he share this information with, and how should he tell them?

Chow thought about approaching Ma. As acting Mountain Master, he had the right to be the first to know and he was empowered to mobilize the gang if he thought it was necessary. But Chow cringed at the thought of how their conversation might go. To begin with, he knew Ma didn't have the same confidence in him that Gao had, and he was sure Ma would demand to know the source of his information. If Chow didn't tell him, whatever trust Ma did have in him would be further eroded. And if he did tell him, he knew Ma was capable of picking up the phone and calling Chin in Wanchai for confirmation. That confirmation might or might not be given, but either way, the call would ruin Chow's reputation in Wanchai.

Then there was the not insignificant matter of Ma's belief that Chow had an ulterior motive for wanting an election. He might think that Chow's anonymous, unconfirmed information was a trap designed to get him to take some ill-considered action that would make him look foolish, and then pretend to agree that there was a danger but sit back and do nothing. And doing nothing, in Chow's view, was being careless in the extreme. *I can't go to him with this,* he thought. *I have to talk to Wang. He's already mentioned his concerns and he has men on the alert. Telling him, rather than Ma, is entirely justifiable.*

It was almost ten when the taxi entered Fanling. Chow knew Wang wouldn't be at home. He worked nearly every night, using several different bars and restaurants as an operations centre, rotating among them. Chow couldn't imagine that his routine had changed much from when he'd worked with him on the street, so he told the cab driver to take him to the Great Wall, a bar about a kilometre from the gang's head office. When they arrived, he told the driver to wait and went inside. There was no sign of Wang, but one of his men told Chow he would probably find him at Lau's Noodle House. It was within walking distance of the bar, so Chow paid the driver and made his way there.

Wang was sitting at a round table near the rear of the restaurant with two men who Chow knew to be forty-niners. Wang faced the entrance and saw Chow as soon as he walked through the door. He raised an eyebrow and frowned when he saw Chow heading towards him.

"What brings you out so late?" Wang asked.

"I need to talk to you."

"Privately?"

"Please."

"You guys can leave," Wang said to his men. "Check on Song. He's at the Double Head Massage Parlour."

"Double Head . . . That's an odd name, and one that's new to me," Chow said as the men rose.

"It opened just last week. The guy who owns it thinks he's funny. He says his girls are specialists in double massage — you know, first the big head and then the little head," he said, pointing to his groin.

"Charming," Chow said, taking a seat and waving down the waiter. "San Miguel, please."

"I'll have another as well," Wang said, and then looked at Chow. "This is Wednesday. I'm surprised that Gao's accident was enough to keep you away from Happy Valley."

"I was there. I left early."

"What prompted that?" Wang asked, his frown returning.

"Wait a minute," Chow said, as he saw the waiter approaching the table. The man put down two bottles of beer and left. Chow picked his up and drained almost half of it in one gulp.

Wang stared at him across the table. "I'm guessing it was something unsettling. I haven't seen you guzzle beer like that in years."

"*Unsettling* is definitely the right word," Chow said, wiping his mouth with the back of his hand. "At the track I met a senior guy from one of the Hong Kong gangs. He told me that Gao's death was no accident. He was targeted."

"Fuck, fuck, fuck!" Wang shouted. Then he lowered his head and his voice. "I didn't want to believe it."

"There's more," Chow said. "Those rumours you mentioned about other gangs having an interest in us are likely a lot more than rumours. The guy also said that Gao's death was organized by one of the gangs in the Territories. He said the same gang is preparing to make a move against us. Weakening our leadership by getting rid of Gao was the first step in its plan."

"Who is this guy who told you?"

"I can't go there," Chow said. "I promised him I won't disclose his name or what gang he's from, so please don't ask me any more questions like that."

"But you know this guy and you trust him?"

"Yes, on both counts," Chow said. "His meeting me at the track wasn't a coincidence. He was sent there specifically for that purpose by his boss, his Mountain Master."

Wang drank from his beer and then slammed the bottle down on the table with a bang. "Uncle, I'd really appreciate a name. Give me a clue — I won't disclose it."

"Sorry. I gave my word."

"You and your goddamn word," Wang said.

"If it makes you feel any better, I don't think knowing who my source is would help anyway," Chow said. "He wouldn't tell me which gang they think is responsible for Gao's death."

"Why not?"

"Well, although they believe they know which one it is, they're not completely certain. And aside from that, he said his boss doesn't want to get involved, even indirectly, with a war in the Territories. In fact, he said the reason he was telling me this stuff was that his boss hopes we can find a way to prevent trouble between ourselves and the other gang."

"Except we don't know who the other gang is."

"I guess they figure we're smart enough to find out."

"We'd better be," Wang said.

"Do you have any idea at all who it might be?"

"It could be any one of four or maybe five. They all have the same stupid mentality. They think the only way to expand their business is to grab someone else's rather than building their own," Wang said. "But what I don't quite get is why this Hong Kong boss is so keen to prevent trouble out here. What does it matter to him what goes on in the Territories?"

"He says that when two gangs start fighting, the cops don't differentiate — a triad is a triad. They go after all the gangs. Shit that hits the fan in the Territories smears everyone in Kowloon and Hong Kong."

"There's a lot of truth in that, and it does kind of explain why they wanted to let us know. But why did they go to you and not Ma? He talked to nearly every Mountain Master earlier today, so there was plenty of opportunity."

"They wanted any communication to remain confidential. They don't want anyone to know they're passing information to us. They don't want to be seen as taking sides."

"But to repeat, why didn't they tell Ma?"

"They don't think he is sufficiently discreet."

"But he's the Mountain Master."

"Acting Mountain Master."

"Right now there isn't any difference," Wang said. "When do you plan to tell him about this?"

"I don't. I thought it over and decided you're the better choice."

"He would disagree with that."

"I have to do what I think is right."

"There you go again doing what you think is right."

"I know I might be a pain in the ass, but that's how it is. If Ma was told about this, what do you think he'd do?"

"What do *you* think he'd do?"

"He'd start calling all the bosses in Hong Kong to find out who knew what. That would only make him look foolish, and it wouldn't do my reputation any good if he spoke to the boss who wanted the information passed along to us. He would also, I'm sure, contact the bosses in the Territories and start asking more questions. Aside from making us look weak and even stupider, it would give whoever's coming after us a heads-up."

Wang sighed. "I have to admit, all of that is possible."

"Which is why I'm not telling him anything, and why I don't want you to say anything either."

"Which leaves us doing what?"

"Before I answer that, let me ask you a question," Chow said. "Assuming everything I've told you is true, when do you think another gang might decide to move against us?"

"Are you talking about timing?"

"Yes. When would be the optimum time?"

"I don't know when exactly, but I have to believe they'd wait until Gao is buried."

"Why would they wait until then?"

"First, they wouldn't want people to connect them to his death. Second, over the next three days there is going to be a steady parade of Mountain Masters and other senior triads coming to Fanling. They wouldn't do anything to interfere with that or focus undue attention on the visitors. I mean, they'd be stupid to piss off ten or fifteen Mountain Masters. Third, they must know that we're on high alert. If they're going to strike, I'm sure they'd prefer to do it when we've started to relax and let down our guard."

"I agree with you," Chow said. "And if that's the case, it gives us some time to find out who has made us their target. With all those people coming and going, it should be easy enough to talk to some of them without drawing attention to ourselves. Someone is bound to have heard something, and given the right approach — and the fact that they're at Gao's funeral — a few may feel inclined to help us. If we don't have any luck, I can always go back to my source and press him a bit harder for some names."

"Would you do that?"

"I would."

"Then I'm okay with that as a short-term plan. But in the meantime, I'll keep the men on high alert. I'll also make some discreet phone calls and I may even visit a few friends. Who knows, maybe they'll be more forthcoming face to face," Wang said. "But listen to me, Uncle, sooner or later we will have to talk to Ma."

"Not if Ren is Mountain Master."

"You won't let go of that, will you."

"No, I won't. And be truthful with me — you have to admit that Ren would be a stronger leader, maybe even strong enough to make that other gang think twice about coming at us."

"I can't deny that."

"So, at the same time as we're trying to find out who killed Gao, I'm going to be working to get Ren elected on Monday," Chow said. "Can I count on your support?"

"Uncle, I told you already that I've avoided gang politics for my entire life. As much as I like you, I'm not going to let you drag me into this," Wang said. "I supported your position on having an election because I think it is the right thing to do. And I may very well vote for Ren, but I won't discuss it with my men and I certainly would never tell them who I'm supporting or who I think they should vote for. That's all you're going to get from me."

11

CHOW SLEPT BADLY. HIS CONVERSATION WITH SAMMY
Wing kept coming back to him, and he was finding it difficult to accept the idea that one gang would deliberately kill the leader of another. It was abhorrent — one brother killing another. He knew his attitude wasn't shared by everyone in the Hung Society, particularly in and around Hong Kong. When gangs grew in size, they needed more income. As Wang had pointed out, one way — the easiest way — to get it was to grab someone else's turf. There hadn't been an all-out war between gangs on any scale for years, but there had been frequent skirmishes that captured a lot of public and police attention. Several times civilians had been caught in the middle and were killed or wounded. Whenever that happened, all hell broke loose and the cops hammered the gangs for weeks.

He was desperate to know who had killed Gao, but unlike Wang, Chow didn't have many ongoing relationships with the neighbouring gangs, or at least he didn't have relationships with the parts of those gangs that could orchestrate a killing or would attempt to take over someone else's territory.

The White Paper Fan was an administrator — a combination of accountant, lawyer, and banker; most of the others, unlike him, had never been on the street or involved in any kind of violence. He talked to those colleagues often. As he tossed and turned, he ran their names through his head, trying to remember if any of them had acted strangely recently or given any hint that something might be amiss. Nothing came to mind.

After being awake for hours, Chow finally got out of bed at five, made an instant coffee, sat in his leather chair, and lit the first cigarette of the day with his old Zippo lighter. He looked out onto the street. It was raining, and the dimly lit sidewalks shone in front of the familiar shops and restaurants. Like the apartment, those businesses were part of his daily life. This was his home, and the idea that someone might try to take away any part of it enraged him. *Calm down,* he told himself. *Wang is a smart, tough, experienced operator. He won't let anyone just walk in and take what they want.*

That thought of Wang triggered another worry that had kept him awake — Ren's election. Chow had been counting on more than Wang's individual support; he had hoped that the Red Pole would actively recruit his men to support Ren. But Wang had shrewdly anticipated Chow's plan and rejected the idea before he could even ask. That was disappointing, since more men reported to Wang than anyone else. Now it would be up to Xu and Fong to work on those they knew. It certainly made getting Ren elected more difficult. During the night, as he'd thought about it, Chow couldn't help but wonder if he'd bitten off more than he could chew.

He held the Zippo in his hand, its faded and chipped black

crackle as familiar to him as his own skin. The memories it invoked were as fresh and painful as if they were five minutes old. He rubbed his thumb over the lighter's surface, slid from the chair, and walked to the window, where his own reflection stared back at him.

"Gui-San, I think I've been rash," he said aloud. "You know it isn't like me to hurry things . . . Remember how long it took for me to tell you that I loved you? But yesterday I was rash. I don't know another word to describe it. Instead of taking the time to think about the situation in which I found myself, I reacted quickly and made a decision that may not have been wise. I've dug a little hole for myself. Not a big hole, but a hole just the same. Now I've got to find a way out of it. Say a little prayer for me. Help me through this, as you've helped me through so many other things."

He put the lighter on the table and lit a second cigarette with the dying embers of the first. When it was finished, he returned to his chair. He tried to focus on the day ahead, but thoughts of Gao and Ren and Ma kept intruding. He closed his eyes, willing them away. The next thing he was aware of was his phone ringing, and he realized he'd nodded off. He picked up the phone, wiping sleep from his eyes with the other hand.

"Uncle, is everything okay?" Xu asked.

"Yes. Why?"

"I'm at the office. It's past nine o'clock. You're usually here before anyone else. I was worried."

"I had a late night. I'll be there in half an hour."

"I probably won't be here when you arrive, and neither will Fong," Xu said. "Pang told the office staff about the election on Monday and gave each of us a list of names that we're to contact. He made it clear that everyone is expected to vote and he wants that message passed along in person — and he wants us to be firm."

"He's taking this seriously. That's a good thing, no?"

"I suppose so, but I've got a list of thirty brothers, and I don't know how long it will take for me to track them all down."

"Are some of them the same men you had on your list?"

"Maybe ten."

"And how about Fong?"

"I haven't had a chance to talk to him about it, but I can't imagine it will be much different."

"Just do the best you can. If you can't talk to the men on your Ren list today, there's still three days before the election."

"Except Pang also told us we're expected to be at the funeral home for the wake tomorrow and the service on Saturday. I'm not sure it would be appropriate, or appreciated, for us to talk up the election of a new Mountain Master at the funeral of our old one."

"That's a good point, but it still leaves a couple of evenings and Sunday."

"Uncle, we'll do what we can."

"I know you will. Keep me updated," Chow said, and ended the call.

He lit yet another cigarette and took a deep drag. Pang's taking up that much of Fong and Xu's time was something he hadn't counted on. What else could go wrong? As that thought crossed his mind, the phone rang again. He reached for it almost hesitantly. "*Wei*," he said.

"This is Ma. I tried to reach you at the office and was told you haven't arrived yet."

"I went to Happy Valley last night. I got back late," Chow said, irritated at the suggestion that he was somehow neglecting his responsibilities. In his five years working with Gao, he'd never been spoken to that way.

"Don't you think it would be better if we all stayed in Fanling for at least the next few days? There's a lot going on."

"Sure," Chow said, biting his tongue again.

"There's the wake, the funeral, the funeral dinner . . . And I know there'll be at least ten Mountain Masters in attendance. We can't expect Gao's family to manage everything by themselves," Ma said. "You're close to the son, Chi, aren't you."

"We're old friends."

"Well, then, I want you to volunteer your services at the funeral home tomorrow and Saturday. I'm sure the family will be glad of the assistance."

"I'll be pleased to give them whatever help they require."

"Good. I'll let Chi and Mrs. Gao know," Ma said. "Now, where do we stand with the flowers and the bands?"

"The flowers have been ordered and will be delivered tomorrow morning before the wake begins, and I've booked three funeral bands."

"Great work. With all the company we're going to have, we need to put our best foot forward."

Chow shook his head. The Mountain Masters were coming to Fanling to honour a colleague they'd respected, not to look at flowers or listen to bands. There would be enough of both even if Fanling did nothing. "We won't be embarrassed," he said.

"What are your plans for the rest of the day?"

"I'll be at the office in about half an hour. I can't ignore our ongoing business," he said.

"Of course not."

"While I'm there, I'll call the florist and the bands to confirm our arrangements and I'll contact Chi."

"Call me if there are any problems or any changes."

"I will."

"And Uncle, you might not know this, but Pang has set the election in motion for Monday. He's scheduled it for between noon and eight at our offices," Ma said. "He's taking it seriously, as am I. In fact, he's trying to make sure that every brother is told in person about the time and place, and he's insisting that every one of them show up to vote or have a solid reason for not being able to."

"Yes, I was told. I have to say that I'm really pleased with the approach he and you are taking."

"Well, I said to him, 'Pang, if we have to have an election, let's make it a good one. Let's run it in a way that leaves no room for complaining about the results.'"

"The men will appreciate your openness."

"That was my thinking."

Chow butted out his cigarette. "I should get going."

"I may see you at the office."

Chow put the phone back on its cradle. He didn't know whether he was pissed off about Ma's management style or pleased about the serious way he was treating the election. But then, maybe Ma thought the greater the number of votes, the better his chance winning. "What the hell," Chow said, and headed to the bathroom to shave and shower.

He reached the office at ten-fifteen and found it empty except for Pang and one of his junior clerks. He went into his private office, closed the door, and looked at the stack of paper on his desk. Xu would have organized it to a point, but Chow took final responsibility for squaring the accounts from the previous day's business. There was nothing exciting or pleasurable about the work, but it was absolutely necessary because the results represented the lifeblood of the gang. Without proper accounting and cash-flow management, nothing would operate it as it should. One reason why the gang's gambling operations were so successful was that they were underpinned by a strong financial structure. No bet was too large for them to take, and no winnings were too large that the debt wouldn't be immediately honoured. The result was that gamblers came from all over the Territories, and even from Hong Kong, to place their bets in Fanling.

The two busiest days of the week were Wednesday and Sunday, obviously because of the racing at Happy Valley on those days. The Hong Kong Jockey Club rigorously controlled all aspects of racing in the colony, and the government generally supported the club without question. One result was that wagering on horse racing was the only form of gambling that was not illegal in Hong Kong. And even then, the only permitted bets on horses were those made by people who were physically at the track on race day. When full to capacity — as it always was — Happy Valley could hold about fifty thousand people. By Chow's calculation, that meant that twice a week, hundreds of thousands of would-be bettors were being denied the chance to gamble. His goal was to accommodate as many of them as he could through Fanling's large, comfortable betting shops. In the two years since he'd started operating the shops, he had discovered two things: he couldn't build enough of them and he couldn't make them big enough.

Even though he shared the same passion for horse racing

as his customers, Chow had never placed a bet in one of the gang's shops. He didn't think it looked right for gang members to play in places they owned and operated. Gao hadn't made that a policy, and some members such as Fong did bet there, but Chow continued to make his twice-weekly trip to Happy Valley, where he could be as manic as he wanted without worrying about keeping up appearances.

He smiled as he went through the numbers from the night before. Revenues kept climbing, from week to week and month to month. Gao used to predict they'd eventually hit a brick wall, but Chow had great faith in the fervour for horse racing — and for every other kind of gambling — in the average Hong Konger. His main fear was that one day the Hong Kong Jockey Club would realize just how much money they were losing through their restrictive betting practices and open their own off-track betting shops. But so far there was no indication they would. Another concern had been that the shops' success would attract the attention of rival gangs, gangs who would prefer to muscle in on Fanling's operations rather than build their own. Although that possibility had been discussed at various meetings, Chow hadn't taken it seriously, until now.

It took several hours to finalize the accounts. Normally he would have given them to Xu, but since he wasn't in the office, Chow put the paperwork in his desk drawer and locked it. He was hungry and it was past his usual lunch hour, but he intended to go to Dong's Kitchen and knew he could be tied up there for a while. So he reached for the phone and called Gao's house. A servant said that neither Mrs. Gao nor Chi was at home. Chow told her to say he'd call back. Then he phoned the florist. The wreaths were on schedule to be delivered to

the Hop Sing Funeral Home the following morning. He called
the three bands and was told they'd be in Fanling Saturday
morning. With those obligations met, he left the office.

Dong's was on San Wan Road, near the centre of Fanling,
about a half-hour's walk from the office. However, Chow's
appetite was getting the best of him, so he took a cab. The
restaurant served Cantonese cuisine and had all-day dim
sum. Chow was primed for the house specialty, chicken feet
marinated in a secret sauce that attacked his taste buds with
varying layers of sweetness, sourness, and the sharp heat of
some unknown chili. But as good as the food was, it wasn't
the main reason he was going there.

On Wednesdays and Sundays Dong's became one of the
gang's betting shops. The operation was managed by Tian
Longwei, Chow's triad mentor, sponsor, and oldest friend.
Tian was semi-retired; he worked only on race days and for
a few hours in the afternoon on Thursdays and Sundays.

Chow hadn't thought of Tian as particularly old when
they were first introduced by Tam, Chow's Wuhan friend
and Tian's cousin. He had been in his late forties or early
fifties then, but the ten years since hadn't been kind to him.
His grey-streaked hair was now completely white, his face
had deep wrinkles, and he bent over when he walked. He had
arthritis and was in constant pain, although some days were
worse than others. On this Thursday when he saw Chow,
Tian immediately stood up and waved; it was plainly one
of his better days.

"What brings the White Paper Fan here? Are my numbers
off?" he said when Chow reached his table.

"I came to see an old friend . . . and I had a yearning for
Dong's chicken feet."

"It was kind of you to mention me in the same sentence as Dong's chicken feet," Tian said, laughing.

The men shook hands and sat down. Chow noticed the bottle of San Miguel in front of Tian. "Are you supposed to be drinking with the medication you're on?"

"I'm having a good day. What's the point of having one if you can't take advantage of it?"

"Have you eaten?"

"No, but I was about to. Are you really going to join me?"

"I am. What's the point of coming to Dong's if you don't eat chicken feet?"

Tian raised an arm in the air and a young woman hurried to their table. "Bring a beer for my friend," he said, "and an order of chicken feet, har gow, *siu mai*, and fried octopus."

"Two orders of chicken feet," Chow said. "And some sticky rice."

"You're going to have to eat most of that," Tian said when the server left. "I'll do the best I can, but like most things in my life now, the gap between what I think I can do and what I can actually do is huge."

"But you never miss a day here, and your numbers are terrific. You're still one of the best operators we have."

"I'm working because if I have to stay home, my wife will drive me crazy with advice about what to eat, drink, do. She's obsessed with my health, and she goes on like she graduated from medical school rather than grade school," he said. "Running this shop is a snap, because everything is above board. The gamblers love it here — nice surroundings, lots of TVs, we post and honour the Happy Valley odds. They're treated with respect when they lose and paid promptly when they win. They'll be our customers for life."

"Or until the Hong Kong Jockey Club opens their own off-track sites."

"Do you think they'll ever do that?"

"They would be stupid not to, but they're so comfortable with their monopoly that I guess they don't see any urgency," Chow said.

"Speaking of stupid, Fong came here last night."

"Did you let him bet?"

"He tried, but I turned him away. He's a terrible gambler, way more obsessed than most."

"I'm worried about his gambling."

"It's like a fever, a sickness. Sometimes it passes," Tian said. "But is that why you came here, to eat chicken feet and ask me about Fong?"

"No, I came to see you. And for the chicken feet."

"Here they come," Tian said.

The server put a cold San Miguel in front of Chow and then two steaming baskets of chicken feet on the table. The feet were a deep red, almost maroon. Chow had never seen them that colour anywhere else. The two men toasted each other, drank some beer, and simultaneously reached into the baskets containing the feet.

Chow gently placed the toes in his mouth and sucked. Meat and skin came away from bone and the flavour exploded in his mouth. Did Dong use vinegar? If he did, what kind? Did he add sugar or some sweet sauce? There was a hint of soy and perhaps some sesame oil, but the chili was now dominating. It was powerful but not sharp, and it washed over him rather than singling out the taste buds. He finished his first foot, spat the bones onto a plate, and took another. As they finished the first basket, the rest of their food arrived.

Twenty minutes later, they put down their chopsticks. There was no food left on the table, and Chow had eaten most of it.

Tian drained the last of his beer and pointed to Chow's empty bottle. "You want another one, Uncle?"

"No, I'm good."

Tian smiled and leaned forward. "So, when are you going to tell me why you came to see me?"

"I was wondering if you've heard from Tam recently. It must be three years since he and I talked last."

"He's happy, his business is going well, and he and his wife have two kids," Tian said. "I must give him credit; he was smart enough to realize he isn't cut out for our life. How long did he last? I don't think it was more than two months."

"Something like that."

"But you — you took to this life like you were born into it."

"This is the second time I've said this in two days, but for me it was like finding a family. I had nothing and no one, and you welcomed me."

Tian spun the beer bottle between the palms of his hands. "I believe you, but I suspect you didn't come here just for the chicken feet and to talk about the old days."

"You obviously know about Gao."

"Yes. That's all anyone has been talking about."

"It's tragic."

"Of course it is, but not dying in your bed is common in our line of work."

Chow looked at Tian. "What do you mean by that?"

"Simply that we are in a dangerous profession, although,

truthfully, it used to be worse. Things are a bit calmer now. I mean, Gao is dead, but the word is he was accidently hit by a van. In the old days, twenty or thirty years ago, it would have been more likely that he would be shot or knifed by a fellow triad."

"I'm glad those days have passed," Chow said. "But however Gao died, he's gone, and we need to replace him."

"I know, and I also know we're having an election. Pang called me this morning to give me a heads-up."

"He called you directly? He didn't send Xu or one of his people to talk to you?"

"I've been around long enough that I guess he thought I warranted a call directly from him."

"Good. That saves me an explanation."

"Is that why you're here, about the election?"

"That's part of it, though I don't want you discounting our friendship or the chicken feet as a motive."

"I won't discount them. I just want you to give me credit for being able to handle three reasons at the same time."

"Sorry."

"*Momentai*," Tian said. "Now, what's the story with the election?"

"How did you react when Pang told you we're having one?"

"I was surprised, and I have to say that many of the brothers will be as well. The assumption was that Ma would become Mountain Master."

"The rules state that there should be an election."

"Except that an election is rarely called. If the Deputy is capable, he almost always gets appointed."

"Maybe some brothers don't think Ma is capable."

"Is that your position?"

"You're as quick to the point as ever," Chow said. "I'll be equally blunt."

"I would expect nothing else from someone who is like a nephew to me. You know you can always say what you want and not worry about it leaving this table."

"I know," said Chow, but he hesitated as he struggled to find the right words. "I believe Ma would be a disaster. No, that's a bit of an exaggeration. I think he would try to maintain the status quo, but the problem is that maintaining the status quo means standing still, and standing still means you get run over."

"That's young man's talk."

"I'm young. What else would you expect from me?"

"I wasn't being critical. Old men just don't like change; we like things as they are. But young men see only the flaws in what you call the status quo that old men prefer to ignore."

"Ma isn't that old, but he certainly doesn't like change."

"He's old enough. I've known him a long time, and I can tell you that even when he was younger, he didn't have much imagination or interest in change."

"That's why I can't vote for him to be Mountain Master."

"Who else is there?"

"Ren."

"Has he put his name forward?" Tian said, his face impassive.

"He's letting it stand, and if he's elected, he'll take the position."

"So he's actively going after it?"

"No. He doesn't want to risk creating an open rift with Ma."

"How do you know this?"

"I discussed it with him. In fact, I encouraged him to

let his name stand. He agreed, but he made it clear that he doesn't want to be seen as taking on Ma directly."

"You don't think that's a bit underhanded?"

"It isn't ideal, I admit, but I also understand why he wants to maintain gang unity."

Tian shook his head. "It isn't my place to question your judgement, but what makes you think Ren would be any better than Ma? He's about the same age, maybe even older."

"For one thing, Ren has been supportive of the changes I've wanted to make. Ma has been dead set against them."

"You got the changes you wanted because Gao supported you. No one else mattered. Gao always put the interests of the gang first. I've never known Ren to care about any interests other than his own."

"If he becomes Mountain Master, I believe he's capable of putting the gang's interests first."

"You can believe all you want, but I wouldn't count on it," Tian said. "Ren will go along with you as long as it doesn't cost him anything. The moment it becomes awkward or difficult, he'll change course. You can't trust him the way you did Gao."

Chow stared at Tian. He hadn't expected this reaction. "I think I'd like another beer. Can you handle one more?" he asked.

"Sure, but if I fall over you have to make sure I get home."

"You can count on that," Chow said, and motioned to the server to bring two beers.

"I don't mean to sound completely negative about Ren," Tian said, as if he realized his opinion had surprised Chow. "But I've been a triad since I was a teenager, and I've had five Mountain Masters, only one of whom was elected, and I was in my twenties then. Of the five, two — including Gao — were really good, two were so-so, and one was terrible. But good, bad, or indifferent, you can't get rid of them once they take the position, unless you shoot them. And me, I don't fancy ten years or more of either Ren or Ma."

"They are the two most senior officers. They are our only options."

"No, they're not. The brothers can vote for anyone they want."

"Who else is there?"

"You," Tian said, pointing at him.

Chow couldn't believe that Tian was serious, but when he laughed at the suggestion, Tian's expression remained stolid.

"What's so funny? Why do you think I'd joke about something this serious?" Tian asked.

"Who would vote for me?"

"All the members who don't want to vote for Ren or Ma. And I'm sure there are quite a few of them."

"Tian, thanks for the suggestion, but you know I'm too young."

"There's no age restriction for the position of Mountain Master."

"And I don't have enough experience to take on that kind of responsibility," Chow said, surprised at how serious Tian seemed.

"No one is ever fully prepared to do the job, and those who think they are learn quickly enough that they're not."

"I'm too junior. I'm only the White Paper Fan."

"There's nothing that says a White Paper Fan, or a Straw Sandal, or an Incense Master can't assume the top job."

"And I'm not from Fanling, or even Hong Kong. I'm still

thought of by some as a mainlander, and that isn't a compliment," Chow said, beginning to feel uncomfortable.

"Other members might think that someone who knows a bit about life outside Fanling could be a positive force."

"Tian, I appreciate the faith you have in me, but I can't put my name forward," Chow said. "I'm not ready to make that kind of leap. Besides, I made a commitment to Ren. I was the one who convinced him to stand for the position."

"I know how much value you put in keeping your word, but this time it may be misplaced. I don't think Ren is worthy. This gang needs a better leader."

"I think you're being too harsh. I've worked side by side with him for years now, and I haven't seen anything that causes me concern."

"Yes, you were working with him, but remember that Gao was alive and running the gang. He kept everyone in line. The Ren you knew was doing whatever Gao wanted. With Gao dead, the leash is off."

Chow leaned towards his friend. "I'm sorry, I don't want to argue with you or question your judgement, but I have to believe that Ren is the man I've experienced and not the one you're talking about."

Tian sipped his beer. As he put down the bottle, his face sagged and he looked tired. "I've made my case," he said. "If at any time between now and Monday you change your mind, let me know. I still have friends. There are still people who will listen to me. I can get you votes if you decide you want them."

Chow got up and walked to the other side of the table. He put his hand on Tian's shoulder and gently squeezed it. "I'm lucky to have friends like you. I can't tell you how much it means to me. But Tian, I'm not going to stand for the position. However, I would appreciate it if you would vote for Ren, and encourage your friends to do the same."

Tian looked up at him with a wry smile." Goddammit, you piss me off — and you've helped me get pissed," he said. "I won't tell you I'll support Ren, because I don't know if I can, but I'm going to take you up on your offer to make sure I get home."

"We'll share a cab. I'll drop you off on the way to my apartment," Chow said. "But no more talk about the election."

"You started it."

"I know, and now I've exhausted it," Chow said. "Tomorrow the focus will be on Gao's wake, and then the funeral on Saturday."

"I'll be at both."

"We've bought ten wreaths and booked three bands. We're told some of the other gangs have booked bands as well."

"That's quite a send-off, but if anyone deserves it, it's Gao," Tian said, struggling to his feet. "The most bands I've ever seen at a funeral is six, so this could be a record."

"That will please him," Chow said, reaching for Tian's arm to offer support.

"What would have pleased him more was having a few more years of life. When you get to my age and have my health problems, staying alive is a job all by itself."

12

CHOW AND TIAN DIDN'T SPEAK MUCH DURING THE CAB
ride. The fatigue Tian had displayed in the restaurant
had intensified, and he sat slumped against the side of
the door. When they got to Tian's apartment building,
Chow helped him out of the taxi and walked with him
to the entrance. He tried to remember how many beers
Tian had consumed, knew it had to be at least three, and
made a mental note not to encourage him to drink the
next time they were together.

When they reached the building door, Tian stopped
suddenly.

"Are you feeling all right?" Chow said.

"I'm just a bit drunk and tired," said Tian. "But I remember
now that I wanted to ask you if you and Zhang have spoken
about Gao's death."

"We did. We agreed it was an accident."

"So you're still communicating?"

"We are."

"Good. I speak to him every week or so, but of course he
is too close-mouthed to talk about you," Tian said. "I respect

him for that, although I can't help feeling curious, since it was me that brought the two of you together."

"We've continued to help each other — within reason, of course."

"He's a superintendent now, the youngest in the Hong Kong Police Force," Tian said. "Who would have thought that would happen? And who knows how much higher he can go?"

"I can't begin to guess where he'll end up."

"I'm sure he is just as uncertain about what your future holds."

"Tian, I have no idea what my future holds. How can he? Or you, for that matter?"

"Forgive an old man for rambling," Tian said, his tiredness becoming more obvious.

Chow opened the door and led Tian to the elevator. When he had seen him safely in, he left the building. He had intended to go back to his own apartment, but it was only late afternoon and too early to call it a day. Heading to the office was an option, but he'd finished his work for the day. He looked down the street that ran past Tian's building and saw a mah-jong parlour that was owned and operated by the gang. He knew there would be at least one brother working inside, so he decided he'd use his time to do some politicking.

There were two triads in the parlour. Chow spent fifteen minutes reminiscing with them about Gao, telling them about the election, and gently lobbying for Ren. He didn't get much of a reaction, but they did direct him to a foot-massage parlour on an adjoining street where another brother hung out. That man was more receptive and, after promising his support, sent Chow to a billiard hall where he could find another three or four triads. And so it went for several more hours as Chow worked his way homeward. By the time he reached his apartment, he had spoken to nine members, making a note of their names so Fong and Xu wouldn't revisit them. All nine had obviously heard about Gao, but none of them had heard about the election until he told them. He got two commitments for Ren and two more seemed to be leaning in that direction. It would have been discouraging, if not for the fact that no one came right out in support of Ma.

It was dark by the time Chow walked into his apartment. He turned on the lights, hung up his jacket, took a beer from fridge, and settled into his chair. He reached for the phone to call Xu, then remembered that he still needed to contact Chi. He dialed Gao's home number, and this time Chi was there.

"I hope this isn't inconveniencing you," Chow said. "If it is, you can call me back."

"No, I'm glad to hear from you. It's been a long and stressful day. We spent most of it at the funeral home making arrangements. The people there have been terrific, but my mother is a mess and needs a lot of my attention, so I wasn't completely focused."

"That's understandable," Chow said. "I'm actually calling to see if I can be of any help tomorrow and Saturday. I can be at the funeral home anytime you want, and I'll do whatever you think is appropriate."

"I'd like that. My mother hardly knows anyone who my father did business with, and I only know locals — people like you. It would be great if you could stand at the door and make sure my mother and I know who we're meeting."

"I'll be pleased to do that. Mrs. Hop said the wake starts at noon. What time should I be there?"

"Eleven should be fine," Chi said. "And Uncle, do you have any idea how many people might be attending?"

"You're going to have a large turnout. Certainly all of our gang, and we've been told to expect up to ten Mountain Masters and other senior officers from gangs in Hong Kong and the Territories. Then, of course, there will be the rest of your family and your father and mother's friends. So it could easily be two hundred people, maybe closer to three hundred."

"Then we'll need your help even more than I anticipated."

"You have it. My time is yours for the next two days," Chow said. "See you in the morning."

He debated between calling Fong or Xu next, and opted for his assistant because there was a greater chance he'd be home. When Xu's wife answered the phone, he heard voices in the background. "It's Chow. Am I interrupting your dinner?" he said.

"Not at all, we just finished," she said. "Let me pass the phone to Xu."

Xu came on the line. "Hey, I've been trying to reach you. I was going to invite you to dinner. Fong is here."

"I went to see Tian and then I walked home from his apartment, stopping along the way to tell some brothers about the election. I have a list of the ones I spoke to, which you can share with Fong."

"How did it go?"

"So-so."

"With Tian or the brothers?"

"The brothers. Tian was quite negative about Ren."

"That's not surprising," Xu said. "They used to be rivals."

"When?"

"Before you came to Fanling. When Gao became Mountain Master, there was talk that Tian would be named his deputy, or at least Vanguard. Instead he was left on the street as an assistant to the Red Pole."

"I never knew that. In all the time I've known Tian, he's never mentioned it or said anything negative about Gao, Ren, or Ma."

"That isn't his style. He's not one to complain."

"How was your day?" Chow asked.

"Fong and I were just comparing notes. Our experiences with the guys we spoke to were much the same as yours, a bit of a mixed bag," Xu said. "There's a lot of sadness about Gao out there. He was really admired. I mean, I knew that, but I was surprised by the extent of it. Most of the guys were more eager to talk about him than the election."

"But they said they're going to vote?"

"Yes, but only after we convinced them there really is going to be an election, and that Pang is insisting that everyone participate," Xu said. "Truthfully, most of them expected that Ma would be appointed, and I think some were disappointed that he wasn't."

"I'm surprised that Ma has that kind of support."

"I'm not convinced he does. I think the brothers are supporting what they think is a tradition. I think they believe Ma has a right to the position," Xu said.

"So they'll vote for Ma?"

"I don't know. We didn't ask anyone outright who they'd vote for, and no one volunteered that information. They were pretty tight-lipped —" Xu said, and then paused. "Just a second, Uncle, Fong is talking to me . . . He says there wasn't much enthusiasm for Ren or Ma, but to be fair, no one openly criticized them either."

"How did Ren's name enter those conversations?"

"You told us not to actively promote him, so we didn't, but when we were asked who the choices might be, we mentioned him and Ma."

"We might have to be a bit more aggressive, a bit more out in the open. But that should wait until after the funeral," Chow said.

"That doesn't give us much time."

"It's all we have, and we have to make our best use of it."

"Changing the subject, Uncle, have you heard from Wang?"

"No."

"He called here about an hour ago, looking for you. He said if I talked to you to tell you to call him at home. He'll be there until nine."

"I'll do that right away," Chow said. "Enjoy the rest of your evening. I'll see you tomorrow at the wake."

"What time are you going?"

"Eleven. It doesn't start until noon, but I told Chi I'd help the family greet the mourners."

"Would you like Fong and me to get there early as well?"

"That might be a good idea," Chow said, and hung up.

He lit a Marlboro and took a deep drag. So far his election plan wasn't working out exactly the way he'd hoped. Chow had thought he could persuade Wang and Tian to throw their support behind Ren, but while he might get Wang's personal vote, Tian's was up in the air, and neither of them was prepared to go out on a limb for Ren. He had also thought that when the men on the street realized they could vote for their Mountain Master, Ma wouldn't be many people's first choice. *Maybe my approach is too subtle,* he thought. *Maybe I have to ask Wang and Tian to support Ren as a personal favour to me. Maybe we have to start pushing Ren as the best man for the job.* But whatever he chose to do, he knew it would have to wait until Sunday.

He reached for the phone again and called Wang.

"Where have you been? I've been trying to reach you all afternoon," Wang said.

"I was with Tian Longwei, and then I spent time with some of the brothers chatting about the election."

"Were you successful?"

"It's hard to say. I wasn't asking people directly who they'd support."

"You didn't ask Tian? He's a friend. He wouldn't have minded."

"I'd rather not get into what Tian and I discussed."

"Knowing how much Tian dislikes Ren, I'm not surprised that you don't want to talk about it," Wang said.

"What I'd rather talk about is why you were trying to reach me," Chow said, ignoring the gibe. "I assume it has something to do with what we talked about last night."

"It does. I made a lot of phone calls this morning. Then I drove to Sai Kun for lunch with their Red Pole, and then I swung over to Mong Kok for a short meeting with my counterpart there. They won't tell anyone why I was meeting with them," Wang said.

"So the meetings were productive?"

"Yes. The phone calls were a waste of time — all I got was the usual bullshit expressions of sympathy for our loss — but the meetings were worth the trip."

"What did you find out?"

"Don't get too excited," Wang said. "I wasn't told anything specific to the degree we want, but I did get independent confirmation that what your Hong Kong contact told you has some basis in fact. The word among the Mountain Masters is that Gao was knocked off and that there's a gang that wants a piece of Fanling. No one is saying which gang that is and no one is asking too many questions. Because, frankly, they don't give a fuck."

"But they at least agree that another gang was responsible for Gao's death?"

"Oh yeah, they'll go that far. They even made it clear that it's a gang near us, a 'neighbour with ambition,' as one of them put it."

"But no possible candidates, no conjecture?"

"My friend in Mong Kok said that if we think about it hard enough we should be able to come up with enough of them on our own."

"It would have to be a bigger gang, so that excludes Fo Tan, Tsuen Wan, and Kam Tin."

"But that leaves Sha Tin, Tai Po, and maybe even Tai Wai," Wang said.

"Do you know anyone in those places you can trust?"

"Trust to ask the type of questions that need to be asked? No, I don't."

"Neither do I. And we can't start stumbling around the same way we were afraid Ma might."

"Listen, Uncle, I was thinking about this on the drive back from Mong Kok. I'm beginning to believe there isn't a hell of a lot we can do to prevent another gang making a move on us," Wang said. "If they've made up their minds and are determined to follow through, who or what will stop them? Even if we find out who they are, what good will that do us if none of the other gangs want to get involved? We're on our own."

"Do we have enough men to take on Sha Tin?"

"No, and not Tai Po either. Tai Wai would be a more even match."

"So we just sit back and do nothing?"

"We have a couple of days to say goodbye to Gao and do a bit more poking around," Wang said. "I suggest we use the time to do some serious thinking as well. It could come down to two options: we negotiate or we fight. And if we negotiate, we'll have to make some decisions about what we're willing to give up. Come Monday, we're going to have a new Mountain Master, and he's going to need our advice. It would be nice if you and I were on the same page."

"That depends what page you're on," Chow said.

"It's a bit soon to talk about that. I'd like to know who we're contending with before making up my mind."

Chow was disappointed with that answer and was about to say so when he caught himself. It was premature to start judging Wang. He needed to know on which side he'd fall before doing that. "So, as you said, we have a few days to figure that out."

"I'll keep digging, and you find out what you can from your end."

"I will, and I'll see you tomorrow," Chow said, ending yet another less-than-satisfying conversation.

Chow stood and walked to the window. He did not like it when things got muddled. He liked clarity, because clarity brought certainty. He hated confusion and its disruption of his sense of order. He knew he couldn't control everything in and around his life, but that had never stopped him from trying. The way he dressed, his daily congee breakfast, the trips to Happy Valley, his work schedule — they were his routines, all part of a structure he'd built that made him comfortable. Now someone was threatening him. Not threatening him personally, but by attacking the gang, they would start tearing down the structure he'd helped to build. And when one part fell away, what was to prevent everything else from crumbling along with it?

The phone rang. It was only a few feet away, but he was mentally so far removed that it didn't register until the third ring.

"*Wei*," he said.

"Ma here."

Not again, Chow thought. "Yes? What can I do for you?"

"I've been on the phone with Mountain Masters for most of the day. Nine have confirmed they're coming to Fanling. Not all of them will be at the wake, but we'll see them at the funeral. That's a remarkable number, given the short notice," he said. "Some of them grumbled about the fact that everything seems rushed, but I explained to them that while Gao insisted on a wake and a funeral, his wife wants it over as quickly as possible. This timing was the best compromise."

"I was wondering why it was happening so quickly."

"Well, that's why. And then, of course, it's better to hold it over the weekend, when more people can attend."

"I can see the logic in that," Chow said. Before Ma could ask, he continued. "I confirmed the flowers and the bands. Then I spoke with Gao Chi about providing the family with some help. He was happy to accept the offer, so I'll be at the funeral home for most of the day tomorrow and Saturday."

"That's great. And did you speak to your people about the white envelopes?"

"I thought that would be Pang's job."

"He prefers that the senior officers deal with their own men."

"That's not a problem. What amounts are recommended?" Chow asked. The money would go into white envelopes that would be given to the Gao family.

"I'm giving fifty thousand dollars, Ren and Pang twenty-five thousand each. You, Wang, and Yu should give ten thousand dollars. Your men should give something between one thousand and five thousand, but nothing less than one thousand."

"I'll let everyone know."

"Then that's that," Ma said, but he stayed on the line.

"Is there something else?" Chow asked.

"Yes. I was wondering," Ma said slowly, "how close are you to Ren?"

"I'm no closer to him than I am to you or Pang or Yu," Chow said cautiously. "Why do you ask?"

"When we had our meeting at the restaurant, I sensed that the two of you had already discussed this election thing."

"We hadn't," Chow said, surprised at Ma's sensitivity.

"He didn't raise the subject with you?"

"No. In fact, I didn't even know about the possibility of having an election until it was mentioned to me."

"By whom?"

"Tian," Chow lied.

"He's been around long enough to remember when we had one."

"He has seen a lot."

"What else did Tian say?"

"What do you mean?"

"Did he say he thinks there should be an election? And if he did, did he say why?"

"He just said it's in the rules. When I remembered that, I thought it might be a good idea to have one, for all the reasons I gave at the meeting," Chow said. "Ma, I hope you don't think my motivation was personally directed at you. I've never been critical of the job you did as Gao's deputy, and I don't doubt your ability to handle the top job."

"I didn't think that was the case. I just thought it was odd that Ren supported your recommendation," Ma said. "And then tonight I started to hear murmurings."

"Murmurings?"

"I've been told that Ren wants to be Mountain Master and that there's a quiet campaign underway to get support for him."

"Have you asked him if he's interested?"

"I don't want to do that; he might misinterpret the question. I don't want him to think I'm discouraging him or that I'm afraid he might run," Ma said. "But I was thinking that you might have heard something."

"I've heard nothing," Chow said.

"Would you tell me if you did?"

"I would be quite uncomfortable about getting into the middle of a contest between my Deputy Mountain Master and the Vanguard."

Ma paused, and Chow wondered if he'd offended him. Then Ma said, "I know that you and I haven't always seen eye to eye on things, but I think you're a bright guy with a terrific future. I expect I'll be making a decision next week about who to appoint as my deputy. You should know that you are on my short list."

"That's a real compliment," Chow said, not believing for a second that anyone other than Yu or Pang would become Ma's deputy.

"But keep it to yourself."

"Of course."

"See you tomorrow. It will be an emotional day for all of us."

When the line went dead, Chow remained standing with the phone pressed against his ear for at least another five seconds. Then he noticed that his palms were sweaty and wiped them on his pants.

Ma had rattled him. He'd never thought of him as being subtle, sensitive, or intuitive, but now he was starting to recalibrate that opinion. The man he'd just spoken with was quite unlike the man he'd known for the past ten years. There had been none of his usual crudeness or bluster, which was even more remarkable given the fact that he might believe Ren was running against him. *Not might believe,* Chow thought. *He does believe it.* Someone hadn't been careful enough in their promotion of Ren. He had no idea who, but once the lid was off that pot, it didn't really matter. Ren needed to be told.

Chow dialled his home number. "This is Chow Tung. I'd like to speak to Ren," he said to the woman who answered.

"He's not here. He's out at dinner and told us not to expect him back until late."

"Do you know where he is?"

"No," she said, in a manner that suggested he was rude to ask.

"Could you please tell him I phoned. I'd appreciate it if he could call me back, regardless of the time."

"I'll tell him," she said.

Chow sat in his chair and lit a cigarette. Three hours later he had smoked his way through half a pack, waiting for a call from Ren that never came.

"Gui-San, I'm more sure than ever that I was rash. And that the hole I dug is a lot deeper than I first thought. I hope you said that prayer for me," he said as he lifted himself out of the chair and headed for his bed.

13

IT WAS SIX-THIRTY WHEN HE LEFT THE APARTMENT TO walk to the congee restaurant. It had rained during the night, but the air was still heavy and Chow knew that the typical hot and humid Hong Kong summer was almost upon them. He stopped at the newsstand to get a copy of the *Oriental Daily News* and then remembered that he hadn't bought it the day before. He asked the vendor if he still had a copy of yesterday's paper. He did. Chow opened it and turned to the racing page. China Doll had won the fifth race at odds of three to one. The bet Chow had left with Sammy Wing would pay him $8,000. It was the kind of start he needed after the way the previous day had gone.

His plan for the day was simple. Breakfast, followed by three hours at the office, and then the rest of the day at the Hop Sing Funeral Home. Since he hadn't heard from Ren the night before, he assumed that the Vanguard had gotten back too late or hadn't received his message. Chow was almost pleased that Ren hadn't called, because it had given him time to rethink his conversation with Ma and put together a proposition for Ren. He would call him when he got to the office.

Chow had congee with sausage, spring onions, and you-tiao while he reviewed Sunday's racing card at Happy Valley. Depending on how the next two days went, he realized it might be wiser for him to spend Sunday in Fanling rather than at the track, but he wouldn't make that decision until he had to. There was no harm in being prepared for either eventuality.

At seven-thirty he climbed the stairs to the offices and was met at the top by Xu. His assistant was wearing a grey suit, white shirt, and black tie. The only other time Chow had seen him in a suit was at his wedding.

"Morning, Uncle," Xu said. "I put the late-night receipts drop on your desk. I'm heading out to pick up the balance."

The door leading from the street to the office entrance had a mail slot cut into it. On the inside was a large metal box with a lock. Before Chow became White Paper Fan, the gang's businesses had sent in their records every few days, and some even weekly. He instituted a daily drop and provided the mailbox so there could be no excuse for not doing it. The practice not only kept their records absolutely current, it limited the possibility that something unpleasant — such as thievery — would go undetected for any length of time.

"I should still be here when you get back. I won't leave for the funeral home until about ten," Chow said.

He waited until Xu had closed the outside door behind him and then walked to his office. He normally dove right into the paperwork, but that wasn't his priority today. He picked up the phone.

The woman who had answered Ren's phone the night

before did so again, but this time she asked Chow to wait while she got him.

"Hey, what's going on?" Ren finally said after several minutes.

"I phoned your house last night and left a message. I wanted you to call me back."

"I didn't get any message. I got home very late and everyone was asleep," Ren said. "What's so urgent that it couldn't wait until morning?"

"I talked to Ma last night. He phoned to ask me about the funeral arrangements, and then he switched gears."

"Ahh."

"Exactly. He wanted to know if you and I conspired to come up with the plan to hold an election. I told him no, but while he didn't come right out and say he didn't believe me, he might as well have," Chow said. "Then he said he'd heard rumours that you want to become Mountain Master and are actively seeking votes. I told him I know nothing about that."

"I can't say I'm shocked," Ren said. "While your idea about being discreet sounded good, I thought it might not work."

"We were very careful. No one was overtly pushing your name."

"I believe you, but some of our guys gossip like girls. All it takes is for one of them to guess right and start blabbing. And guess what, it took only one day," Ren said. "Also, Ma isn't stupid and has a keen sense of self-preservation. When he chooses to pay attention, he can be very sensitive to what's going on around him. This election obviously has his attention."

"Well, at this point I guess it doesn't matter who said what or what Ma actually knows. We need to make a decision."

"About what?"

"Whether or not you should come out in the open and formally declare."

"Why would I do that?"

"Why not? The cat is as good as out of the bag anyway," Chow said. "If people know you're in the running then we can do some real campaigning for you."

"How did the lobbying go yesterday?"

"Not bad."

"What does that mean?"

"Pang asked Fong and Xu to tell a list of brothers that an election is going to be held and that they're expected to vote," Chow said. "There was some confusion about why an election is needed, how it will be conducted, and who they can vote for. That took up a lot of their time."

"But once they got past that and things were made clear, who did the brothers indicate they were going to support?"

"Many of them were noncommittal. But then, they don't know that you're actually in the game."

"Are you telling me you have no idea which direction this could go in?"

"The way things stand, I guess I am. But if you declare, we'll know very quickly."

"It sounds to me that you're saying I could lose whether I declare or not."

"I think the sooner the men know you're in the race, the better our chances."

"But you can't guarantee I'll win."

"Of course not, but I believe your chances will improve dramatically once the men know they have a strong alternative to Ma."

Ren became quiet. Chow waited, unsure of what he was thinking.

"Let me ask you this," Ren said finally. "As things stand, do you think it's likely that Ma will win?"

"Anything is possible."

"That's not an answer. That's an evasion."

"Yes, it is, and I apologize," Chow said, gathering his thoughts. "What I should have said is now that Ma suspects he has competition, he'll bring persuasion and pressure to bear. And if he's the only one out there really running and you're still sitting on the sidelines, you'll have to assume that he can pick up enough support to win."

"But if I get off the sidelines, there's still no guarantee I'll win."

"Correct."

"Then why in hell would I bother doing that?"

"I thought you wanted to be Mountain Master."

"I do — more than you know — but at what cost? If I oppose him publicly and I lose, I'm going to be humiliated, I'll have made an enemy of Ma, and my power is certain to be cut back," Ren said. "One of the main reasons I went along with your idea was that I could stay in the background. Now, after only one fucking day, you want me to be out on centre stage."

"I think that may be necessary if you want to win."

"But, to repeat, it still isn't a guarantee that I will win."

"That's correct."

"Tell me, Uncle, if I don't declare, if I decide to stay on the sidelines, will you and your friends keep lobbying for me?"

"Only if you want us to."

"You didn't say that with much conviction."

"To be blunt, we seem to have as much — if not more — conviction than you do right now."

"That's a fair comment," Ren said with an abrupt laugh. "So, what this means is that I have a decision to make about whether I'm in or out. I'm going to have to think about it. And don't worry; I know I don't have a lot of time, so I won't leave you dangling. But until I decide, why don't you guys give it a rest."

"You're right about not having a lot of time."

"I don't mean to sound unappreciative; I know you've stuck your neck out for me," Ren said. "And I promise you this, Uncle, if I'm in, I'll go at it full bore. If I'm not, then I'll simply tell Ma I'm supporting him and you can do the same."

"I hope you're in."

"Right now, honestly, it's a fifty-fifty proposition," Ren said. "Now, what time are you going to the wake?"

"It starts at noon, but I want to be there early to make sure our wreaths have arrived. And I'll be there until it ends at five, because I promised to help Chi and his mother."

"I don't imagine I'll get there until midafternoon. By then I should have an answer for you."

Chow put down the phone with a thud. Ren might be more capable than Ma, but he was also more slippery. Whatever enthusiasm he'd originally had for Ren's candidacy had almost evaporated. Tian's opinion of Ren had made an impact, as had the fact that the rank and file didn't seem that keen on him. On top of all that, the conversation they'd just had was deflating. If Ren's condition for staying in the race was a guaranteed job without his having to make any effort, then maybe it was better if he didn't run.

That would leave Ma as Mountain Master, and if Chow's

recent talks with him were any indication, Ma had more respect for him than he'd previously thought. He didn't believe that Ma would ever make him his deputy, but maybe, just maybe, he was prepared to be more open-minded where business was concerned.

"Things may work out better than I thought. Gui-San must be praying for me," Chow said quietly to himself as he took the first sheet of paper from the pile.

14

WHEN CHOW ARRIVED AT THE HOP SING FUNERAL HOME and Crematorium at five to eleven, there were already people milling about in the courtyard. It confirmed his expectations of how large the event was going to be.

This was not his first visit to Hop Sing and he knew his way around the place. He walked through the courtyard and down the side of the building to a door marked "staff." He opened it and was met by a small, grey-haired woman wearing a black pantsuit and a badge that read "mrs. hop."

"Good morning, Mrs. Hop. I'm Chow Tung. I'm not sure you remember me from previous visits, but I worked with Mr. Gao," he said. "I'm here to check on our wreaths."

"I remember you now that I see you," she said. "Your wreaths arrived at seven this morning. You shouldn't have sent so many. With the others we've received, we've hardly any room for the mourners."

"Gao Lok was greatly respected."

"So I'm aware."

"Is the family here?"

"They came at midnight and spent the night here in vigil."

"All of them?"

"They took shifts."

"Where can I find them?"

"The Iris Room, but we expect it will fill up very quickly, so we're using an adjacent room as a place where people can wait."

"Can I go through? The family is expecting me. I'm going to be helping as a greeter."

"Go ahead. If we have as many people as I think we'll have, they'll need you."

Chow went to the double doors with the name Iris stencilled in gold on each, and entered a long, narrow room. Gao's open coffin was at the far end. It was surrounded by wreaths and flanked by a large formal photo. Chi sat to the left of it, near the shoulder of the coffin. Gao's wife sat on the right. She and Chi were dressed completely in white, the traditional colour of mourning. A saffron-robed monk stood several metres behind her. Off to one side was another monk, wearing a black cone hat, black robes with silver trim, and a black-and-white pendant around his neck depicting yin and yang. Chow knew that the man in black was a Taoist and the man in saffron a Buddhist. Gao was covering all his bases. It was quiet inside the room just then, but once the public wake began, Chow knew the monks would start chanting from their respective scriptures.

Two rows of chairs on the left were already occupied by various in-laws and other relatives. Like Chow, they were wearing a mixture of black and white. The walls were lined with wreaths, so many of them they were in double rows. At the foot of the coffin was an altar covered with white candles and burning incense. Chow walked to it, lit a joss stick, placed it between the palms of his hands, and bowed deeply to Gao's photo. When the stick burned out, he put it in a receptacle that already had many in it, turned to Gao's wife, and bowed three times. He then took a white envelope from his pocket and put it into the donations box.

At a wake, mourners were not expected to speak to the bereaved family, but given the relationship between him and Chi and the role he was expected to play during the day, Chow approached Gao's son. Chi nodded a welcome and then handed Chow a white armband. "We really appreciate your doing this."

"It's going to be very busy here today. The courtyard is already full of people," Chow said. "I think I should go to the entrance and help with organization."

"Thanks. We'll see you later."

Mrs. Hop met Chow as he left the Iris Room. "I'm glad you're doing this. The room is going to be crowded and there could be some shoving and pushing. You are better equipped to deal with it than my staff. Your people intimidate them."

"Mrs. Hop, I've been here for other funerals and I've never seen our people act badly."

"Have you been to a wake for a man of Mr. Gao's stature?"

"No."

"I have, including Mr. Gao's predecessor. It was chaotic."

"I'll keep order."

She placed her hand on his arm. "I know you'll do the best you can, but can I make a suggestion?"

"Sure."

"It might be better if you let only a handful of people, say six to eight, into the Iris Room at one time. That way people can pay their respects in a proper way and not feel rushed or pressured.

You can use our anteroom to hold more people, and the rest you can leave in the courtyard until it is their turn."

"That sounds reasonable enough. Let me see what I can do."

"I also think we should open the doors a bit earlier than planned."

"Yes, let's do that. In fact, let's open them now."

Chow left Mrs. Hop and walked into the courtyard. In the time he'd been inside, the crowd had increased by at least a third. He eyed it and spotted Xu in his suit and Fong, wearing black slacks and a white shirt, standing in the throng. "Come over here," he called.

"I'm recruiting the two of you," Chow said when they reached him. "We're going to act as traffic cops today. We're going to allow only eight people at a time into the Iris Room, where the wake is being held. We have the use of an anteroom next to it, where another twenty can wait their turn. Everyone else will have to wait in the courtyard. I'm going to explain this to the crowd and then I'm going to ask them to get in line."

"No one's going to like that idea," Fong said.

"I don't care. Besides, it will move quickly enough. People won't linger; they'll pay their respects and then leave."

"What are you going to do when Ma and Ren get here, or the Mountain Masters from other gangs? You can't make them line up," Xu said.

"No one will complain if they go directly inside, so I don't think that's a worry," Chow said. "Now come and stand next to me while I tell everyone how things are going to be run."

He had to shout to get everyone's attention, but eventually people listened. When Fong and Xu directed them to form lines, there weren't any problems.

The morning and the early hours of the afternoon flew by as a steady parade of people entered the funeral home. There was a half-hour break at two, and shortly after the wake resumed, the first Mountain Master arrived.

His name was Johnny Kang and he ran Sha Tin. Chow knew he was a cousin of Sammy Wing, which immediately triggered the thought that maybe Wing hadn't wanted to name Sha Tin as the threat to Fanling because of that relationship. Before he could pursue the thought any further, Kang approached.

"Is Ma here yet?" he asked, his voice sombre.

"No."

"He told me he'd be coming at two-thirty."

"He must be running late."

"How about Jen? Have you seen him?" he said, referring to the boss from Mong Kok.

"No. You are the first Mountain Master to arrive."

"The plan was for the three of us to go in together. Ma thought it would make a nice impression on Mrs. Gao."

"I'm sure it will," Chow said. He looked past Kang to see Ma entering the courtyard with Jen. "And Ma and Jen have just arrived."

Kang turned to look. The triads in the courtyard moved aside to let Ma and Jen pass, and then stood back as the three Mountain Masters converged. They shook hands and muttered something to each other.

Ma walked to the door, with Kang and Jen just behind him. "How's it going in there?" he said to Chow.

"It's been busy but not crazy. We've been allowing only a handful of people in at a time. That's why you see these lines out here."

"Uncle is always efficient," Ma said to his two colleagues. "Gao used to say, 'If you want to be sure a job gets done well, you should give it to Uncle.'"

"I appreciate your efficiency, but we don't have to get into one of your lines, do we?" Kang said.

"Of course not. Follow me," Chow said.

Most of the people in line were triads, which wasn't surprising, since Gao had few friends outside the society. As Chow led the three Mountain Masters past the queue and towards the Iris Room, there were no protests from those who were waiting. Everyone understood the pecking order. Even if they didn't, Kang and Jen were such fierce-looking men — squat, muscular, and scarred — only a fool would get in their way. Chow thought Ma looked soft and meek by comparison.

Chow led them into the Iris Room. "Mrs. Gao, Mountain Masters Kang, Jen, and Ma are here to pay their respects."

The men already in line stepped aside to let them pass. The Mountain Masters walked towards the coffin. They lit joss sticks, bowed once to the coffin, three times to Mrs. Gao, and then deposited their envelopes.

"Your husband was a great man and a great friend," Kang said to her.

"He will be missed by all," Jen added.

Mrs. Gao lowered her head, and Chow could see that she was more uncomfortable than pleased with the compliments. Chi had told him many times that his mother was embarrassed by her husband's profession. It was her pressure, along with his own distaste for violence, that had motivated Chi's decision to leave the triads.

"I will be here tomorrow, and Sha Tin has engaged a funeral band," Kang said.

"The same is true for Mong Kok," said Jen.

"Mrs. Gao, I'm told there could be as many as ten bands tomorrow," Ma said. "No one can remember a funeral where there were so many."

Mrs. Gao began to sob.

"My mother appreciates that you came to honour my father," Chi said. "We will certainly welcome you tomorrow."

The three Mountain Masters turned to leave. Chow walked beside them and escorted them out of the room. Just as they got to the exit, Ren stepped inside. Everyone came to a halt.

"Ma, I've been waiting to talk to you all day. Do you have a minute now?" Ren asked.

Ma glanced enquiringly at Kang and Jen. "Go ahead," Kang said. "We'll wait outside."

Chow walked with Kang and Jen into the courtyard. The crowd was beginning to thin but there were still lines. The two Mountain Masters shifted their feet and looked absent-mindedly around. Chow knew they wanted to be gone but were committed to stay until Ma joined them. It was five minutes before the door opened and Ma came out.

"We can go now," Ma said to his colleagues, and smiled.

Chow watched them leave and waited for Ren. He had a good idea what had caused Ma's smile, but he needed to hear it.

Ren came out and looked at Chow. "Bad news, Uncle. I've told Ma he has my full support," he said without hesitation. "I told him I've heard rumours that I want to become Mountain Master and assured him that isn't the case. I said I will do whatever he wants to help him get the job."

"Thanks for being direct," Chow said. "But I wish you'd told me first. I thought we agreed on that."

"What difference does it make who I told first? Ma was here. Why not take advantage of it?"

"You seem very relaxed about the decision."

"It's a load off my mind. The less I have to worry about, the happier I am."

"I thought that was Ma's objective in life."

"Maybe it is, but he's caught up in the moment."

"And when reality bites?"

"Don't be too harsh in your judgement of him. And don't forget that we have a good team here in Fanling to support him."

"Did you tell him I urged you to put your name forward?"

Ren stepped forward and put a hand on Chow's shoulder. "I did not. I've appreciated your support and would never do anything to disrespect it," he said. "Look, Uncle, you're young; you'll have your own chance one day. Maybe this was mine and maybe it wasn't. All I know is that I wasn't prepared to lose. Now I've got to go. I'll see you tomorrow at the funeral."

Chow watched him leave, almost more annoyed with the way Ren had handled things than with the decision itself.

"What was that about?" Xu asked, coming to Chow's side.

"Ren just told Ma that he has no interest in becoming Mountain Master and that Ma has his full support."

"Was that bullshit?"

"No, he meant it."

"What the hell?"

"I had a hunch he was leaning that way. The only good thing about his decision is that it was made before we were too far out on a limb."

"Will there still be an election?"

"Sure, why not? Ma will be officially endorsed, so no one

can question his legitimacy, and the men will feel that their opinions have counted. It's all positive."

Xu move closer to Chow and said, "I have to tell you, I thought Ma had a great chance of winning anyway."

"I know. Ren and I talked about that this morning. That's why he withdrew. He didn't want to risk losing."

"You'd better tell Fong," Xu said, pointing to their friend, who was still playing traffic cop in the courtyard.

"I'll tell him now," Chow said, and began to walk over to Fong. He had almost reached him when he heard his name called. Looking towards the back of the line, he saw Tian.

"I tried to reach you at the office earlier," Tian said.

"I left early. I've been here all day."

"We need to talk."

"What's going on?"

"I don't want to discuss it here."

"We can move to one side."

"I would prefer real privacy," Tian said. "Can you meet me at Dong's Kitchen?"

"When?"

"What time does the wake end?"

"Five."

"Can you make it there for six?"

"I don't see why not, but can you give me some idea of what this is about?"

"I'll see you at six," Tian said with a vigorous shake of his head.

15

ATTENDANCE AT THE WAKE BEGAN TO THIN BY LATE afternoon, and the people who came to pay their respects seemed to be mainly friends of Mrs. Gao and Chi, so there was less of a need to keep order. Chow knew he could have left Hop Sing at four and not been missed, but a combination of wanting to fulfill his commitment and not knowing what he would do until six o'clock kept him on duty.

A few minutes after five, he re-entered the Iris Room. Chi was standing at the foot of the coffin with his arms wrapped around his mother. Chow hadn't looked closely at the dead man when he'd been there earlier. Now he did and saw Gao dressed in a black suit, white shirt, and black tie. His face was pale and waxy, except for his lips, which were an unnatural bright red. Chow didn't understand why morticians thought red lips were necessary. Gao's body was covered with photos, flowers, money, and a few personal items.

"We're about to close the coffin," Chi said.

"Do you want me to leave?"

"No."

Mrs. Hop was in the room and approached the coffin with an assistant. "Is it time?" she asked.

Chi nodded.

Mrs. Gao pried herself free from her son, went to the coffin, and gripped the side with both hands. She bent over and kissed her husband on the lips, then ran her hand over his forehead and hair. Her body convulsed as she began to sob. Chi put his arms around her again and gently pulled her back. The coffin was closed.

"Thanks for everything you did today," Chi said to Chow.

"It was my honour."

"Will you join us for the wake dinner? We've been eating nothing but *jai*, rice, and fruit for the past three days. Tonight we're having roast pig, chicken, and duck."

"I appreciate the invitation, but I have a business dinner to attend."

"But we will see you tomorrow?"

"I'll be here by eleven," Chow said, and then turned to go.

Chi stopped him. "You haven't received your envelope," he said, pressing it into Chow's hand.

Chow waited until he had left the room to open it. It contained a white handkerchief to wipe his tears, a piece of candy to remove the bitter taste of death, a Hong Kong ten-dollar note to bring him luck, and a string of red thread that symbolized good fortune. He put the candy in his mouth and the handkerchief and money in his pocket, then tied the string around his wrist. He stood quietly for a moment, taking deep breaths as he tried to gather himself. When he felt under control, he went outside.

Fong and Xu were waiting for him in the courtyard.

"Want to grab some dinner?" Xu asked.

"I've love to, but I promised Tian I'd see him at six."

"What's going on?"

"I don't know. All he said was that he needs to talk to me."

"If you finish early, call me."

"I will," Chow said, and then looked at his two friends. "I owe both of you an apology for dragging you into this Ren election business."

"Forget about it," Fong said.

"I don't need an apology either," Xu said. "I thought the idea made sense. And besides, we hardly spent any time on it. My only regret is that we're going to be stuck with Ma, and I can't help thinking that he's going to be a weak leader."

"Maybe he is, but Ren didn't have the guts to take him on, so what does that say about him?" Chow said. "The bottom line is that we're going to end up with Ma, so we should start getting used to the idea. And I have to say, my last conversation with him wasn't that bad. It actually gave me some hope that he can be convinced to support some of our proposals."

"I guess stranger things have happened," Xu said.

Chow looked at his watch. "I think I need to get going."

"Where are you meeting Tian?"

"At Dong's Kitchen."

"Where else? It is his second home, after all," Xu said. "How are you getting there? Do you want a ride?"

"No, I'm going to walk. I need to clear my head."

"Will you need us here tomorrow?" Fong asked.

"Yes. Thanks for reminding me, and thanks for your help today. I know the Gao family appreciated it," Chow said. "Can you be here by eleven to play the same role?"

"Sure," Fong said.

"I'll be here," Xu said.

"Great. I'll see you both then," Chow said, and turned and walked across the courtyard.

Dong's was a three-kilometre walk from the funeral home, and Chow figured it would take him about forty-five minutes to get there. Hop Sing was halfway up a hill that rose gradually from the town and ended at the cemetery, so the first part of his walk was downhill. The way would be relatively flat when he reached the centre of town, but he knew he'd be slowed down by traffic and stoplights. It would have been easier for him to have accepted a ride with Xu, but he really did need to clear his head and hadn't wanted any company. He'd been struggling all day to keep painful thoughts of the loved ones he'd lost from overpowering him. He'd done well until he opened the envelope that Chi had given him. As simple as the gifts were, every one of them was more than he'd been able to give when the people he'd loved had left his life.

He had watched his grandmother, father, sister, and mother die, all within ten days. The village doctor, such as he was, had shaken his head in pity when Chow's mother told him what roots and greens she had been feeding to her starving family. He then sold Chow a bag of herbs that, when boiled, was supposed to be a liquid antidote. His grandmother died the day after he made her drink some. He threw the rest away. With his entire family bedridden, it fell to Chow to dig his grandmother's grave, on the edge of the land that his father had farmed until the Communists took it from him. When the hole was dug, he wrapped her body in a sheet and carried her to it. With help from a neighbour, he lowered her into the ground and covered her body with dirt.

His father died next. He was probably the strongest of

them all physically, but his spirit was broken and he had little will to live. In some ways, Chow thought, death might have been a relief for him, although certainly not the agony that accompanied it. Another grave was dug, another body lowered into the ground.

His sister and mother both fought to hang on, desperate to outlive the poison that was making them retch and soil themselves so often that keeping them hydrated was almost impossible. His sister went first, silently, in the middle of the night. His mother died the next day, screaming in agony and grief. He buried them next to his grandmother and father. The entire family was resting together, separated by dirt walls only a metre thick.

The only thing that had kept him from disintegrating, from giving in to the pain that threatened to consume him, was Gui-San. She had taken his despair and helplessness and turned them into hope. Then she was gone, and there was no one to ease that pain. Not then, not since, and, he imagined, not ever.

Despite Chow's experiencing so much death, it hadn't hardened him. What it had done, slowly but relentlessly, was make him realize how precious life was, and how important it was to live in a way that honoured it. For him, honouring life did not mean preserving it at any cost. Life had to have meaning, and that meaning came with the values he believed in and clung to. There were lines he would not cross. When his values came into conflict with the prospect of death, he never backed down. To do that, in his mind, would have been a betrayal of everyone he'd loved.

As he walked to Dong's, Chow stopped several times to wipe his eyes with the hankie that had been in the envelope.

But by the time he reached the restaurant, the worst was over. For the thirtieth, fiftieth, or hundredth time since he'd been in Fanling, he'd relived the memories of the events that had brought him there and put them back in their mental boxes.

Tian was at his usual seat and waved as Chow came through the restaurant door. "Are you hungry?" he asked when Chow reached the table.

"Yes," Chow said, noticing that Tian had a pot of tea in front of him. "No San Miguel today?"

"Not today — and probably not for quite a few days — but don't let that stop you."

"I've never had dinner here. What do you recommend?" Chow asked as he sat down.

"I like their *dau miu*, and they have good barbecued pork and duck."

"I'll have some of each, and a San Miguel."

Tian called for the waiter and gave him the order. When the server left, he said, "That was a tremendous crowd today. Gao is getting one hell of a send-off."

"Don't you think he deserves it?"

"He deserves all of it. How many bands will there be tomorrow?"

"Seven, maybe more. But I think I told you that yesterday."

"My memory isn't what it used to be."

"Bullshit."

"Yeah, bullshit," Tian said, and smiled. "I have something to tell you, but I'm still trying to organize my thoughts."

"What could possibly require that amount of thinking?"

"Your friend Ren."

"Ah, back to him again."

"It wasn't anything I planned. It was forced on me."

"I'm listening," Chow said, noticing that Tian had become serious.

"One of my men phoned me at home this morning, which I thought was a bit unusual. We talked some business — nothing special — until he asked me who I was going to vote for in the election," Tian said. "I told him I didn't know, and then he said Fong had paid him a visit yesterday and was indirectly promoting Ren. He said he'd thought about it and had decided he would vote for Ma."

"Did he tell you why?"

"He said he doesn't trust Ren."

"Why not?"

"He'd received a call from an old friend who told him that Ren had dinner in Kowloon last night."

"Since when is dining in Kowloon a problem?"

"It isn't, but Ren wasn't alone."

"My dear Tian, I'm sure this is leading somewhere, but I do wish you'd get to the point instead of dragging it out."

"Ren was having dinner with Tso Qiao."

"The Mountain Master in Tai Po?"

"The very same," Tian said. "You do know that Ren has roots in Tai Po."

"So I've been told."

"Well, it's true. And he and Tso have been friends for years."

"I still don't see why two old friends having dinner in Kowloon should be a concern."

"Why would they meet in Kowloon? Why not in Tai Po or Fanling? It's as if they didn't want anyone to know."

"You don't think you're reading too much into this?"

Tian leaned forward. "I think Ren was trying to enlist Tso's help to become Mountain Master."

"How could Tso help?"

"The Tai Po gang has connections in Fanling that Tso could call on. And if he did and Ren won, then he'd be indebted to Tso, and that would mean we'd be indebted to Tai Po. I can't think of anything good coming from that," he said. "Gao was always careful to keep Tso at arm's length, and he had his reasons."

"I heard Gao recite those reasons more than once," Chow said.

"Was Gao wrong or misdirected?"

"I never thought he was."

"If he wasn't, what has changed that justifies Ren's cozying up to Tso?"

The server brought Chow's beer and a plate of barbecued pork. Chow waited until he'd left before saying, "Is your concern based solely on your belief that Ren is seeking Tso's help to get himself elected?"

"Isn't that enough?"

"I imagine it might be if Ren were actually running. But he isn't."

"You told me yesterday that he is."

"He changed his mind this afternoon. He even told Ma he has his full support."

"Are you serious?"

"Completely."

"Then why did Ren meet with Tso in Kowloon?"

"I don't know, and neither do you. So let's keep this conspiracy theory of yours strictly between us."

Tian shook his head. "He really withdrew?"

"He did. Now let's enjoy our dinner and not spend any more time worrying about Ren and Tso."

As the men ate, their conversation dwindled. Chow thought Tian looked dejected, as if disappointed that his suspicions about Ren had been wrong. For his part, Chow looked calmer than he felt. Tian's last question had hit a nerve. Why had Ren met with Tso in Kowloon? There were probably many good reasons, and a long friendship was a perfectly reasonable explanation. But what if Ren had met with Tso to talk about the election? *No,* Chow thought, *it makes no sense. Why would he do that and then withdraw?*

Chow and Tian shared a taxi again, but this time after dropping off his friend, Chow rode it home. It was still early; he thought about calling Xu, then discarded the idea. He didn't feel like reliving the day, and he certainly didn't want to talk about Ren.

Why did Ren meet with Tso in Kowloon? The question just wouldn't let go. The one sure way to get some kind of answer was to call Ren and ask him, but that would be an awkward conversation. How could he frame the question without it sounding like an accusation? How could he even raise the issue without it looking like he was spying on Ren or poking his nose into matters that didn't concern him? And even if he could find a way to ask the question and Ren gave him an answer, how in hell could he verify it? *And verify what? I'm getting as paranoid as Tian.*

There was one thing he could do, he thought, and without reflection reached for the phone.

"This is Uncle," he said when his call was answered. "I'm sorry to call you at home, but I was wondering how you felt the day went, and if you had any thoughts about tomorrow."

"It was a good day. The other Mountain Masters were impressed with the turnout and the way things were

organized," Ma said. "If we have that many people tomorrow and all the bands show up and the Mountain Masters
who've told me they're coming do, it will be even better."

"I think tomorrow will do well by Gao," Chow said. Then
he paused.

"Is there something else you want to tell me?" Ma asked.
"Is there a problem with the bands?"

"No, but I've been thinking all day about our talk last night,
specifically the rumours you heard about Ren manoeuvring
to become Mountain Master," Chow said. "I made a point of
speaking to him today and asked him directly if he's angling
for the job. He told me he isn't, and I have no reason not to
believe him."

"You didn't have to do that, but I am glad you took my concerns seriously instead of thinking I was just being insecure,"
Ma said. "I spoke to him as well — or I should say he spoke to
me. Without any prompting, he told me he'd heard the same
rumour and wanted me to know I have his full support."

"I'm glad that's been put to rest."

"Me too. Now all that's left is to put Gao to rest, and then
to start a new chapter in the history of the gang."

Chow put down the phone, lit a cigarette, and slid into his
chair. As trivial as it might seem, knowing for certain that
Ren had pledged his support to Ma took the edge of Chow's
unease. Ma was correct; it was time to start a new chapter.

16

AS IT HAD BEEN THE DAY BEFORE, THE HOP SING Funeral Home was a busy place when Chow got there at quarter to eleven on Saturday morning. The courtyard was almost full and there were people congregating on the street, mingling with clusters of uniformed band members. Chow walked among the bands until he found the three he'd hired. He asked them how they planned to organize themselves and was told to leave things in their hands. The bands all knew each other and had worked together before, although not with so many at one time.

"This was an important guy, huh?" one of the band leaders said.

"He was a Mountain Master — he ran the triads here in Fanling. There will be a lot of other senior triads here today," Chow said.

"We'd better play well then, with no fuck-ups."

"Not fucking up is a very good plan," Chow said.

Fong and Xu were waiting for him in the courtyard. He hadn't spoken to either of them since the day before, and he expected questions about his dinner with Tian, but after greeting him, all Xu said was, "It is going to be crazy today."

"I know. I'll find out from Mrs. Hop how many chairs they're setting up inside. The Iris Room can be opened up to accommodate more than two hundred people. We should probably start forming lines now, so that when the doors open, people can enter in an orderly way. It will also make it easier to count them. We don't want to let in more than she thinks the home can handle."

"We'll get started," Xu said.

Chow climbed the steps to the front door. It opened before he got there and he saw Chi standing in the entrance.

"It looks like another huge crowd," Chi said.

"There will be more people than yesterday. You can count on most of our gang and a lot of senior people from the Hong Kong, Kowloon, and Territorial gangs. I hope they don't overwhelm your mother. Yesterday she looked uncomfortable with Kang and Jen."

"She's still in shock."

"Who can blame her? Your father's passing was so sudden and unexpected."

"The girlfriend didn't help either," Chi said. "She knew about her, of course, but it's hard for Mom to accept that the girlfriend was the last person to see my father alive."

"The Mountain Masters who come will want to pay their respects to her. Will that be okay?" Chow asked, not wanting to pursue the topic of the girlfriend.

"Yes. She's not as sensitive as she appeared yesterday. In fact, when I was young and my father was the Red Pole, we had gang members coming and going from the house all the time. She used to make them tea," he said, and smiled. "That changed when I became a Blue Lantern. She wouldn't allow any talk about the gang in the house, and she told my father that his friends were no longer welcome. She never changed that attitude, not even after I quit."

"What about the rest of your family, and the family friends? Will they be comfortable sitting among a sea of triads?"

"I'm sure they'll be fine. They're mostly here to support my mother. Triads don't mean anything to them."

Chow pointed to the Iris Room. "How many seats are inside?"

"I counted them when I got here this morning. There are 260 in the room itself and they can put another sixty in the anteroom."

"Are there reserved seats?"

"We've put aside seats on the right for the family, and part of the front row on the left is for some close friends."

"Do you think you could reserve about twenty seats for some of your father's senior associates?"

"Of course. I'll ask Mrs. Hop to do that."

"If the service starts at noon, what time do you expect it will end?" Chow asked.

"We'll greet people for two hours. The service will last for another hour, and then we'll walk to the cemetery from here. It's less than a kilometre away. We've arranged for monks to be at the gravesite for three-thirty. I figured it might take us half an hour to get out of here and up the hill."

"It might take longer than that. There are nine bands outside."

"Was it necessary to have so many?"

"It wasn't deliberate. People simply want to show their respect. And you know what some of the gangs are like — if one hires a band, the others feel they have to as well. And in this case, Ma told me to get three."

"That sounds like Ma. He always went overboard where my father was concerned," Chi said. "Well, I'd better warn my mother about the bands, and I'll talk to Mrs. Hop about the reserved seating."

Chow returned to the courtyard. A long line had already formed and the men were waiting politely. "Nice job," he said to Xu.

"Thanks," Xu said. "And you should know that Wang is here. He's at the back of the line."

Chow went to meet him. "You don't have to stand in line," he said when he reached him. "You can wait inside in the anteroom."

"I'll stay in line. I have men here; it's good for them to see us all treated the same."

"Will they object to your having a reserved seat?"

"No. This is sufficient as a show of solidarity."

Chow paused, wondering for a few seconds if he should mention his dinner with Tian, but then he saw that quite a few sets of eyes and ears were turned in their direction. "I'll see you inside," he said.

The doors opened promptly at noon and people began to file into the Iris Room. As they had at the wake, they burned joss paper, bowed to the coffin and the family, and in a few cases spoke to Mrs. Gao and Chi. But after paying their respects, this time everyone stayed. When the coffin left the funeral home for the journey to the cemetery, most of them would follow it on foot. The line moved steadily, and Chow was sure that by two o'clock everyone who had come would have had a chance to pay their respects.

Chow stood by the entrance for the entire time. Wang was the first senior triad he greeted, quickly followed by Yu, Ren, and Pang. Around one o'clock, the Mountain Masters began to arrive. Chin, the Wanchai boss, was the first; he had brought Sammy Wing and his Red Pole with him. Jen and Kang again came together. Tse from Happy Valley, Yin from Kowloon, La from Central, Tso from Tai Po, Go from Sai Kung, and Tong from Tuen Mun all arrived with one or more men, and the seats that had been reserved for the triad leaders were quickly filled.

Conspicuously absent was Ma. At one-fifteen, Chow approached Yu.

"Have you heard from Ma?"

"No. He should have been here by now. This doesn't look good in front of the others."

"I know. It's become embarrassing," Chow said. "I'm going to phone him."

"Please," Yu said, concern flitting across his face.

Chow made his way to the funeral home office. "I need to make a call," he said to a young woman. She turned her phone towards him.

He dialed Ma's number and waited. He didn't hang up until the phone had rung ten times. His anxiety increasing, he left the office and hurried towards the entrance, where Xu was shepherding the last of the mourners into the building.

"Any sign of Ma?" he asked.

"No. Fong and I were just talking about him."

"I just called his house and no one answered. Do you know where he lives?"

"Yes, it's only a short cab ride from here."

Chow looked out at the street. In front of the funeral

home it was crowded with sixty or seventy band members, their instruments at the ready and their funeral banners fluttering in the light wind. On all sides of the home, cars were parked and double-parked; the only open path seemed to be a single lane that ran to the cemetery.

"We don't have time to wait for a cab, and I don't know how one would get here anyway. Run to his place and check on him."

"It will take me as least twenty minutes to get there and back," Xu said.

"Then you'd better get going."

Xu nodded and sped from the courtyard.

"What's going on?" Fong asked.

"No one has seen Ma. I've sent Xu to his house."

"What the fuck do we do if he doesn't get here in time for the funeral procession?"

"We'll have the funeral procession without him."

"We'll look like idiots. The gang will look like shit."

"This day isn't about Ma."

"If he doesn't show, that's all anyone is going to talk about."

"He will be here," Chow said. "When he arrives, hustle him right inside."

Chow left the courtyard and re-entered the Iris Room. Yu looked at him questioningly. Chow shook his head and resumed his marshalling duties. Fifteen minutes later, after the last of the mourners had paid their respects to the Gao family, there was still no sign of Ma.

Chow approached Mrs. Hop. "There is no one else left to greet," he said. "The bands have been waiting to warm up. Can I tell them to start?"

"I'll talk to the family."

He watched as she spoke with Chi, her head nodding constantly. When she returned, he wasn't surprised when she said, "We're a few minutes early but the family has agreed to start now. I'll make the announcement."

"I'll let the bands know."

"We'll take the coffin through the side door. The bands should move to that side of the building. The road there leads directly to the cemetery."

Fong was sitting on the entrance steps when Chow went outside. "We'll be heading up to the cemetery in a few minutes. The bands have to move to the side of the building. I'm going to talk to them."

"Still no fucking Ma, and Xu isn't back yet," Fong said.

"It is getting so late that it's beginning not to matter," Chow said, and then headed towards the bands.

His experience with funeral bands was limited to two other triad funerals, but those bands shared similarities with the nine in front of Hop Sing. They had between six and ten members, wearing a variety of uniforms that were primarily white and topped by a white peaked cap, and each band carried elaborate silk banners embroidered with couplets and sayings that praised and honoured the dead. Where the bands differed somewhat was in the instruments they played. Aside from a large bass drum, which they all had, the other instruments were an eclectic mix. The bands on the street in front of Hop Sing were carrying trumpets, French horns, flutes, trombones, clarinets, cymbals, and bells of various sizes. The mixture didn't matter from a musical viewpoint because the bands were not there to make real music; they were there to make a noise intended to drive away ghosts and demons.

"You can move now to the side street that leads directly to the cemetery," he told the band leaders. "The hearse will be exiting the home from the side entrance."

As the bands gathered themselves and began to march raggedly towards the starting point, Chow saw Xu running up the hill from town. He was alone.

Chow went to meet him. "What did you find out?"

"There was no one at the house. I talked to a neighbour, who told me Ma's wife left the house early this morning and Ma left a couple of hours ago."

"Was he alone?"

"He was picked up by a driver. I asked the neighbour to describe him. It sounded like Peng."

"Did the neighbour have any idea where Ma could have gone?"

"He didn't have a clue."

"This is getting stranger and stranger."

"Uncle, what the hell is going on?" Xu asked. "No matter what I think of Ma, this doesn't make sense. He would never deliberately insult the Gao family like this."

"I agree."

"So?"

Chow drew a deep breath. "We have a Mountain Master to bury. Until that's done, I don't want to hear Ma's name again."

17

THE NINE BANDS MADE MORE NOISE THAN CHOW HAD imagined was possible. The overall sound was loud, shrill, discordant — a musical rendering of raw emotions. *But what else*, he thought, *could drive away any evil spirits and ghosts? What else could express so adequately the pain and sense of loss the Gao family must feel?*

The bands led the procession, followed by the hearse and the mourners. Chow was among the fourth tier of mourners, behind the immediate family, close family friends, and the senior triads. Fong walked with him while Xu stayed behind to look for some friends of Peng.

"When I die, I want to have a band at my funeral," Chow said to Fong.

"If I'm alive when you die, I'll make sure you have one," Fong said. "Will you do the same for me?"

"I will."

As the procession continued towards the cemetery, the citizens of Fanling lined the street to watch. For them the funeral was entertainment for a Saturday afternoon and not much more than that. Chow didn't imagine that many of the onlookers knew who Gao was, and if they did, he doubted they would feel any sadness about his passing. He couldn't blame them; the relationship between triads and citizens was complicated.

With the exception of the protection business, which he despised, Chow liked to think that the gang provided services to the town. The fact that the British authorities classified those services as illegal didn't bother him, because he believed that what the Brits defined as crime was in a constant state of flux, subject to time, place, and circumstance. Basically, most things that ran contrary to the status quo were labelled criminal, and since the British had imposed — and rigorously defended — their version of the status quo on a Chinese culture with a different set of values, there was a disconnect.

British and Chinese attitudes towards gambling was one example. Chow thought the government's policy was idiotic, and the thousands of people who quite happily made their way to Fanling's mah-jong parlours, small casinos, and betting shops were proof of that. He felt the same way about the policies regarding massage parlours and brothels, as long as they were run in a way that was fair to both client and practitioner. He saw them as services that were wanted and needed. He even imagined that the day would come when they would be legal.

"I still can't see any sign of Ma," Fong said, interrupting Chow's thoughts.

"I told you, I don't want to talk about him."

"I just thought he might have come directly here, but all I can see are the monks."

Chow looked through the gates and saw a cluster of

orange-robed men standing on the hill. "It looks like Gao's grave is at the highest point of the cemetery. That's good feng shui."

"The man is dead. What does it matter where they put the body?" Fong said.

"What's got into you? You're not usually this negative," Chow said.

"I'm pissed off about Ma. There's no excuse for his not being here," Fong said. He paused before adding, "The truth is, I played mah-jong last night and lost my ass."

"Is this more about Ma or about you losing?"

Fong looked uncomfortable.

"How much did you lose?"

"Thirty thousand."

"And you don't have it?"

"No."

"I'll lend it to you. I just wish I didn't have to."

"We all have our vices," Fong said.

"What's mine?"

"You always think you're right."

"I was wrong about Ren, and I've been wrong often enough before. But I agree that when I do believe in something, I tend to act as if there's no other way to think," Chow said. "Part of that stems from the fact that I don't like indecision. When you can't decide something for yourself, someone else will always decide it for you. If I'm going to make mistakes, I want no one to blame but myself."

"I don't think Ren was a mistake," Fong said. "How could you have known he didn't have the balls to see it through?"

"Obviously I didn't know him well enough."

The bands reached the entrance to the cemetery and

the procession backed up behind them as they slowly funnelled through the narrow gateway. As the line of mourners compressed, Chow found himself only a few metres behind the Mountain Masters. Ren was among them, standing between Kang and Tso. The two Mountain Masters were talking, and Ren was nodding in agreement to whatever was being said.

A few minutes later they cleared the gate and continued uphill to the gravesite. The coffin was laid on ropes next to the grave while the mourners took their positions around it. The family and their friends were closest to the grave, the triads formed a secondary circle, and the bands stood on the fringes, their instruments momentarily silent. The monks began to chant. Chow felt a chill and lowered his head.

When the monks had finished, six male friends of the family stepped forward and, with the help of cemetery staff, lowered the coffin into the ground. As they did, the family and the other mourners turned their backs on the grave. When the coffin reached the bottom, Chi took his mother gently by the elbow, picked up a handful of dirt, and pressed some into her hand. They both turned and the two of them threw the dirt onto the coffin.

Everyone else followed suit, some saying a few words over the grave, others throwing money or joss paper with the dirt. When the last mourner had paid his respects, the monks approached the grave and began to chant again. Chi put his arm around his mother's shoulder and led her away from the grave to begin the journey back to the funeral home.

As they were leaving, Mrs. Hop stepped forward. "I have

been asked by the family to invite everyone to join them at the Good Fortune Restaurant for the funeral dinner," she said. "Dinner will be at six; drinks will be served starting at five."

"What do you want to do?" Xu said to Chow.

"We'll go to the dinner."

The crowd began to make its way down the hill in the same order it had ascended. The bands were no longer playing and there wasn't a lot of conversation among the mourners. The journey downhill should have been faster than the one up, but halfway down, progress began to slow. The crowd was brought to a full stop several times, for reasons that Chow couldn't fathom.

"What the hell is going on?" Fong asked in frustration.

"I have no idea," Chow said, shuffling forward until he met a wall of people who had come to a standstill.

The crowd stirred again but only inched forward. Then shouts could be heard from the direction of the funeral home. Chow tried unsuccessfully to see over the throng.

"Xu, find a way through. Something is going on down there that's causing this."

Xu pushed his way to the far right. He had gone about twenty metres before he came to a stop and began talking to a young man Chow recognized as a Blue Lantern. The young man was waving his arms in the air.

"I have a bad feeling about this," Fong said.

"Don't jump to conclusions," Chow said.

Xu started walking back towards them, his face grim.

"What did that guy tell you?" Chow said.

"He said cops have cordoned off the funeral home."

"Why in hell would they do that?" Chow asked.

"There are two bodies in the courtyard."

"Does he know who they are?" Chow asked, dreading the answer.

"He says it's Ma and Peng," Xu said. "He also says their bodies are riddled with bullet holes."

18

IT WAS CHAOTIC ON THE STREET. THE POLICE HAD blocked access to the courtyard and the funeral home and had closed the road that led to the cemetery. A Saracen armoured car cut off any vehicular access between the cemetery and the town.

"How did so many cops get here so fast?" Fong asked, as he, Chow, and Xu finally threaded their way through the crowd to the police barrier.

"I imagine they were on standby. They knew Gao was being buried today and they knew the brotherhood would be out in force. Maybe they suspected trouble," Chow said, peering through the courtyard's wrought iron fence at the two bodies covered in sheets. "And it looks like they found it."

"Are we sure it's Ma and Peng?" Fong asked.

"Shan, the Blue Lantern I spoke to, saw the bodies before they were covered," Xu said. "He was certain."

"This is a disaster," Chow said.

"What the hell is going on here? What's happened?" a voice said.

Chow turned to see Chi looking distraught. He hesitated, uncertain what to say.

"There are bodies in the courtyard of the funeral home," Chi went on. "My mother and the rest of our family are being stopped by armed police. For god's sake, Uncle, tell me what is going on."

"We've been told that the bodies are those of Ma and a Blue Lantern named Peng," Chow said.

"Oh my god. Are you sure?"

"Sure enough."

"This is terrible, in so many ways," Chi said.

Chow moved close to him. "You should leave with your mother as fast as you can. There's no reason for you to stay here. I'm sure the police will let you pass."

"Our car is blocked in."

"Then walk into town. It isn't far."

"You say that so calmly."

"My hands are sweaty, my stomach is in knots, and my head is ready to explode with questions," Chow said. "I'm far from calm."

Chi shook his head. "We have the funeral dinner tonight."

"I'd cancel it," Chow said. "People will understand."

"But the restaurant is booked."

"Then talk to them about rescheduling to a time when things have calmed down and we can pay proper respects to your father. I'm sure they'll be reasonable," Chow said. "If not, I'll handle it."

"I'll have to talk to my mother, but I think she'll agree about rescheduling."

"Please tell her I'm sorry the day had to end like this," Chow said.

"She understands the life. That's why she wanted me out."

"The life doesn't have to be this way."

"Perhaps, but it too often is," Chi said. "And I have to tell you that, as sad as my father's death is, my mother and I take comfort from the fact that it was accidental."

"Excuse me," Xu interrupted. "Yu is heading this way."

"I think I should get going," Chi said.

"The dinner?" Chow said.

"We'll reschedule it. I'll ask Mrs. Hop to tell people, and maybe you can pass along the word as well."

"Gladly."

Chi shook Chow's hand, nodded at Xu, and then brushed past the approaching Yu, whose face was so pale and drawn he seemed to have aged ten years in ten minutes.

"The word is that it's Ma in the courtyard," Yu announced.

"We've been told the same thing," Chow said.

"This is so awful, so fucking awful."

"That does sum it up."

Yu put his hand on Chow's forearm and pulled himself close, his breath blanketing Chow's face. "Do you have any idea who might have done this?"

"I don't have a clue. Who could be so vicious and degenerate as to do this on a day that should be dedicated to honouring Gao?"

"Lau and Ng aren't at the funeral," Yu said, referring to the Mountain Masters from Tsim Sha Tsui and Tsing Yi.

"If we start listing people who aren't here, there will be no end to it," Chow said.

"Okay, then let's talk about who is here."

"What are you suggesting?"

"Nothing that I'd want repeated."

"Then maybe you shouldn't say anything at all," Chow said. "It seems to me that the last thing we need right now is unfounded speculation."

Yu looked like he wanted to argue but shook his head. "I came over to tell you that there's going to be an executive meeting at the office at seven o'clock tonight."

"Ren called a meeting?"

"He is the Vanguard, and he is next in line," Yu said. "He might expect to be named Mountain Master."

"My position hasn't changed. I don't want anyone to be appointed; I want an election."

"Well, now that Ma is dead, Ren has a clear path to the job," Yu said. "I know he was running for it, but I have to tell you he would never have won."

"Actually, Ren told Ma yesterday that he wasn't running. In fact, he told Ma he had his full support."

"You don't think that could have been a ploy?"

"I don't like what you're hinting at, and I don't want to listen to any more of your shit right now," Chow said.

"I'm just stating the obvious."

"We're all in shock and maybe not thinking clearly. That includes you," Chow said. "Have you told Pang and Wang about the meeting?"

"They're next on my list."

"Don't spin the same conspiracy theories when you talk to them."

"Pang supports the boss, or whoever he thinks will be boss. He will already have swung his support from Ma to Ren. I won't waste my time with him," Yu said. "Wang is more objective."

"He's also the Red Pole. If Ma's death is to be avenged, he's the one who has to do it. I'd be careful about how much you wind him up."

Yu stared at Chow and then turned back in the direction from which he'd come.

Chow, Xu, and Fong stayed where they were for another thirty minutes. The crowd began to thin as people lost interest in the courtyard and began to find their way back to town. Chow looked for familiar faces, but there was no sign of Ren, Pang, Yu, or Wang. Chi and his mother had left, and so had all the Mountain Masters. The only face he recognized was that of a police officer inside the courtyard, and he knew this wasn't the time or place for them to talk.

"Let's get out of here," he said to Xu and Fong. "Nothing else is going to happen, and there's nothing more to be done."

19

FONG AND XU WALKED INTO TOWN WITH CHOW. THEY tried to spark a conversation, but he wasn't in the mood for speculation and stayed quiet. When he'd told Yu they were all in shock, he wasn't excluding himself. The reality of Ma's death was clear enough but hard to stomach. Now he had to come to grips with the ramifications, and he had only a few hours to do so before the executive meeting. It was a process best completed alone.

He left Xu and Fong near the office, promising to call them after the meeting, and walked to his apartment alone. Once inside, he took off his jacket, got a beer from the fridge, turned the leather easy chair so that it gave him a clear view of the street, and settled in. Positioning the chair that way was a subconscious reaction. He didn't expect to be attacked in his home, but he wasn't a careless man, and being diligent was something that came naturally to him. He lit a cigarette and leaned back. There were two questions that needed to be answered: Why was Ma killed? And who had ordered it to be done?

The who question was the easiest to answer, at least on

the surface. The public display of the body with its multiple bullet holes was a clear sign that this was a triad execution. When the triads shot to kill, one bullet was never enough and ten was never too many. And it was impossible to think of a location that would have been more public that afternoon than the funeral home where a Mountain Master was being laid to rest.

But if Ma had been killed by triads, who had ordered it done? Given his position, it was unlikely that the decision to kill him could have been made by anyone below the rank of Mountain Master. But if he had been fingered, was it by someone from another gang or, as Yu had implied, by Ren or someone connected to him? Could that have been the object of Ren's dinner with Tso in Kowloon? Again that dinner tormented him. Given the events of the week, how could it have been just two old friends meeting for a meal?

Chow began to replay the conversations he'd had with Ren over the past few days. Had there been a clue, even the smallest hint, that this was his work? Chow believed that one of his strengths was his ability to discern when he was being lied to or strung along. He parsed his talks with Ren. The Vanguard had gone from being a nonplayer to a reluctant recruit to a possible front-runner before completely reversing his position. Why had he changed his mind? Ren had said he didn't want to face the prospect of losing. How much truth was there in that? Had Ren played him and then played Ma? Was that possible? It was Chow who had approached Ren and convinced him to run, and Ren's response every step of the way had been reasonable, if slightly guarded. So, despite Yu's veiled accusation, Chow found it hard to believe that Ren was behind the killing.

But if it wasn't Ren, then who? Once he'd discounted Ren, the list became rather long. Ma had been a triad for his entire adult life. How many enemies had he made during that time? How many of them would be unhappy enough about the prospect of his becoming Mountain Master that they would take action? There was too much hatred, jealousy, and rivalry among gang members to discount the possibility that his death had been triggered by personal animosity.

Then there were the gangs around Fanling who coveted their turf. Was taking out Ma another message, another step towards an attempted takeover? Was killing Ma an attempt to make them more vulnerable, to soften their resolve? What sense did that make? Anyone who knew anything about the gang would know that Ma was no fighter, and that killing him would only put Fanling more on guard.

Chow needed to talk to Sammy Wing again, he decided. He reached for a notebook he kept by the chair, found Wing's number, and dialled.

"*Wei*," Sammy said.

"It's Uncle."

"I thought you'd call."

"I wanted to talk to you at the funeral home, but you left rather quickly."

"We all left quickly. No one wanted to be around that mess."

"How did your boss react?"

"Uncle, I'm not sure we should be having this talk."

"I didn't start this conversation. You did, at Happy Valley. I'm simply trying to continue it."

"You have a point," Sammy said.

"And the agreement to keep you out of it is still binding

from my end," Chow said. "So please, tell me how your boss reacted to the killing."

Sammy hesitated and then said, "He was as angry as I've ever seen him. He was pissed off about the disrespect it showed to Gao. And that was compounded by the fact that he and the other Mountain Masters found themselves surrounded by what looked like half of the Hong Kong Police Force and confronted by a fucking Saracen."

"You're exaggerating about the number of cops."

"But not about Chin's anger."

"Sammy, who did it?" Chow asked.

"I'm not going there, Uncle. I told you that at Happy Valley and I'm telling you the same thing now."

"Are you telling me that you know but won't tell me, or that you don't know and don't want to speculate?"

"I don't know."

"Chin must have talked with you about it."

"I'm not going to share with you what the boss and I have discussed."

"Sammy, please," Chow said. "You know I have tremendous regard for Chin — he's one of the smartest Mountain Masters I've ever encountered. I'm just curious about his reaction. You don't have to name names."

"All I'll say is that the boss thinks the killing may have nothing to do with Ma. He was a lightweight, hardly considered a threat by anyone. Gao, though, was a man everyone took seriously. He kept Fanling secure, but over the years that made him a lot of enemies. There were people who would be happy to see him die, and maybe that wasn't enough for someone. Perhaps they wanted to ruin his funeral, shit on his memory."

"That doesn't make sense," Chow said.

"You asked me how the boss reacted."

"I'm more inclined to think that what you told me at Happy Valley has more bearing."

"You can think whatever you want," Sammy said. "The only thing I'll stress is that the boss's determination to stay out of feuds in the Territories has been strengthened threefold. He will not get dragged into whatever is going on out there."

"I get that, and that wasn't my intention. I haven't mentioned your names or Wanchai since we talked," Chow said. "I'm just wondering if you've heard anything else that might be helpful. And Sammy, like I said, my promise to keep it between us is still good."

"Haven't I told you enough, then and now?"

"You didn't tell me Ma was a target."

"But I did say there was danger on your borders. It was up to you to take precautions."

"That's true, and obviously we didn't do enough," Chow said. "What more can we expect?"

"How would I know?"

"I suspect you know something."

"Chin did say something you should pay attention to. He said that once there's fresh meat on the ground, the vultures will descend to pick at the carcass."

"Who are the vultures?"

"He didn't say. Even if he had, I wouldn't repeat it."

"Who do you think they are?"

"Fuck off, Uncle," Sammy said.

"Not even a hint?"

"No."

"Tso?"

"You can throw ten more names at me but I won't guess. And guessing is what it would be, because I don't know."

"Well, whoever it is, I want you to tell your boss that we won't just sit back and let someone run over us."

"Who is 'we'? When did you become Mountain Master of Fanling?"

"You know that will never happen."

"Right. Chin assumes it will be Ren."

"That's a safe assumption."

"If it is Ren, what makes you think he won't just sit back? He's never been particularly aggressive."

"We have Wang."

"Wang is a good man, but who's going to give him the orders?"

"What makes you think Ren won't?"

Sammy Wing hesitated. "I've said too much already. You always get me going."

"As you said at the track, we young guys have to stick together."

"There will be no more sticking tonight."

Chow lit another cigarette, inhaled deeply, and blew smoke towards the window. "Thanks for taking my call, Sammy. I appreciate it."

"As I said at the track, the boss has a lot of time for you. But Uncle, stay out of trouble."

"I won't go looking for it, but I won't run if it finds me," Chow said, and ended the conversation.

He stared out at the street. Sammy Wing couldn't have made it clearer that Fanling had enemies on its borders and that men as senior as Chin doubted its ability to defeat them. He reached for the phone again and dialled.

"This is the Zhang residence," a woman answered.

Chow recognized the voice of Zhang's housekeeper. "This is Chow Tung. Is the Superintendent home yet?"

"No, he isn't."

Chow was disappointed but not surprised. He was sure the day's events at the Hop Sing Funeral Home were keeping Zhang busy. "When he gets home, could you please tell him that I called, and that I would like to speak to him tonight. I'll be out myself until nine or ten. He can call any time after that. I don't care how late it is."

"I'll let him know," she said.

Chow checked the time. If he was going to get something to eat before the meeting, he needed to leave the apartment right away. He started to rise out of the chair but was stopped by the phone ringing.

"It's Wang."

"I looked for you at the funeral home," Chow said. "How are you doing?"

"I'm still stunned. You would think that after all these years I'd be beyond that. I guess not."

"Who do you think is responsible?"

"I have no idea. The reason I left so quickly was that I wanted to grab some of the other Red Poles before they could disappear. They were as stunned and surprised as me, and they all claimed to know absolutely nothing about what happened."

"Do you believe them?"

"What difference does it make? Either way, we don't have a name to attach to the killing."

"I spoke to my contact from Hong Kong, the one who approached me at Happy Valley," Chow said. "He danced around the subject and didn't say anything specific, but he implied that it could be connected to the move against us."

"I'm thinking along the same lines. I have all my men on the streets right now, and they'll be there all night."

"I wasn't suggesting that you aren't on top of things."

"I didn't take it that way. Who could have expected this? Who takes out a second Mountain Master during the funeral service for the first?"

"Did Yu speak to you?"

"He did."

"Did he spin his conspiracy theory about Ren?"

"He did. I listened and said nothing."

"Do you think there could be any substance to what he thinks?"

"It's dangerous to speculate along those lines. He needs to be careful about what he says and to whom. We need to be united right now, and that kind of talk is divisive."

"Still, between us, you can't deny that even if Ren wasn't involved in this, he is the one who benefits most from it."

"Of course I can't deny it, but we don't have any facts. This is a time to keep our ears and minds wide open," Wang said. "And that brings me to the reason I called you. How are we going to handle the meeting tonight?"

"What do you mean?"

"Ren is acting Mountain Master, and he's not wasting any time making decisions."

"What kind of decisions?"

"He intends to promote Pang to acting Vanguard and he's going to name Hou as Incense Master. I expect that once that's done, he'll propose to the committee that we postpone Monday's election indefinitely or ask us to confirm him as permanent Mountain Master. With Pang and Hou, he has three votes. All he needs is one more."

"He won't get my vote. He might get it on Monday, but not tonight."

"Under any circumstances?"

"What are you trying to say?"

"I heard he's also thinking about making you Deputy Mountain Master."

"Who told you this?"

"Forty-niners tend to stay loyal to their Red Pole. I can't say more than that."

Chow sighed, not sure how much he should believe. "Listen to me, Wang. Ren hasn't offered me anything, and if he does, I'll tell him no. I'm not going to be bought off."

"I thought that would be the case, but I'm still pleased to hear you say it," Wang said. "But what do you think about the idea of postponing the vote?"

"Postponing it would only leave things hanging and create uncertainty. Outsiders need to know that we have stable, long-term leadership and that we're unified. The longer we wait, the more vulnerable we'll appear. We need to re-establish some semblance of normalcy."

"Even if we're trying to unify behind a man we have doubts about?"

"Tian Longwei said something to me a few days ago that struck home. He said you can't predict what kind of Mountain Master someone will be until he is in the job and facing its challenges. Let's hope Ren rises to those challenges."

"Amen to that," Wang said. "I'll see you tonight."

"Assuming that neither of us gets shot before seven."

20

AT SIX-THIRTY, CHOW SLID FROM HIS CHAIR AND WENT
to the bathroom to freshen up. He hadn't eaten, but his conversation with Wang had ruined whatever appetite he had.
His focus was now entirely on the evening's meeting.

The sun had almost set and it would be dark by seven.
Darkness suited his mood. Ma's murder had changed the
dynamic. A vague outside threat had turned into reality.
The continuity that Ma had represented, at least in theory,
had been badly disrupted. Doubts about Ren filled his head,
among them renewed suspicion about Ren's dinner with Tso
in Kowloon. Then it dawned on him that he hadn't mentioned anything about it to Wang. Ma's announcement that
Ren had pledged his support had put those concerns briefly
to rest. Ma's death had resurrected them, but only gradually, and not until he'd finished his phone call with Wang.
He made a mental note to tell Wang the first chance he had.

Chow thought about the meeting. He wondered if Wang
was right about Ren's plans, and if he was, how aggressively
Ren would push them. They couldn't prevent Ren from promoting Pang or appointing Hou, but they could stop him

from hijacking the election. And what about the election? Despite his fears about Ren, Chow could not bring himself to believe he had anything to do with Ma's death, or Gao's for that matter, because the two could be linked. The two men had been Ren's colleagues for decades. Chow had never heard Ren say anything negative about either of them, and he had never heard Ren talk or act in any way that suggested he had secret ambitions.

Ren deserved the benefit of the doubt, Chow thought — but only up to a point, and that point was how he conducted himself at the meeting. *What do I want from him? Some thoughtful reasoning about who might be behind Ma's killing, why it might have happened, what it means for the gang, and what plans he has to stabilize the situation. Give me those things and I'll find a way to convince myself to support him.*

Chow was so absorbed in his own thoughts that he was startled when someone spoke his name. He was about a hundred metres from the office, and a forty-niner was standing in a shop doorway. "I hope I didn't disturb you, Uncle."

"No, not at all," Chow said, and then looked closer at his surroundings. The street was peppered with forty-niners. Wang wasn't taking any chances.

Chow entered the office building. As he climbed the stairs he heard voices, several of them sounding stressed and excited. When he walked into the common area, he saw that the boardroom door was open and that he was the last to arrive. He took a seat next to Wang. Then he noticed a new face at the table.

"You know Hou?" Ren asked.

"We were Blue Lanterns and forty-niners together."

"I've appointed him acting Incense Master. I don't think

he should be confirmed as permanent until we have a new permanent Mountain Master."

"Still, congratulations," Chow said to Hou, a tall, thin man with a long nose, pointed chin, and shaved head. He wore a long-sleeved black shirt. Under the shirt, Chow knew, his arms were heavily tattooed.

"I'm honoured," Hou said.

"Since Hou is to be Incense Master, I assume Pang has become either the acting Vanguard or Deputy Mountain Master."

"Vanguard," Ren said.

"Great choice," Chow said.

Ren looked at him from across the table. "I've decided to hold off naming a new Deputy Mountain Master for now."

If that was an attempt to be subtle, Chow thought, it wasn't very well done. "That seems like the right decision," he said.

Ren nodded and then lowered his head. "Now, unfortunately, we have to talk about what happened today at the funeral. It was shocking and tragic, it made a mockery of Gao's funeral, and, to be blunt, it didn't do us any credit."

"Are you suggesting it could have been prevented?" Wang said, leaning forward.

"I'm not the Red Pole. That is your responsibility and your area of expertise — as much as anyone can be an expert in such matters," Ren said. "But no, I'm not suggesting it could have been prevented. I'm simply pointing out that it was regrettable on so many levels that it wasn't."

"The only question I have is, who was behind this? Who killed Ma?" Yu said.

No one answered, but Chow saw Pang glance at Ren.

"I believe Ren may have some information for us in that regard," Pang said finally.

Ren raised his head, put his hands in front of his mouth, spread his fingers, and put their tips together. It was a mannerism Chow had seen Gao display many times, but never Ren, until now. "I spoke with some of the Mountain Masters at the funeral home, then about an hour ago I called others I know well. They told me they think Ma's death was an aberration. They think it was most likely an act of personal vengeance and nothing more. It's still a terrible thing, but —"

"Which Mountain Masters did you speak to?" Yu interrupted.

"Sha Tin, Kowloon, Central, Tai Po, and Mong Kok."

"And they all said that?"

"Two of them did. I won't be any more specific."

"We're expected to accept that at face value?" Yu asked.

"Yes, you are," Ren said.

"And why wouldn't you?" Pang said.

"Because I want to know who killed Ma."

"They don't know or they wouldn't say. I'm not sure there's anything to be gained by pursuing that right now," Ren said.

"Is that your decision?"

"It's my suggestion."

"And if I disagree?"

"Then it can be my decision," Ren said.

"That's shit."

"Listen, I know we're all upset about what happened today, but we can't let it cloud our judgement," Ren said. "If this is an isolated event, as I'm told it is, we need to stay calm and not start lashing out wildly and blindly."

"What if it isn't isolated?" Chow asked.

"What are you getting at?" Ren said.

"What if Gao's death was deliberate? What if it wasn't an accident?"

"The police have ruled it an accident. Knowing that it was Gao who was involved, I can't imagine them making that decision unless they were completely certain," Ren said.

"Wang, I know you have men stationed all over town. Have there been any warning signs, any alarms since this afternoon?" Pang asked.

"No."

"Do you have any reason to be worried about our security?"

"Not right now, but I share Uncle's concerns about this not being an isolated incident."

"You wouldn't be doing your job if you didn't take every possibility into account," Pang said. "But is there anything concrete that you can report?"

"Only rumours that a neighbouring gang or gangs are organizing to move onto our turf."

"Those are rumours you've been reporting for months," Ren said. "But what's actually happened?"

"Gao and Ma are dead."

A heavy silence fell over the table. Chow could feel Yu's anger and hoped he would restrain himself.

After an awkward few minutes, Pang said, "I have a suggestion to make."

"Yes, what is it?" Ren said.

"Ren, I know you haven't asked me to do this, and you may not want me to, but under the circumstances I believe it's exactly the right thing to do," Pang said, and then looked pointedly at everyone sitting around the table. "I believe we should confirm Ren as Mountain Master."

"Not that again," Chow said.

"What do you mean?" Pang asked.

"We just had this discussion. Ma wanted to be confirmed and we — which includes both you and Ren — agreed that we should have an election. I haven't changed my mind."

"The circumstances have changed."

"What's changed? Wang tells us that the streets are quiet and his men are in control," Chow said. "Ren says he believes Ma's death was an aberration. What circumstances are you talking about? You're talking out of both sides of your mouth."

"The men are uneasy. We need to let them know that things are normalizing."

"To my way of thinking, 'normal' would be letting them vote as planned on Monday," Chow said.

"Don't you think that having a vote now would be a distraction, not to mention a colossal waste of time? We need to show the men that we're unified in how we respond to Ma's death," Pang said.

"The only response I've heard you and Ren make is that we shouldn't bother trying to find out who killed him," Yu said.

"What good would that do? It would only lead to revenge killings. Where would that end?"

"We can't just ignore the fact that our acting Mountain Master and one of our Blue Lanterns were shot and left dead and on display in the courtyard of the funeral home where we were honouring our long-term Mountain Master," Yu said.

"Yu makes a valid point," Chow said. "I believe we have an obligation to Ma, to his family, and to the gang to correct what's happened. We can't appear not to care and we can't risk looking weak."

Ren leaned towards Chow. "All the other Mountain Masters know that we care; I made that clear enough to them. And they were the ones who advised a cautious approach until things settle. In their minds — and mine — being cautious right now is smart, not a sign of weakness. We should also remember how many policemen were there today. I'm sure they're waiting for us to retaliate, for us to escalate the violence, so they have an excuse for bringing down the hammer on us and all the other gangs."

"I can understand why the other gangs would advise us to be cautious, but I'm also sure they're doing that for reasons that serve their best interests," Chow said.

"I still say we need to find out who killed Ma," Yu said. "We can't ignore it."

"I'm not ignoring it," Ren said. "All I'm suggesting is that we let things sit for a little while. At some point we'll find out who did this and we'll settle with them. But for now, we need to stay calm and not run around like chickens with their heads cut off."

"And stop acting like you're the only person who's upset about this," Pang said to Yu.

Yu started to respond but Chow interrupted. "Where does this leave us?"

"I think Ren should be confirmed as Mountain Master. We have the authority to make that decision and I think it's exactly what we should do," Pang said.

"We know where you stand," Chow said. "What does everyone else think?"

"I'm for it," Hou said.

"I'm against," Yu said.

Chow looked at Ren. "Are you going to vote for yourself?"

"Do you think I should?"

"No. Ma didn't, and it was the right and honourable decision."

"Then I won't."

"So that leaves Uncle and Wang," Pang said. "I'm hoping one of you is going to be sensible."

"I've already told you I want an election," Chow said. "Why would you think I've changed my mind?"

"I was hoping that Ren might have convinced you otherwise."

"He hasn't."

"I'm not convinced either," Wang said, and then looked at Ren. "I can see no harm in making you wait for two days to become Mountain Master. I'll cast my vote on Monday, and not before."

21

CHOW, YU, AND WANG LEFT THE OFFICE TOGETHER AND then separated. Chow started walking home but had gone only several hundred metres when he heard Wang shout, "Wait!"

He stopped walking until Wang caught up, two forty-niners trailing about ten metres behind him. "I didn't want to talk in front of Yu," said Wang.

"He is excitable."

"Do you want to grab a beer?" Wang asked. "There's a bar just down the street."

"Sure."

Wang led them to a place that Chow, despite having been up and down the street countless times, had never noticed before. There was no sign indicating that it was a bar, or indeed a business of any kind. It was simply a long, narrow room that ran off the street, with a bar on the left and a shelf where you could rest your drink on the right. There were six stools at the bar but Wang went right past them to the far end of the room, where it was dark. He leaned on the bar. Chow joined him; when he looked back towards the entrance, he saw that the two forty-niners were flanking it.

"This is a strange little place," Chow said.

"I've been coming here for years. It's private, the beer is cold, and I like their fried grasshoppers."

"Fried grasshoppers?"

"It's a house specialty. They remind me of Guangzhou."

A small, grey-haired man wearing a blue apron left two customers at the front of the bar and came to them. "Good to see you," he said to Wang.

"San Miguel and grasshoppers," Wang said.

"San Miguel," Chow said.

"You have to try some of my grasshoppers. They go perfectly with beer," Wang said. He waited for the man to leave before adding, "Well, that meeting was crap."

"Why do you sound surprised? It went exactly as you predicted."

"But I didn't expect him to spin that bullshit story about Ma's death being an act of personal vengeance."

"You didn't believe him? Not even a little?"

"Did you?"

"It is convenient, and it's the same story my Happy Valley contact tried to convince me is possible. At least, it was one of his scenarios. The other one, which he hasn't abandoned, is that we have nasty neighbours."

"Maybe you and Ren were talking to the same person."

"I doubt it. Perhaps that's what he was told and he just wants to believe it."

"Well, I'm not buying it," Wang said. "You're right that it's what he may have been told, but it's insulting to expect us to believe it. Having nasty neighbours makes far more sense."

The barman approached with the two beers.

"*Ganbei*," Wang said.

They tapped bottles and drank.

"What do you really think happened to Ma?" Wang said after a second slug.

"The way you ask that question reminds me of Yu."

"The fact that Yu has a theory neither of us wants to believe doesn't make him wrong," Wang said. "I was neutral, or leaning towards not believing him, until I heard Ren's bullshit story. It made me stop and think that maybe Yu has a point."

"But you don't know that what Ren said is bullshit."

"Be truthful," Wang said, lightly touching Chow's arm. "Do you really believe Ma was killed in an act of personal vengeance?"

"No."

"Then why would someone with as much experience as Ren believe it, or at least pretend that he does?"

"I think it's likely that he spoke to some other Mountain Masters. I think it's possible that one or more of them threw out the personal vengeance idea. After that, I don't know."

"I know you don't want to think the worst of Ren — neither do I — but let me ask you again. Do you really think he believes Ma's death was an act of personal vengeance?"

"That is an incredibly difficult question to answer."

"But that's where we are."

The barman reappeared, carrying a large bowl. He put it in front of Wang.

"Bring two more beers in about five minutes," Wang said.

Chow looked into the bowl and saw what were clearly grasshoppers, their wrinkled bodies brown and crispy, their legs thin and frail-looking.

Wang reached into the bowl and started to eat, the insects

crunching audibly in his mouth. "The only thing I don't like about eating these is that the legs get stuck between your teeth," he said. "Try some."

"I'll pass," Chow said.

"Are you also going to pass on my question about Ren?"

"No, I'm not. I don't think he really believes it was an act of vengeance, but it's a reason and it's convenient," Chow said.

"So how are we supposed to believe anything else he tells us?"

"I'm not sure. In fact, I have something to tell you that adds to my doubts," Chow said, watching Wang prepare to put several grasshoppers into his mouth.

"What?" Wang said, squeezing the fried insects between his fingers.

"The night before Gao's wake, one of Tian's men was in Kowloon and saw Ren having dinner with Tso."

"Tai Po Tso? Mountain Master Tso?"

"The very same."

"Fuck . . . Tian's man was sure about this? He saw them together on that specific night?"

"That's what Tian told me, and I have no reason not to believe him."

"It's hard to think that was a coincidence."

"Although it may be one. They are old friends, so having dinner together wouldn't be so odd."

"Except for the timing," Wang said. "Have you asked Ren about this?"

Chow shook his head. "The man was having dinner with a friend. What business is that of mine? What excuse could I have for asking him about it? I'd just sound foolish."

"I'm going to call some friends tomorrow, do a bit of

poking around," Wang said. He finished his beer and slammed the empty bottle onto the bar. The barman hurried towards them with two fresh bottles.

"This will be the last one for me," Chow said. "I won't be staying much longer. I'm an early riser."

"And tomorrow is Sunday, so that usually means Happy Valley for you, correct?"

"Yes."

"Do you intend to go tomorrow?"

"Yes. I think it will take my mind off things," Chow said.

"Any chance you might bump into that source of yours and pump him for more information?"

"If he's there, you can count on me trying. But I don't think he'll be particularly forthcoming. He made it clear that he's said all he's going to say."

"I hate being in the fucking dark," Wang said angrily. "We need someone to tell us the truth."

"I'm not sure it's possible to find someone who both knows the truth and is willing to tell it to us."

"I know, but that doesn't make it any less frustrating."

"So where does that leave us?"

"It leaves us having to put up with the situation as it is," Wang said. "There's the election on Monday, but that won't change anything. Ren is the natural successor, and one sure thing I know about our men is that they respect the chain of command. Even when you were trying to promote Ren over Ma for Mountain Master, I never believed the rank and file would bring themselves to vote against Ma."

"That seems like a long time ago," Chow said.

"Doesn't it."

Chow drained his beer. "I should get going."

"If you need me tomorrow, I'll be at one of the betting shops. As you know, it's our busiest day of the week. I generally circulate among them to keep an eye on things. Tomorrow I'll have more reason than usual to do that."

"Do you want me to stay in Fanling?" Chow asked, feeling guilty.

"No, go to the track. There would be nothing for you to do here. The men know their jobs. You'd only get in the way."

"Will you have extra men on duty tomorrow?"

"I'll have everyone I can get, both in the shops and on the street. We should be able to handle whatever pops up."

"The gang needs to add more men," Chow said.

"So Gao kept saying, but he never did anything about it. We're too limited in manpower compared to Tai Po and Sha Tin. Right now, I sure wish we weren't."

22

CHOW BOUGHT A RACING FORM ON HIS WAY HOME from the bar. He was tired and emotionally spent but he knew sleep wouldn't be coming easily, if it came at all; the form would provide some distraction.

It was a typically busy Saturday night in the restaurants and bars he passed, and there were lots of people out on the street. He saw a steady stream of green taxis, their colour identifying them as coming from the New Territories, and an unusually large number of red taxis, which were registered in Hong Kong. Red taxis weren't an uncommon sight in Fanling, but he couldn't help wondering why there were so many. Then he realized he was being a touch paranoid.

When he entered his apartment, Chow put the racing form on the table by his chair and went to the fridge to get a beer. He walked back to the chair but, rather than sitting down, he opened the window, lit a cigarette, and stood looking out onto the street as he smoked and drank. He had promised to call Xu and Fong and wished he hadn't. His two friends would be looking for answers, for some level of certainty from him, and he didn't have much to give. He phoned them anyway.

The conversations were brief as he told them about Hou's appointment, Pang's promotion, and the decision to proceed with the election on Monday. He didn't mention the concerns that he, Yu, and Wang shared about Ren, and when asked about Ma's death, he said there had been a lot of speculation that wasn't worth repeating. Fong took Chow's answers, as he always did, at face value. Xu pushed for more detail about Ma.

"Look, Ma is dead. I'm sure we'll find out more about what happened, and why, in the coming days. For now, leave it alone," Chow said, knowing Xu would be frustrated by his answer.

Xu hesitated as if he wanted to argue but then switched topics. "What are your plans for tomorrow?"

"Unless something dramatic happens, the same as usual; I'll be going to Happy Valley. I volunteered to stay in Fanling, but Wang told me there isn't any need."

"I can't remember you missing a single day at the races."

"And I can't remember a stranger day than today. Maybe this is a weekend for firsts."

After he ended the call with Xu, Chow went to the fridge for another beer. He was getting close to his capacity. He fell back into his chair, reached for the phone again, and dialled Sammy Wing's number. He got an answering machine. "Sammy, it's Uncle calling. I'd like to follow up on the talk we had today. I plan to be at Happy Valley tomorrow, and I'd appreciate it if you could meet me there at the same spot as before."

He picked up the form and opened it to the first race.

Before he could complete even a rudimentary analysis, the phone rang. He answered, thinking it would be Sammy Wing.

"Uncle, it's Zhang. My housekeeper told me you called earlier. I'm glad you didn't make me reach out to you first, or I would be even angrier than I am," he said. "Now tell me, what the fuck are you people doing? Do you have any idea how big a mess you've created, first with Gao and now with Ma and that young man?"

Zhang's full name was Zhang Delun. He was now, as Tian had mentioned the night before, a superintendent with the Hong Kong police. Specifically, he was in charge of the Fanling/Sha Tin District within the New Territories Northern Division.

"We don't like it any more than you do, and we didn't create this mess," Chow said. He was accustomed to Zhang's direct style.

The two men had been friends — or associates, as Zhang preferred to say — for almost nine years. Zhang was several years older than Chow. When Tian had brought them together initially, Zhang was already well into a promising career, while Chow was just beginning his.

Zhang's father had been a triad in Guangzhou; he had escaped with his family to Hong Kong when Mao began his purge of the triads. He died shortly after his arrival, before he could really establish himself within the Fanling gang. Tian had known him only briefly but, following the edict of the first of the Thirty-Six Oaths, he'd provided for the wife and son.

Tian had no children of his own, but he didn't try to play father to young Zhang. He was more like an uncle, there for a helping hand or advice whenever it was needed. When Zhang came to him and said he intended to join the Hong Kong Police Force, Tian was surprised but genuinely wished him every success.

Tian had taken a similar interest in the young Chow Tung when he joined the Fanling triads, and eventually he brought his two charges together. "You are two young men who can help each other," he told them. "You don't have to be friends, but you also don't have to be enemies. Find a middle ground where you can coexist without betraying your primary obligations."

Both Zhang and Chow were honest, straightforward, smart, and dedicated to their respective organizations. What made them useful to each other — which Tian had shrewdly observed — was that while they were dedicated, they weren't blind to the weaknesses of their organizations or the strengths of the opposition. Zhang knew enough about the triads and their history to understand that they weren't simply criminals, and he also understood that the regulations enforced by the Hong Kong police were sometimes out of step with the reality of Chinese culture and customs. Chow, for his part, accepted the need for policing; when his gang or others he knew first-hand failed to manage their affairs in a way that met his standards of human decency, he didn't feel compelled to defend or protect them.

So, over the years, Zhang and Chow had traded information when their interests aligned, but no money had ever changed hands. If that had even been suggested by Zhang, Chow would have ended their relationship. He was certain Zhang would have reacted the same way if the suggestion had come from him.

Initially, given their relatively junior status in their organizations, the information they exchanged was basic. Zhang would warn Chow about raids on gambling dens or massage parlours; Chow would identify known rapists, pedophiles, and men who couldn't contain their rage and took it out on innocents. When Zhang joined the Organized Crime and Triad Bureau, their mutual conflict of interest was so obvious that they communicated infrequently. But after he was assigned to regular police work in the New Territories Northern District, Zhang had contacted Chow. The two men had met at Tian's apartment to hammer out an agreement over a few beers. Chow would do everything he could to keep the Fanling gang out of human trafficking, drugs, and loan sharking. Zhang agreed to turn a blind eye to the betting shops, mah-jong parlours, and massage parlours. They also agreed to share information that didn't compromise their organizations.

Chow's police contacts were the envy of the gang's senior executives, and he'd been asked many times to reveal them. He never had and never would. The only person who knew of the relationship between Zhang and Chow was Tian. Not even Gao had known.

"If you didn't create this mess, who did?" Zhang asked.

"We don't know."

"Do you know how stupid I look now because I classified Gao's death as an accident?"

"It was a reasonable conclusion at the time."

"But not now. My bosses are convinced that the deaths of Gao and Ma are linked. They want me to reopen Gao's case."

"And if you do?"

"The presumption will be that there is a gangland war

going on, and we'll be forced to assign more resources to combat it."

"There is no war," Chow said. "And speaking of resources, how did it happen that half the Hong Kong Police Force was at the funeral home today?"

"How often does a Mountain Master get buried? It was a chance to see who would attend and what kind of nonsense might go on. We were on standby, nothing more. And you should know by now that even on standby, we come out in numbers. But there was no expectation that there would be trouble, especially the kind we ended up with. If we'd known that, our numbers would have been double."

"Can you calm things down on your end?"

"Under what pretext?"

"Not a pretext, but the fact that Gao's death was an accident, Ma was killed in an act of personal vengeance, and there is no gang war."

"Are those really facts?"

"No, but it will be better for all concerned if you treat them as such until I can confirm or deny them."

"Do you have any idea who killed Ma and the other man?"

"No, not yet."

Zhang hesitated and then said, "There's a feeling at Headquarters that events are getting out of control in the New Territories. The last thing they want is for civilians to get caught in the middle."

"You know that's the last thing I want to happen."

"I do, but it doesn't mean you can prevent it."

"Well, if we can't, who will? If you get involved, it will be after the fact. Give us a chance to sort this out."

"Sort out what? How?"

"Look, Gao's death caught everyone by surprise. He was a strong, stabilizing figure. His departure left a leadership void that other gangs might have thought they could take advantage of. But we'll have a new Mountain Master by Monday, and the first thing he'll do is calm the waters."

"Uncle, you aren't raising my comfort level when you imply that another gang might have been responsible for these deaths."

"Look, even if it was another gang, we don't want the violence to escalate. We have businesses that we don't want disrupted. We understand that when gangs fight each other, everyone loses. That's why, for the past five years, we've managed to keep peace in this part of the Territories. It wasn't always easy. There were provocations and disputes, but we managed to settle them without calling attention to ourselves or involving the police."

"I know you did, and that's why I give you as much rope as I do. Don't disappoint me this time."

"I won't," Chow said. "So, where does that leave us with regard to Headquarters?"

"I'll tell them I still think Gao's death was an accident and that Ma's killing was a personal act of vengeance," Zhang said. "They may not entirely believe me, but it should buy you some time to stabilize your situation. Once it is stable, the questions will stop. Did you say you'll have a new Mountain Master by Monday?"

"Yes. We're having an election."

"Who's most likely to win?"

"Ren."

"I know the name but I don't know much about him. What kind of man is he?"

The question caught Chow slightly off guard, and he struggled for a few seconds to find the right answer. Finally he said, "Solid."

"That's a good word to hear," Zhang said.

"Well, he's a good man."

"Stay in touch, Uncle," Zhang said. "I need to know if anything changes."

"You'll hear from me," Chow said.

He sighed in relief as he put down the phone. Chow didn't take Zhang's support for granted. He treated every conversation as if it were their first, as if they had to find common ground and determine how much trust could be extended. He had never knowingly lied to Zhang, and he'd never felt lied to. There had been times when he couldn't tell the entire truth, and he knew that cut both ways. Even so, he understood that this was a relationship that could end in a heartbeat; it amazed him that it had lasted as long as it had.

Chow got out of his chair and went to the bathroom. When he came back, he debated having one last beer but decided against it. His head was already feeling a bit woolly and he hadn't done any handicapping yet. He sat down, picked up the racing form, and focused his attention on the first race, a thousand-metre sprint for colts and geldings four years and older. He worked diligently on that race and then the others for several hours, the form's facts and figures displacing the worries that had filled his head. When he started to yawn and his eyes began to close, he put down the form and headed to the bedroom before he could fall asleep in the chair one more time.

He slept unusually well, and if he dreamed, he wasn't

aware of it. When he woke, the sun was streaming through the window onto his face. He blinked, shook a head that felt groggy, and licked lips that were dry. He went into the kitchen, drank two glasses of water, and then went to get his cigarettes and black Zippo lighter, which had been left with his watch and the racing form on the table by the chair. He lit up and looked at his watch. It was almost nine o'clock. This was the second time in less than a week that he'd slept well into the morning; his normal Sunday schedule was already off-kilter.

Half an hour later he walked out of his building with the racing form tucked under his arm and headed for the congee restaurant. The restaurant was a busy place every day of the week, but particularly on Sundays. He was about a hundred metres from the door when he saw there was a lineup outside. He groaned and debated whether to join the line, go to another restaurant, or take his chances on getting seated. He walked into the restaurant, squeezed past some waiting customers, and almost ran into Jia.

"There you are," she said. "I was getting worried about you. You're rarely this late."

"I had too much to drink last night."

"That's not like you either."

"Well, there have been things going on."

She leaned close. "I heard. That's one more reason why I was worried about you."

"I'm fine, but I'm hungry. Any chance of getting a seat?"

"I'll give you the next available table, or you can sit now if you don't mind sharing one."

"I'll wait," he said. "I want to be able to spread out my form."

"Shouldn't be more than a few minutes. You can stand by the cash register."

Chow leaned against the counter and opened his form, forming a barrier between himself and the other customers, who were visibly annoyed by the preference he was being shown. That didn't actually bother him. Jumping the queue wasn't something he did as a rule, but in this case he regarded it as a reward for the loyalty he'd shown to Jia and her husband over so many years. He read over the form, his notes in the margins from the night before a messy scrawl.

"Your table is ready," Jia said before he could finish re-handicapping the first race.

He followed her to the back of the restaurant and slipped into a booth for four. "I'll have my congee with sausage, scallions, duck eggs, and youtiao," he said.

When she left, he buried his head in the form again. There was a big-money stakes race that day, and a well-known jockey had been flown in from Australia to ride one of the favourites. The jockey had also been booked to ride in some earlier races; Chow was keen to see how he did in them before deciding to back him in the big race. It was generally believed that Hong Kong jockeys weren't of the same calibre as the top riders from Australia and Europe, but Chow thought there was something to be said for local course knowledge. He wanted to see how well the jockey adapted to Happy Valley.

Although he was now operating according to his usual routine, things weren't seamless. Flickering on the edge of his consciousness were the events from the day before, and as much as he tried to focus on the race card, he couldn't stop them from intruding. When the memory of Ma's body in the Hop Sing courtyard entered his mind's eye, he put down his pen for a moment and stared blankly at the seat across from him.

"Here's your breakfast," Jia said, interrupting his thoughts.

Chow poured tea and then sprinkled white pepper over his congee. He added the small slices of red sausage and slivers of green scallion and dipped his spoon into the bowl. For once he didn't eat in a hurry. His mind was still racing and he needed to slow it down. Eating slowly, he thought, might calm him, so he moved the spoon from the bowl to his mouth very deliberately, waited until the congee had been swallowed, and then painstakingly repeated the process. Fifteen minutes later, feeling calmer, he pushed the bowl to one side, spread the paper across the table, and made ready to delve into the high-stakes race. Before he could, he heard a familiar voice. Looking towards the front of the restaurant, he saw a grim-faced Xu walking quickly towards him.

"Thank god I found you," Xu said. "I tried the apartment, and when you weren't there, I was afraid you had already left for Happy Valley."

"What's going on?"

"Tian has been trying to phone you. When he couldn't get hold of you, he called me."

"He must have just missed me," Chow said. "But you still haven't told me what's going on."

"There's some shit going down at Dong's Restaurant. He didn't give me any details. He said he needed to talk to you."

"Why me? Why hasn't he spoken to Wang or Ren?"

"Uncle, I don't know any more than I've told you, except that he sounded desperate."

Chow looked for Jia and saw her coming out of the kitchen. He waved at her. "I have to make an urgent call. Do you have a phone I can use?"

She nodded in the direction of the kitchen. "Our office is behind the door on the left. The phone is on the desk, probably buried under a pile of papers. Excuse the mess."

"Wait here," Chow said to Xu. He left the booth and headed for the office. He opened the door and stepped into a room that had space for only a desk, a chair, and a filing cabinet. Jia hadn't exaggerated about the mess. Papers were strewn everywhere. He lifted some bills off the phone, put them to one side, and then called directory assistance for Dong's number. As he dialled the number he'd been given, he braced himself for bad news in one form or another. Tian wasn't a man often described as desperate.

The line was busy. Chow hung up, waited, and redialled. Tian answered on the fourth ring with a terse "*Wei.*"

"This is Uncle. What's going on over there?"

"It's what's not going on that has me pissed off," Tian said.

"I don't understand."

"Normally at this time on a Sunday morning, this place is filled with horse bettors. Today it's empty, because our horse players are out on the street and can't get in."

"Why the hell not?"

"Uncle, the entire fucking place is surrounded. About twenty men arrived about half an hour ago; they aren't letting anyone in and they won't let us out. They told me we won't be opening for business until they give the okay."

"Who are they?"

"Tai Po forty-niners and Blue Lanterns."

"Are you sure about that?"

"They told me, and I know a few of them anyway. One of them apologized for what they're doing."

"Are they armed?"

"They are."

"Has anyone alerted the cops?"

"Not that I know of."

"That's probably just as well. We don't want to involve them in this," Chow said. "But Tian, doesn't Wang have men in your area?"

"There were two of them, but they disappeared when the Tai Po guys arrived," Tian said. "Can't say I blame them, given how badly they were outnumbered."

"You need to contact Wang."

"He was the first person I called, but I can't reach him."

"He wouldn't be at home on a Sunday morning. He'll be making the rounds of the betting shops."

"I know that. After I couldn't reach him at home, I phoned three of our shops. No one answered at any of them. I just tried again a few minutes ago."

"How come they're letting you use a phone?" Chow asked.

"They locked me in the restaurant office by myself. No one noticed there's a phone here, but I guess the guys running the other shops weren't as lucky," Tian said. "I'm guessing that all those shops are shut down."

"It's too soon to jump to that conclusion," Chow said, even though the same thought was in his head. "How about Ren? Did you try him?"

"The woman he lives with told me she has no idea where he is."

"Did you leave a message?"

"Of course I did, and I stressed how urgent it is that he get it."

"Shit."

"Uncle, Tai Po is making a play for us. I know they are," Tian said. "That fucker Ren has sold us out. I told you that dinner with Tso in Kowloon was suspicious."

"I'm not saying you're wrong about Tai Po, but you should stop that kind of talk about Ren," Chow said. "The first thing we have to do is be certain about what's going on. Once we are, I'm sure Wang and Ren will find a way to deal with it."

"You have to get hold of them first."

"I will, one way or another."

"Uncle, we can't let them do this to us," Tian said. "We can't let them take over like this."

"No one is going to take over."

"Then someone had better do something, and quickly."

Chow drew a deep breath. "Stay close to the phone, and for god's sake don't do anything stupid. I'll get back to you as soon as I can." He ended the call and then immediately dialed Wang's number. He hung up when he heard the answering machine. He phoned Ren. No one answered. Pang was next on his list.

"This is a bit of a surprise," Pang said as soon as he heard Chow's voice.

"Have you heard what's going on?"

"There's nothing to worry about," Pang said.

"What the hell do you mean?"

"It is true that the cops picked up Ren early this morning and took him to Hong Kong for questioning about yesterday's killings, but there's nothing to it. It's just the cops trying to show that they're doing something. I spoke to Ren's lawyer half an hour ago. He said Ren should be released in time for lunch."

"That isn't what I'm talking about," Chow said. "Tai Po is making a move on us. They've already closed down some of our betting shops."

"What? How do you know that?"

"I just spoke to Tian. Dong's Kitchen is surrounded by twenty guys from Tai Po, and they're not letting anyone in or out. He hasn't been able to make contact with the other shops, so I think it's logical to assume that the same thing is going on there."

"Are you absolutely sure about this?"

"I don't doubt Tian. He said the guys are from Tai Po. He said he's shut down. What's not to believe?"

"No, you're right, Tian is not a man to exaggerate," Pang said. "What does Wang say about this? This is his responsibility."

"We haven't been able to contact him and we have no idea where he is," Chow said. "It would be helpful if you could help in that regard — by making some calls, I mean."

"Of course."

"But I think the first call you should make is to Ren's lawyer in Hong Kong. Tell him what's going on and get him to pass word to Ren. We need Ren to phone his friend Tso and tell him to back off."

"Tso and he aren't really that close."

"That's not what I've heard, but that doesn't matter. What's important is that Ren contact him and they sort this out," Chow said. "In the meantime, I'll keep trying to find Wang."

"Don't do anything rash, and keep me informed," Pang said.

"The same advice to you," Chow said, not willing to concede an ounce of leadership. "Now go call Hong Kong."

Chow tried Wang's number one more time, with the same result. He called directory assistance again and got the numbers for two more betting shops. No one picked up the phone at either shop. He called Dong's. This time Tian didn't answer.

Chow left the office, frustrated and anxious in equal measure. Xu was sitting in the booth when he reappeared, but quickly stood up. "What's going on?" he said.

"It appears that Tai Po is making a run at us, or at least at our gambling operations," Chow said. "They've shut down Dong's and, I think it's safe to assume, at least a couple of our other shops."

"Holy fuck."

"There's more," Chow said. "Ren is in Hong Kong being interviewed by the police about yesterday's killings, so he's out of touch. No one has been able to contact Wang. He isn't answering his home phone, probably because he's out on the street somewhere. We need to find him. Do you know where Fong is?"

"I imagine he's at home."

"Get hold of him. I need both of you on the street looking for Wang. You take the western part of town and tell Fong to look in the east. I'm going to see if I can find him around here."

"How do we reach you if we do find him?"

"Let's meet back here at the restaurant in an hour. Hopefully, when we do, one of us will have found Wang."

23

CHOW FOUND WANG SITTING IN THE LUCKY EIGHT MAH-
jong parlour, which did extra business as a betting shop for
the Happy Valley races. It was the third business Chow had
gone to after a restaurant and a massage parlour, and it was
markedly different from the others because a dozen tough-
looking armed men formed a wall in front of it. Chow saw
gun butts sticking out of waistbands and the outlines of guns
under several shirts; one man was openly carrying a machete.

A larger group — maybe fifty or sixty men — was milling about on the street, talking to each other and pointing
to the parlour. Chow assumed they were frustrated bettors.
Moving closer to the toughs, he looked into the Lucky Eight.
Through a plate-glass window he could see Wang sitting at a
table with three other men, two of whom Chow knew were
betting clerks. The third man had his hand on a gun that
was lying on the table, pointed in the direction of Wang.

"I'd like to go inside to place a bet," Chow said to one of
the toughs.

"The place is closed."

"When will it open? The races start soon."

"I don't know."

"Well, could I talk to one of the guys inside? They must know."

"Move along."

"What's going on here?"

"You should mind your own fucking business and move on like I told you."

"This isn't right," Chow said, staring through the window and trying to get Wang's attention. But the Red Pole's head was lowered and his eyes were focused on the table.

"I'm not telling you again . . ." the man said, taking a step towards Chow and pointing at him.

"Okay, I get it. I'm leaving," Chow said.

He checked his watch as he moved away from the Lucky Eight and saw that he had fifteen minutes to get to the congee restaurant to meet Xu and Fong. He hurried along the street, his mind turning over calculations. There wasn't any doubt that Tian was correct about their gambling establishments being targeted, but was it just Tai Po or were other gangs involved? Logically he thought it would be Tai Po alone, but he kicked himself for not trying to find out where the man with the machete was from. Assuming that it was Tai Po, what was their end game? As he struggled to answer that question, he saw two men standing on the next street corner whom he recognized as Fanling forty-niners.

"Hey!" he shouted as he drew near to them.

They saw him and immediately looked uncomfortable.

"Where are you guys supposed to be? Not here, I bet," Chow said.

"We were at the Lucky Eight. We were outside when that gang arrived. They ran us off," the taller of the men said.

"They outnumber us five to one, and they're armed to the teeth," the other said.

"I saw how many of them there are," Chow said. "Where was Wang when they showed up?"

"He was inside the parlour. They trapped him. They wouldn't let him leave."

"And what did you do then? Go for tea?" Chow said.

"We didn't know what to do. We didn't want to do anything that might put Wang at risk. We didn't know who to talk to. We've been standing here trying to figure out something," the tall one said, his discomfort growing. "It hasn't been that long since those guys moved in on us."

Chow shook his head. "You know who I am, right?"

"Uncle."

"Are you armed?"

"We don't have guns on us. That's part of the problem."

"But you do have guns?"

"Yeah."

"How long would it take for you to get them and come back here?"

"Half an hour, more or less."

"Then go right now, and get back here as fast as you can," Chow said. "If I'm not here, you wait. Do not leave."

"Okay."

"And if you see any of our forty-niners or Blue Lanterns on the way, or if you can get hold of some, I want them to get their weapons as well and meet us here. Tell them that's an order, not a request."

"Uncle, are we going to war against those guys?" the tall one asked.

He seemed to ask out of curiosity rather than fear, and

Chow began to feel better disposed towards them. "What we're going to do first is free Wang. I'm not sure what we'll have to do to accomplish that, but whatever it is, we'll do it. After that's done, who knows?"

The tall man nodded. "We'll see you back here soon."

Chow watched them leave, then continued towards the restaurant with an increased sense of purpose. When he got closer, he saw that Xu and Fong were already there, pacing back and forth on the sidewalk.

"I found Wang," he said before either of them could speak. "He's in the Lucky Eight mah-jong parlour. I think it's fair to say that he's being held prisoner, because he's sitting at a table with a gun pointed at him and the place is surrounded by a gang of thugs who won't let anyone in or out. It's exactly the same scenario as at Dong's."

"Do they know who Wang is?" Xu asked.

"I expect they do."

"He must be going nuts."

"He didn't look happy."

"What are we going to do?"

"Get him out of there."

"How?"

"I met two forty-niners on the way here. They were outside the Lucky Eight when the gang arrived and got run off. I've sent them to get guns and as many other men as they can."

"Are we really going to resort to weapons?" Fong said.

"We are. Do you still have that Russian submachine gun?"

"No, but I have a slightly improved Chinese knock-off version of the same gun."

"Get it. Do you have a pistol?"

"The Chinese Type 54 — another knock-off."

"Bring it for me."

"I have a pistol as well," Xu said.

"Great. How many men do you think you can locate in the next half-hour?"

"Maybe two or three," Xu said.

"A few," Fong added.

"They don't all have to be armed," Chow said.

"Most of them will be," Fong said.

"The more men we can get and the more weapons they have, the less bloody this should be. My first objective is to free Wang. After that, we'll play it by ear."

"What about the cops?" Xu asked.

"I didn't see any there and there weren't any at Dong's. As long as things don't get out of hand, they have no reason to get involved."

"How can you prevent things from getting out of hand?" Xu said.

"I'll figure that out when I see how many men we have to go with us to the Lucky Eight. Right now, the priority is for you to get your weapons and find as many men as you can. I'll be waiting here for you."

As soon as they left, Chow went back into the congee restaurant. There was still a line of people outside and a throng inside the door. He squeezed past them and waved at Jia. "Can I use your phone again?" he asked.

"Go ahead."

He entered the office, sat behind the desk, and made his first call. As the phone was ringing, he quietly prayed that it be answered.

"This is Superintendent Zhang."

"This is Chow."

"Two phone calls in less than twenty-four hours. Something must have happened."

"It has, and I'm calling you to ask for something I've never requested before — a favour."

Zhang hesitated. "What kind of favour?"

"For the next three or four hours, I'd like you to keep the police away from all of our betting shops."

"Uncle, you know that we always give your shops a wide berth on Sunday."

"Yes, but that's because they're normally open and operating. Right now our shops are closed. They're surrounded by triads who I think are from Tai Po, and they're not letting anyone in or out. Unless I'm badly mistaken, our bettors are going to start getting fractious as post time gets nearer, and that won't be a good thing. They'll either initiate some kind of confrontation with the Tai Po boys or start flooding your phone lines with complaints."

"Instead of keeping our force away from the shops, why shouldn't I do the opposite and send some of my men?"

"How would the police intervening to help keep open illegal betting shops look to your superiors?"

"I could massage it."

"Maybe you could, but I still don't want you involved," Chow said. "We've been hearing for months about another gang possibly trying to muscle their way onto our turf. Now it's happened. We're the ones who need to respond to it. We have to send a clear message that we're capable of defending our own interests. If we don't, they'll just keep coming at us. They won't stop and you'll get that escalating violence we talked about last night."

"Could this gang be behind the killings?"

"Possibly, which is another reason why you want us to make sure Tai Po doesn't get a foothold in Fanling. They don't hesitate to use violence against anyone, including civilians."

"If that's the case, how can you remove them without violence?"

"I believe I can do it, but I can't promise that. I'll do everything I can to avoid violence, and if it can't be avoided, I'll try to keep it to the absolute minimum. And I'll make sure that no civilians get involved," Chow said. "Zhang, you need to trust me on this one."

"Uncle, I have never not trusted you. But you're right, you've never asked me for a favour before, and I'm trying to figure out how this fits into the structure of our relationship."

"If I'm granted this favour, it can only strengthen our relationship. And I'll owe you a very large favour in return."

"And if I don't grant it?"

"I don't want to consider that possibility."

Zhang became quiet. Chow waited; he'd stated his case and saw no reason to expand on it.

"I'll tell my men to stay away from all your betting shops until this evening. That should give you enough time to do whatever you have to," Zhang finally said. "But Uncle, if things get out of control, you understand that I'll have no choice but to move in. And if I do, it will be in numbers large enough to take care of both the Fanling and Tai Po gangs."

"Thank you."

"Good luck. And I sincerely hope I won't hear your name for at least the rest of today."

Chow sat back in the chair, feeling relieved and thankful.

Then he took several deep breaths and reached for the phone again.

"Who is this?" Pang said.

"Uncle. I've located Wang."

"Where is he?"

"At the Lucky Eight mah-jong parlour."

"That's good."

"No, it isn't. The place is surrounded by goons, and just like at Dong's, they aren't letting anyone in or out."

"Are they from Tai Po?"

"I didn't ask, but I assume so."

"Is Wang hurt?"

"I couldn't talk to him but he looked okay, other than being pissed off," Chow said. "But if we don't open the shops, our business is going to take a beating today. We all know that Sunday is our most profitable day of the week."

"I care less about that than I do about keeping everything calm, and Ren feels the same way."

"You spoke to him?"

"Not directly, but I did talk to his lawyer. I explained to him what was going on and he passed the message to Ren. Then he called me back with Ren's orders."

"And those are?"

"Do nothing. He'll be back in Fanling this afternoon. He'll find out what's really going on and then he'll deal with it."

"Did you tell the lawyer we believe Tai Po is behind this?"

"I did. He told me that Ren said we aren't to jump to any conclusions until he's had a chance to speak to several people. I assume Tso will be one of them."

"Or the only one."

"It's Ren's decision," Pang said.

Chow found himself staring at a calendar on the office wall. The photo was of horses barrelling down the stretch of a racetrack that looked like Happy Valley. "If we don't open for business today, we're going to lose a lot of income. As far as I'm concerned, it's money that will have been stolen from us by Tai Po."

"That's ridiculous."

"And I can't sit back and allow Wang to be held hostage."

"No one has made any demands. How is he a hostage?"

"He's being held at gunpoint and they won't let him leave. That fits my definition."

"Maybe they don't know who he is."

"Do you really believe that's possible? Of course they know who he is."

"Leave it alone, Uncle," Pang said, sidestepping Chow's question. "Let Ren look after things when he gets back from Hong Kong."

"Wang is our Red Pole, for god's sake. I imagine he's going crazy being stuck in this humiliating situation. It makes him — and us — look ridiculous."

"He should have been more careful."

"That's bullshit."

"Ren told him more than once to be on the alert."

"I'm quite sure he had as many men on the street as possible, and I'm equally sure he allocated them as best he could."

"Well, his best wasn't good enough."

"Fuck you, Pang," Chow said. "I'm not leaving him in their hands and I'm not going to let them steal an entire day's income from us."

"What are you talking about?"

"I'm going to get him and I'm going to open up our shops so our customers can bet like they do every Sunday."

"No!" Pang shouted. "Leave it alone! Do as Ren says. Give him a chance to negotiate some kind of settlement."

"If they're still holding Wang, we'll lose negotiating leverage. He runs our guys on the ground."

"We can manage the guys on the ground without Wang."

Chow started to argue and then stopped. It was pointless. "Whatever," he said.

"Ren will be back here by midafternoon. He'll get this settled in no time."

"I'm sure he will."

"So you'll leave this alone?"

"Look, I'm using an outside phone right now. Later today I'll be at my apartment or at the office. Call me when Ren gets back."

"That's a sound decision. We'll talk to you then," Pang said.

Chow ended the call and immediately dialled Sammy Wing. He got the answering machine again. "Sammy, this is Chow. Change of plans — I won't be at Happy Valley today. Tai Po has made a move on us. Tell your boss I hope he keeps his word and doesn't take sides."

He stared at the calendar again. *If I'm going to miss a Sunday afternoon at the races*, he thought, *I'm going to make it worth it.*

24

CHOW WAITED OUTSIDE THE RESTAURANT FOR XU AND
Fong. Fong lived closest but it was Xu who arrived first,
with a man he recognized as the operator of three massage
parlours. As they exchanged greetings, Fong approached
from the opposite direction with two men whom Chow
had worked with as Blue Lanterns. One now owned a restaurant and the other was on the fringes of the "insurance
business" — Ma's term for protection money. Fong and the
restaurant owner were carrying large leather bags.

"What's in the bags?" Chow asked.

"Your pistol and a submachine gun are in my bag. Cho
has an SMG in his."

"Is everyone else armed?" Chow asked.

Xu and the massage parlour operator nodded.

"Does everyone know the plan?"

"All I told them is that we have a problem and need their
help," Fong said.

Chow smiled, pleased that the men had so willingly
shown their loyalty. "The situation is simple enough. The Tai
Po gang has decided to shut down our gambling operations

and is holding some of our men hostage, including Wang. Our first job is to free Wang. He's at the Lucky Eight mahjong parlour, and that's where we're headed."

"How many Tai Po men?" Cho asked.

"About a dozen."

"We're only six."

"We're meeting more men on the way. We're also going to have more firepower and the element of surprise on our side," Chow said. "I don't want to say anything else until our whole group is together."

"Then let's get going," Fong said.

Chow led the way. When they neared the corner where he'd told Wang's men he'd meet them, there were now four men looking towards him. "Thanks for coming," he said as he approached. "Does everyone have a weapon?"

"We all do," the tall man said.

"What's the plan?" Xu asked.

"Can I have the pistol?" Chow said to Fong.

Fong reached into his bag and passed it to him. Chow stuck it into his right-hand jacket pocket.

"The plan is to go to the Lucky Eight mah-jong parlour, get Wang out of there, and open the place for business," Chow said. "The problem is that some triads from Tai Po are controlling it and holding Wang. They've formed a wall in front of the place and are preventing anyone from getting in or out. We're going to take down that wall."

Chow saw the men glance at each other, and a couple of them shuffled their feet. "There is no reason to look uncomfortable," he said. "I'm not suggesting we go charging at them. I want to do this in a way that stops them from reacting until it's too late to do anything, and in a way that hopefully avoids violence. We don't want the police to get involved, and if there's much gunplay, they will be. So we need to be smarter than the guys from Tai Po."

"How are we going to do all that?" Fong asked.

"Like this," Chow said, and then proceeded to explain how he wanted the operation to be run.

"What if they don't co-operate? What if they want to fight?" Fong said when Chow had finished.

"Then there will be a fight and we'll take our chances with the cops. There's no backing down. There's no walking away. Does anyone have a problem with that?"

"I think we're all good," Fong said, looking at each man in turn. None of them indicated otherwise.

"In that case, let's go free Wang."

As they approached the betting shop, Chow saw that the crowd had grown and had become more agitated. Those were all positive signs in his mind. He stepped into the middle of the throng while his men spread out. He waited until he was sure they were all in place, then held up his arm and began to ease his way towards the men blocking the entrance to the Lucky Eight. He stopped just short of the man with the machete and then looked left and right to make sure everyone was in place. When he could see them all, he stepped directly in front of the Tai Po triad.

"Hey, remember me?" Chow said. "Any chance of getting inside yet?"

"Fuck off."

"Pardon?" Chow said, putting his hand in his jacket pocket and moving even closer.

"I said fuck off."

Chow pressed forward, slid the gun from his pocket, and

dug the barrel into the man's belly. "Make one move and I'll shoot you right here and now," he said.

The man stared at him in disbelief, then looked to his right as if expecting help. The Tai Po men on that side had three pistols and a submachine gun trained on them. He looked left and saw a similar sight.

"We could take you all out in ten seconds," Chow said. "But we'd rather not, and I'm sure you feel the same way."

"You don't know what you're doing."

"I know exactly what I'm doing. Now I'd like you to drop the machete and for the rest of your group to drop their weapons. Do you want to tell them, or should I?"

The man seemed distracted, his eyes shifting in all directions. Chow tensed as he sensed this wouldn't be ending as peaceably as he'd hoped. "Drop the machete," he repeated.

The man nodded, and then Chow saw the arm holding the machete twitch and the steel blade suddenly start rising into a striking position. Without a second thought, he lowered his gun and fired. The bullet ripped into the man's inner thigh, near his genitals. The machete fell from his hand and the man's body followed it to the ground. He writhed in pain, his knees pulled up and his arms wrapped around his legs.

Chow picked up the weapon and waved it at the Tai Po men. "All of you, hand over your weapons. If you don't, we'll shoot you one by one. I don't think I shot off his balls, but I came close. Maybe I can do better with a second chance. Does anyone want to try me?"

In a matter of seconds the Fanling men were in possession of all the Tai Po guns and knives.

"Was this guy in charge?" Chow asked, pointing the machete at the prostrate body.

"No, I am," a tall, lean man said.

"What's your name?"

"Li."

"Where are you from?"

Li hesitated.

"I'm not going to ask again."

"Tai Po."

"Well, Mr. Li from Tai Po, here's what we're going to do," Chow said. "We're going into the parlour and you're going to tell the guy in there with the gun to hand it over. If he doesn't, I'll shoot you and then him."

"That won't be necessary. We'll co-operate," Li said. Then he motioned to the man on the ground. "You didn't have to do that."

"Just like you didn't have to bring an armed gang to Fanling and attempt to take over our businesses. Let's go inside," Chow said, prodding him with the gun. He shouted to Xu, "Come with us."

The men at the table stood up as soon as the door opened. Chow, Xu, and Li entered the room. "Hand over your gun to the guy you've been guarding," Li said to the man.

"Do you know who he is?" Chow said, pointing to Wang.

"No. Should I?"

Wang took the gun from the man, stuck it into his waist-band, and came towards them. Without acknowledging Chow and without uttering a word, he drove his fist into Li's face. Chow heard a crack and saw blood spatter. Li fell back and almost keeled over.

"I know that must have felt good, but that's enough," Chow said.

Wang rubbed his fist. "I'm over it now."

"Is there a room in this place where we can lock up these guys, plus another ten or so that are outside?" Chow asked.

"There's a supply room in the back."

"Any windows? Any way for them to get out?"

"No, they'd have to come through the door, but you can lock it."

"We can also leave a couple of guys with guns outside the door just in case."

Li removed his hand from his bloody nose. "The man you shot needs a doctor. He needs treatment. You can't put him in a supply room. We're not animals."

Chow turned to Wang. "Is there a local doctor we can use? One who knows how to keep his mouth shut?"

"There's one five minutes from here."

"Then let's get that guy into a cab with one of your men from outside and send him to see the doctor. Your man shouldn't leave his side. When the guy is fixed, he should bring him back here," Chow said, and then looked at Li. "We're not animals either."

"I'll do that in a minute," Wang said. "First you need to tell me what the hell has been going on this morning."

"It looks like Tai Po is trying to take over our gambling operations, and maybe more than that," Chow said. "Tian called me to say Dong's has been shut down, and we haven't been able to make contact with the other shops."

"How many places did you target?" Wang said to Li.

"I don't know. I had nothing to do with the planning of this. I was told to come here and just make sure no one went in or out."

"Told by whom?"

"Tan, our Red Pole."

"That fucker," Wang said, and then shook his head. "I blame myself for this. I shouldn't have spread our men so thinly."

"You can only do so much with what you have," Chow said. "Speaking of which, how many forty-niners can you get to join us in the next half-hour?"

"There were two here with me, but they took off."

"They're outside now. They came with us and they were terrific."

"That's good to hear; I was ready to beat the shit out of both of them," Wang said. He paused as he thought. "There are about ten more in the vicinity."

"We'll need them all."

"What are we going to do?"

"After we've put these guys in the supply room, we need to open up Lucky Eight and get back to business. We'll leave two guards. They can double as security," Chow said. "Then I want to head directly to Dong's. There's an even bigger Tai Po crew there, but if we take the same approach, and if they have any respect for submachine guns, we should be able to take back control."

"What is Ren saying about all this?"

"I have no idea. He's in Hong Kong. The police picked him up early this morning for questioning. He should be released this afternoon."

"So he doesn't know what's going on?"

"I wouldn't go that far. I talked to Pang. He told me he talked to Ren's lawyer and the lawyer briefed Ren."

"Do we know how Ren reacted? Did he say anything through the lawyer?"

"According to Pang, Ren's instructions were for us to stay

calm and do nothing until he gets back to Fanling this afternoon. Pang said Ren and Tso would sort things out."

"Doing nothing isn't exactly what you just did."

"The instructions were shit."

"He's still the boss."

"Maybe I misunderstood what I was told," Chow said.
"That's the problem with second- and third-hand conversations — things get misconstrued. Besides, if Ren is serious
about negotiating, I thought it would be better if we were
the ones holding hostages."

"I can't argue with your logic," Wang said, and then shook
his head. "I can't remember the last time I felt so stupid and
useless. At least now we have a chance to turn this thing
around."

"Are you ready to go to Dong's?"

"Am I ever," Wang said. "Do we need to let Pang know
what's gone down?"

"No, not until we're completely finished."

"Then let's go."

"Xu, stay here with Li until we send in the other men.
Once they're in the supply room and we have the guards in
place, I'd like you to come to Dong's."

"Sure thing, Uncle."

Chow and Wang had begun to walk towards the door
when Wang stopped. "How come there aren't any cops here?"
he asked. "I've just noticed there isn't a single one. I thought
the crowd outside would have caught their attention, and if
not that, then your gunshot."

"I talked to my friends in the police department. I managed to convince them to allow our Fanling gang to resolve
our differences with Tai Po on our own, without any outside

interference. As long as we maintain public order, they'll leave us alone until the end of the day. And nothing I know of will maintain public order better than getting our betting shops open."

"Uncle, you are one smart son of a bitch."

"Thank you, Wang."

"And I'd forgotten what a tough son of a bitch you are too," Wang said. "It's good to see that all those years of working in the office haven't softened you."

25

THEY RODE IN CARS FROM THE LUCKY EIGHT TO DONG'S
Restaurant, but they got out about half a kilometre away and walked the rest of the distance. They heard the crowd at the same time they caught sight of it. It was larger than the one at the Lucky Eight and appeared to be even more agitated. Chow looked at his watch. It was twelve-thirty, and post time for the first race at Happy Valley was one o'clock. No wonder the gamblers were restless.

They had agreed to use the same strategy as at the Lucky Eight. As soon as they reached the crowd, the men spread out and began to work their way towards the line of Tai Po men blocking the entrance to Dong's. Wang was five metres to Chow's immediate right, trying to be as inconspicuous as possible, but as they neared the restaurant he stopped and said, "Uncle, that's Min in the middle of the Tai Po group. He's Tan's assistant. He'll recognize me for sure, and he might know you."

"I don't think I've ever met him. He doesn't look familiar."

"Okay, but I'm going to hang back until you can put a gun in his belly."

Chow nodded and continued to fight his way through the men standing shoulder to shoulder as they complained about the closed betting shop.

Min was short and broad-shouldered and had tattoos on his bare arms and down the side of his neck. Chow cleared the crowd and approached him. Min stared at him with eyes that were narrow slits. "What do you think you're doing?" he said.

"I want to place a bet. Why is the shop not open?"

"It's closed."

"Until when?"

"Until we're told it isn't."

"And who will tell you that?"

"None of your fucking business."

"But this *is* my business," Chow said, taking two quick steps forward and pressing the gun into Min's side. "I'm Chow. I'm with the Fanling gang. Please don't move or try anything silly. We have all your men covered."

"You should believe him," Wang said, moving into their line of sight. "He will shoot."

Min looked at Wang and then back at Chow, his face registering confusion. "What's going on?"

"How can you ask that, you asshole?" Wang said. "You've shut down our businesses, you're on our turf, and we're real close to having a war."

"I don't know what you're talking about," Min said. "I was told to put men around this place, the Lucky Eight mah-jong parlour, the Red Sun Restaurant, and your betting shop in Shek Wu Hui, and that's what I did. You need to talk to your bosses — whoever they are these days. They'll explain."

"What do our bosses have to do with this? I spoke to one

of them a few hours ago, and he knew nothing about this," Chow said.

"I don't know who's talking to who, and I don't care. I was told to put men around these four places and make sure no one went in or out, and that's what I did."

"We've just come from the Lucky Eight. Your men were holding me prisoner there," Wang said. "And you're holding Tian inside Dong's."

"Like I said, I was told not to let anyone in or out. Were you inside when my men arrived?"

"Yes."

"Then that explains it. My men follow orders, just like I do," Min said. "You know what it's like. The bosses tell us the absolute minimum and we tell our men even less. We expect them to do exactly what they're told. They don't need explanations and we don't want them to start thinking for themselves. I'm sorry if you got caught up in it, but you know how it works."

"How what works? This is our territory. You have no right to be here," Wang said.

"I was told we were coming here to provide protection," Min said.

"Are you crazy? Protection from what? From whom?"

"I don't know and I didn't ask. Like I said, I was given an order to seal off these businesses until I'm told they can open."

"Well, whoever or whatever we're supposed to be protected from, we obviously don't need it anymore. So why don't you tell your men to drop their weapons," Chow said.

"Are you sure about that?" Min asked.

"Just tell them to do it," said Wang.

Min stared at Wang. Wang stared back, unblinking, his jaw clenched.

"Put your weapons down," Min shouted to his men.

"Collect them and take them back to my car," Wang said to one of his forty-niners, and then turned back to Min. "Now tell your men to stand by that bakery over there. I'll send some men to keep them company. No one is leaving here yet, and that includes you. We need to talk."

"Sure," Min said, and then spoke to his men.

As he was doing so, Chow stepped past him and went into the restaurant. Tian and five other men were waiting for him. "You're open for business again," Chow said. "But this crowd is going to be crazy. Do you need help?"

"We can handle them," Tian said, and smiled. "I knew you'd get here sooner or later."

"Sit over there," Wang said as he entered with Min.

The two men went to a corner table. Chow joined them.

"So what's this crap about you being sent here to protect us?" Wang said.

"That's what I was told. I can't tell you anything more than that because I don't know anything else."

"And it was Tan who told you that, correct?" Chow said.

"Yeah."

"If someone or something was a threat to Fanling, why wouldn't he call me? I'm the Red Pole," Wang said.

"I don't know. You'll have to ask your bosses. Or you can talk to Tan."

"I intend to."

"In the meantime, can my men and I leave?"

Wang looked at Chow. "What do you think?"

"We can't risk them coming back. Keep five of his men

here. Put them somewhere out of the way and under guard. The rest of them can leave," Chow said, and then leaned towards Min. "If you or anyone else from Tai Po comes back here, we'll kill all five of them."

Min glared at Chow. "I'm just realizing that I don't know who you are."

"His name is Uncle. He's our White Paper Fan," Wang said. "But he can do a lot more than push paper."

"We also have ten of your men locked up at the Lucky Eight. The same thing will happen to them if you try anything," Chow said. "We have a problem that needs to be resolved, and until it is, I'm not letting any of those men go."

"None of that's necessary — we won't be back," Min said. "But I get what you're doing."

"Good. Now, you said you have men at the Red Sun and in Shek Wu Hui?"

"Eight at the restaurant and a dozen at the shop."

"We have a car nearby. I want you to go to both places and tell your men to go home. I'll send Xu, one of our senior guys, with you. Then I want you to come back here with him. You okay with that?"

"That's fine."

"Then I have nothing more to discuss with you," Chow said, and turned to Wang. "I'd appreciate it if you could introduce Min to Xu and let Xu know what we expect to happen. I have to make some phone calls."

He waited until both men had left the restaurant before he got up from the table. The restaurant had filled quickly; there were long lines leading from the door to the rear, where Tian and his assistants sat behind two tables taking money and writing betting slips. Chow walked around the lines, having to repeat several times that he wasn't trying to cut in to place a bet.

"I need to use a phone," he said to Tian.

"There's one on the wall just inside the kitchen," Tian said, barely looking up.

Chow found the phone easily enough and was pleased to see that the kitchen was closed, so he wouldn't have to worry about privacy or noise. He reached for the phone and dialled.

"*Wei*," Pang said.

"This is Chow. Any word from Ren?"

"I spoke to him about five minutes ago. He's been released. He should be in Fanling in about an hour."

"We need to meet when he gets here."

"He's ahead of you on that score. He's already told me to organize a meeting. Can you make it to the office for three?"

"I'll be there. And I'll let Wang know that Ren is back in Fanling and has called for a meeting."

"Wang? I thought you said he was at the Lucky Eight."

"He was, but the guys who were holding him had a change of heart and let him leave."

"What happened?"

"You can ask him when you see him."

"Whatever the reason, that's great news."

"And you'll be happy to know that all our betting shops will be open for business shortly."

"How?"

"Another change of heart, I guess."

"This is all very strange."

"Which part? The fact that they were closed down in the first place or that they're now operating normally?"

"All of it," Pang said, and paused. "Ren will be thrilled to hear this, but we still need to meet. The fact that things seem to have normalized doesn't mean we don't have a problem that could return and bite us on the ass."

"My feelings exactly."

"So we'll see you and Wang at three?"

"You will indeed," Chow said, hanging up. He quickly dialled another number.

"Zhang residence," a woman answered.

"Can I speak to the Superintendent, please?" he said.

"Who is calling?"

"Chow Tung."

"Just one moment."

He heard voices in the background and imagined that the policeman wouldn't be happy about his calling again.

"Uncle," Zhang said. "What's gone wrong?"

"Nothing. I swear to you, things couldn't have gone more smoothly. I resolved our problem and life in Fanling is proceeding as it should on a Sunday afternoon."

"Then why are you phoning me?"

"I need to confirm something."

"Are you asking for another favour?"

"If you want to classify it as a favour, I won't object."

"Tell me what you want first."

"It isn't complicated. I was told that Ren was picked up by the police this morning and taken to Hong Kong for questioning about Ma's death. Is that true?"

"Who told you that?"

"One of our people."

"And you doubt him?"

"I simply want the truth, and I think you're a more reliable source than him."

"I don't know if that's a compliment or an insult."

"A badly worded compliment."

"Well, the truth is I don't know, but that doesn't mean he wasn't," Zhang said. "Those killings yesterday caused considerable concern in Hong Kong. The octb might have wanted to talk to him."

"The Organized Crime and Triad Bureau?"

"Yes."

"Could they have pulled him in without talking to you?"

"It is possible."

"Can you find out if they did?"

Zhang hesitated.

"I would really appreciate it," Chow said.

Another hesitation, and then Zhang said, "Are things truly calm in town? I haven't heard otherwise, but I assume you know better than anyone."

"Completely calm."

"Then I'll make a call. How do I get in touch with you?"

Chow read him the number written on the phone, and then said, "How long do you think this will take? I'm using the phone in a restaurant kitchen, and I can't stay here indefinitely."

"I'll get back to you in a few minutes."

26

CHOW AND WANG LEFT DONG'S TOGETHER TO GO TO the meeting at the office. They hadn't spoken much since taking back Dong's. Wang was worried about the other betting shops, and even after Xu and Min had returned from the Red Sun Restaurant and Shek Wu Hui, he kept calling them to make sure they were open and running. When he finally accepted that they were, he pulled Min aside and grilled him again. Min's story didn't change.

Chow had other concerns. Zhang had called back as promised, and after their conversation, Chow struggled to understand what it meant. He sat by himself in a far corner of the restaurant and replayed various conversations from the previous three days. He still hadn't decided what he believed when Wang approached. "We should get going."

As Wang's car wound its way to the centre of Fanling, Chow said, "This meeting could become a bit awkward."

"Why?"

"I'm not prepared to accept everything I've been told."

"So you aren't buying the Tai-Po-coming-to-our-defence story?"

"Are you?"

"No. And I would like to understand why it was told in the first place."

"I expect we'll hear some kind of explanation from Ren."

"It sounds like you're expecting the worst."

"I have my doubts, but I'm prepared to listen to what Ren has to say. I think you should do the same."

"I have no problem doing that, but do you think Yu will be able to restrain himself?"

"I don't think Ren cares about Yu. He'll be more concerned about us. You control our men on the ground and I manage the money."

"We'll see about that," Wang said, and then said to the driver, "Pull over for a minute."

"Why did you do that?" Chow asked as the car stopped.

"There are a couple of things I'd like to understand," Wang said.

"Like what?"

"I know you told Pang that I'm active again and that our shops are open, but does he know what we did — what you did?"

"No."

"Does he know we're still holding fifteen men from Tai Po?"

"No."

"Why not?"

"I thought it would be interesting to learn what he and Ren know."

"What makes you think they'll just tell us?"

"I don't know if they will, but I'm all ears."

Wang shook his head. "Let's leave it at that," he said, and then tapped the driver on the shoulder. "Okay, head for the office."

Five minutes later, the car stopped out front. Yu was already there, leaning against a wall. When he saw them, he rushed to the car. "Where have you been? I've been trying to reach you both all day. Do you know what's been going on?"

"We've been in the middle of it," Wang said. "You can relax. It's been resolved."

"I know that fucker Ren was somehow involved."

"Do us a favour, will you," Chow said, touching the older man lightly on the forearm. "Let Ren explain what he thinks happened before you start making accusations."

"That fucker —"

"Listen to me," Chow said, his voice sharpening. "Losing control will help nothing, and it could even be hurtful."

"What do you want me to do? Keep quiet while he throws bullshit at us?"

"That's exactly what I want you to do."

"And Yu, Uncle is speaking for me as well. Please control yourself."

Yu looked at them. "Okay," he said grudgingly, "I'll do my best."

"Thank you," Chow said. "Now let's go upstairs and find out what we're expected to believe."

The three men climbed the stairs to the office. Ren, Pang, and Hu were already there, sitting in the boardroom.

"There's beer in the fridge and water for tea," Pang said.

"I'd rather get down to business," Chow said, taking a seat.

"I think we all would," Ren agreed.

Wang and Yu sat on either side of Chow. The men looked warily at each other across the table. Chow waited for Ren to start, but Ren was sipping his beer as if waiting for them to do so.

"Can someone explain what took place in Fanling this morning?" Chow finally said.

"Before we talk about that, perhaps you could bring us up to date on what happened to you this morning," Pang said to Ren.

Ren looked questioningly at Chow.

"Go ahead," Chow said.

"As I believe Pang has told you, the police paid a visit to my house this morning and asked me to accompany them to Hong Kong for a chat about Ma. I saw no reason not to co-operate, so I went. I ended up spending a good part of my day there. It was the usual nonsense. They don't have any leads about Ma, so they went fishing. 'Are there any ongoing feuds among gangs? Was anyone pissed off that Ma was going to become Mountain Master? Did Ma have any enemies inside or outside Fanling who could have done it?' Like I said, they were fishing."

"Are they going to release the body?" Pang asked.

"Not any time soon, so any funeral arrangements will have to be delayed," Ren said.

"That's just as well," Pang said. "I don't think any of us is ready for another one."

"I'm surprised that you were taken to Hong Kong," Chow said. "I would have thought you'd be interviewed by the regional cops first."

"I was a guest of the Organized Crime and Triad Bureau."

"Ah. And it led to nothing?" Chow said.

"It was an absolute waste of their time and mine. I should have been here," Ren said.

"But you weren't. And while you were in Hong Kong, Tai Po made a move on us," Chow said.

"No, no, no," Ren said, waving a hand. "You've got that all wrong."

"They shut down four of our betting shops this morning."

"They only closed them temporarily."

"What the hell is the difference?" Wang asked, irritation showing in his voice.

"The difference is that they came to Fanling to provide us with some extra protection. They weren't here to harm us or our businesses."

"I don't understand," Chow said.

"And if I'd been here, even that wouldn't have been necessary."

"I still don't understand."

"I met with Tso, the Tai Po Mountain Master, last week — you all know that he and I are old friends. He told me, as a friend, that the Sha Tin gang has their eyes on us. He said they're eager to expand and think we're an easy target. When I told him I don't think we have enough men to fight off a gang of that size, he said Tai Po is prepared to stand with us in exchange for our ongoing co-operation," Ren said. "I immediately went to see Ma and we talked it through. He thought working closer with Tai Po made sense. He said that after he officially became Mountain Master, he was prepared to meet with Tso and begin formulating an agreement. But of course he never had the chance."

"What was supposed to be in this agreement?" Chow asked.

"I'll come back to that in a minute," Ren said. "Before I do, I want to explain what happened this morning."

"We were ambushed," Yu said.

Chow looked at him. "I'd rather hear from Ren," he said.

Yu glared back but fell silent.

"We were not ambushed," Ren said. "Early this morning, Tso got a call from a source inside Sha Tin. He was told that the gang is preparing to come at us sometime in the next few days, perhaps as soon as today. Going after our gambling operations is their first priority. Tso tried to call me, but by then I was on my way to Hong Kong with my police escorts. When he couldn't reach me, he decided the safest course of action was to send his men to protect our interests."

"Why didn't he call me?" Wang said. "Given the threat, I would have been the next logical choice."

"Other than Ma, Tso had no idea who else knew anything about our arrangement. He didn't want to make assumptions and he didn't want to interfere in our chain of command," Ren said. "He figured he'd reach me soon enough and that sending in his men would be strictly a stopgap measure until he did. And, as my housekeeper can tell you, he tried multiple times to contact me."

"We should be thanking Tso," Pang said.

"Did you know anything about this arrangement?" Chow asked Pang.

"Of course not. If I had, I would have told you."

"So let me get this straight," Chow said. "Because you were in police custody in Hong Kong and Tso couldn't get hold of you, he sent forty men to Fanling to protect our assets, out of the goodness of his heart."

"I detect a touch of sarcasm in that remark," Ren said.

"I just find it odd."

"It isn't that odd if you understand that helping us protect our assets also benefits Tai Po."

"How so?"

"The working relationship we've been discussing, and that Ma was warm to, involved giving Tai Po a financial interest in some of our operations in exchange for access to some of their supply chains and — whenever we need it — their firepower."

"Our gambling operations?" Chow asked in disbelief.

"That is their main interest."

"What level of financial interest?"

"We've only had preliminary talks. We haven't gone into the details. That was to be the main purpose of the next meeting between Ma and Tso."

Chow saw Yu began to bristle again and said quickly, "What supply-chain access were we supposed to get in return?"

"Drugs and liquor."

"I'm not sure why we need to expand our liquor trade, and drugs only create problems with the cops," Chow said. "And I don't know why you'd think we need their firepower."

"Sha Tin is more than twice our size. Do you really think we could fend them off if they decided to come at us in force?"

"We sure as fuck could," Wang said.

"Okay, maybe we could, but then what?" Ren said. "We'd have cops all over us. We'd lose business. We'd lose men. We'd be weakened and become an even easier target for some other gang. Nothing good could possibly come from going to war with Sha Tin. Ma understood that, and that's why he was willing to make a deal with Tso. He knew that aligning with Tai Po would provide a strong deterrent."

"You said things would have been handled differently if you had been here. How would they have been different?" Chow asked.

"The instant I heard from Tso, I would have contacted all

of you and we would have had our own internal conversation. We could have made a collective decision whether or not to involve Tai Po. Instead it was sprung on you, and it seems that some wrong conclusions were drawn."

"How could they not be?" Chow said.

"They wouldn't let anyone in or out of our betting shops," added Wang. "Our men, including myself, were held as fucking prisoners. What other conclusion can you draw from that?"

"No one was hurt, were they?"

"No."

"And Pang tells me the betting shops are now open."

"They are, but not because Tai Po voluntarily withdrew," Wang said. "Uncle put a team together and made them step down."

"How did you do that?" Ren said.

"Tso hasn't told you?"

"I haven't spoken to him."

"Given the circumstances, I thought he would have been your first phone call."

"He was, but we haven't connected yet."

"Uncle, I told you to wait for Ren to get back from Hong Kong," Pang interrupted. "I told you not to do anything. I was very specific."

"I'm responsible for our cash flow. I didn't want to lose Sunday's Happy Valley money."

"What did you do to get the shops reopened?" Ren said.

"I had ten men, two submachine guns, a whole bunch of pistols, and the element of surprise."

"Which led to what kind of confrontation?" Ren asked.

"Well, obviously it was an armed one, but it was controlled. There was minimal violence."

"Minimal?"

"Wang punched one of Tso's men on the nose and probably broke it. I shot another one, but he'll live."

"I'll have to explain this to Tso."

"Don't apologize to him for anything we did," Chow said.

"Of course not; you didn't know any better. But you can understand that he won't be pleased that you attacked the men he sent here to help us."

"And we're still holding about fifteen of them," Wang said.

"What?" Ren said.

"We thought we should keep them for insurance, that it might strengthen your hand if we're forced to negotiate with Tso."

"Let them go," Ren said angrily.

"If we do, will they be staying at the shops or going back to Tai Po?" asked Wang.

Ren looked at him across the table. "If Sha Tin does pose a threat to us today, are you certain you can handle it?"

"We can."

"In that case, I'll make sure anyone you release goes back to Tai Po."

Wang glanced at Chow, who nodded his head. "I'll tell my men to release them," Wang said. "Do you want us to give them their weapons back?"

"Naturally," Ren said, and then shifted his attention to Chow. "I do wish you'd done what Pang asked of you. I thought the instructions I passed to him through my lawyer were clear. It's fortunate that things turned out as well as they have, because today could have been a disaster for us."

"Except it wasn't."

"Don't say that so quickly. I still have to talk to Tso. I'm not sure how he's going to react. On top of everything else, you may have put our proposed alliance at risk."

"From what I'm hearing, I could have killed ten men and not done that."

"What do mean?"

"It sounds to me like the deal is already done."

"It isn't."

"No?"

"Is the prospect of us doing a deal with Tai Po that terrible to you?"

"That depends on the details you haven't worked out yet."

Ren leaned towards Chow. "You're the one who's always saying we need to change, that we need to adapt. Now what, you're singing a new tune?" he said. "Please understand that this is something Ma and I thought was worthy of consideration. I think you owe it to him and to me to wait till you understand what the deal could do for both parties before you decide to oppose it. That would be a fitting legacy for Ma."

"Assuming he actually wanted to do a deal. But we'll never know that, will we?"

27

CHOW, WANG, AND YU LEFT THE OFFICES TOGETHER and walked to the small bar where Chow and Wang had drunk the night before. It was empty when they arrived, but Wang still led them to the farthest point from the door. After the barman had taken their order for three San Miguels, Wang told him, "We need privacy. If anyone else comes in, keep them down at the other end."

"What do you think about all that shit Ren was throwing at us?" Yu said as soon as they were alone.

"As much as I don't want to admit it, Ren is right about how hard it would be to take on Sha Tin by ourselves," Wang said. "In terms of fighting men, they'd outnumber us three to one."

"Okay, but what I don't get is, if Sha Tin is the threat, why aren't we talking to them? Why can't we handle our own negotiations? Why do we need Tai Po in the middle?" Yu said.

"Talking to Sha Tin would make perfect sense if Sha Tin was actually a threat," Chow said as their drinks arrived.

"What do you mean by that?" Yu asked.

Chow picked up his beer. "*Ganbei*," he said, tapping bottles with his colleagues, and then took a long swig.

"What do you mean?" Yu repeated.

"Was there anyone in the gang closer to Ma than you?" Chow said.

"I don't think so."

"Did he ever mention to you the possibility of doing some kind of deal with Tai Po?"

"No. But I didn't talk to him on Thursday, and only very briefly on Friday."

Chow paused. "Wang, I remember you telling me that you have a decent relationship with the Red Pole in Sha Tin. Is my memory faulty?"

"No, we're close enough."

"Then do me a favour and call him. Use the phone at the end of the bar. Tell him you've heard that they're going to make a grab for our territory. Ask him if it's true."

"If they are, why would he tell me?"

"He wouldn't, but you've always been someone who can read people. If he lies, I suspect you'll sense that."

"Have you talked to the White Paper Fan in Sha Tin?"

"No. I don't know him well enough to have that kind of conversation."

"Go ahead and make the call," Yu said to Wang. "I'm curious about what he'll say."

Wang looked at them, shrugged, and walked to the bar entrance. He picked up the phone and turned his back.

"I suspect you know something you're not telling us," Yu said quietly.

"Let's wait for Wang."

They watched Wang's head bob up and down as his free

hand swung in the air. This went on for several minutes. When he put down the phone and came back to face them, he looked grim.

"Well?" Chow said.

"He swears up and down — and I mean *swears* — that Sha Tin has zero interest in us. He said that if anyone claims something different, they're lying."

"Do you believe him?"

"I do."

"Good, because then everything fits," Chow said.

"Explain that, please," said Yu.

"Sorry, I don't mean to be vague. The truth is that Ren lied to us today. He wasn't being held in police custody in Hong Kong. He might have been in Hong Kong, but it had nothing to do with the police or with Ma."

"How can you know that?" Wang asked.

"I asked my source — my senior source — inside the department. He made some calls for me. No one at any level in the Hong Kong Police Force met with Ren this morning, let alone took him into custody."

"Who is this source?" Yu said.

"You know better than to ask me that."

"But you trust him?"

"I'd trust him with my life, if it came to that."

Yu shook his head. "Shit. What does this say about Ren?"

"What it says is that there are a lot of questions that need answers," Chow said. "For starters, if Ren wasn't with the cops, where was he? And more important, if he wasn't with the cops, why does he want us to believe he was?"

"That son of a bitch."

"I believe that he and Tso are playing us," Chow said.

"Ren said Tso sent his men into Fanling because Tso couldn't reach him. That's nonsense. They were just looking for an excuse to do it."

"But they really didn't do anything except block entry to our betting shops," Wang said. "What was the purpose of that?"

"They wanted to create the impression that we're vulnerable, so they came up with that bullshit Sha Tin attack scenario," Chow said. "Then they wanted us to believe that Tai Po came to our aid by sending in their men. Now the story Ren is spinning is that we aren't capable of surviving on our own and need to form an alliance. And who better to ally with than our friends in Tai Po, who have already demonstrated their commitment to us?"

"It wouldn't be an alliance. This is all about Tai Po taking over Fanling," Yu said.

"I think that would be the reality eventually, though they might do it incrementally," Chow said. "I do have to admit that the way they've tried to structure it is clever. Tai Po wouldn't really be taking anything — we'd be handing it over to them."

"Why would Ren do that?"

"That's where it gets murky."

"Do you think he had a hand in Ma's death?"

"I don't want to."

"But?"

Chow sipped his beer and then looked at Yu and Wang. "Ren met with Tso in Kowloon on Thursday night. They had dinner, just the two of them. There's nothing sinister about two old friends having dinner, except for the fact that it was in Kowloon and therefore meant to be private. On Friday morning I spoke to Ren. He didn't mention the dinner — I didn't actually learn about it until Friday night, so it wasn't discussed. What we did talk about was the election. As you both know, I was promoting him, with his agreement, to become our next Mountain Master. When I told him my people were getting a less than enthusiastic response, he didn't seem surprised. And truthfully he didn't seem to care. I think he was already prepared to pull out."

"During the brief conversation I had with Ma on Friday, he told me Ren was going to support him," said Yu.

"That's what he told me too, but I'm beginning to think Ren knew all along that he couldn't win and was concocting another plan."

"With Tso?" Yu asked.

"Sadly, that makes sense."

"Are you suggesting that Tso arranged to have Ma killed so Ren would have a clear run at becoming Mountain Master?"

"Why not? They're friends and they would both benefit. Ren becomes Mountain Master and Tso gets to put his hand in our pockets — and could end up controlling us down the road."

"That's a lot of conjecture," Wang said.

"I know."

"Do you have any proof that they conspired? Do you have any way of proving they were responsible for Ma's death?"

"No, but can either of you come up with another explanation?"

"No. I just don't want to think that it's possible," Yu said.

"I feel the same, but I'm not about to start accusing a Mountain Master and a potential Mountain Master of murder. Both of you should be cautious about what you say to whom about this. There could be serious repercussions if a man like Tso hears we're blaming him for Ma's death," Wang said.

"I'm having a drink with two friends in a bar. I wouldn't have said anything at all if I thought it would leave this room," Chow said.

"Sorry. I just wanted to be clear," Wang said. "I've known people who got whacked for saying less."

Yu slammed his bottle onto the bar. "Even if we're not going to talk about them killing Ma, they can't prevent us from trying to stop Ren from cutting a deal with Tai Po."

"I agree. That's where our focus should be," Chow said.

"More beer for everyone," Yu shouted to the bartender, and then stared at Chow. "Uncle, I have a couple of questions for you."

"I've told you everything I know."

"My questions have nothing to do with Ren and Tso."

"Then ask away."

"What would you have done this morning if the men from Tai Po had resisted?"

"One did. I shot him."

"No, I mean what if all of them had resisted?"

"There wasn't much chance of that. We surprised them and we had them outgunned."

Yu shook his head. "Let me come at this from another direction. Are you in favour of doing a deal with Tai Po or Sha Tin, or anyone else, for that matter?"

"Not if it means giving up the tiniest piece of our territory or independence, because once we do that, there'll be no end to it. If we give an inch, they'll want a foot. We'll get taken over bit by bit until we're completely absorbed into someone else's gang."

"But what if Ren is right? What if Sha Tin does decide to come at us?"

"Sha Tin has no interest in us."

"I mean theoretically."

"Then we'll fight Sha Tin."

"Even though they're more than twice our size? One of the few things Ren said in that meeting that I agree with is his description of the fallout that would result from that kind of gang war."

"If you're afraid to go to war, war will find you," Chow said. "You can't show fear. You can't leave any doubt that you'll defend yourself, that you'll do absolutely everything to win, and that you'll never quit. You have to make the other side stop and think, 'Do I really want to take those guys on? I may beat them, but they're going to do me a lot of damage. Is it worth it?'"

"Do you agree with him?" Yu asked Wang.

"I do," Wang said.

"But it should never come to a war," Chow said.

"How would you prevent it?"

"You have to be proactive. You can't sit back and wait for things to come at you. You need to send a very clear message, not just to Tai Po but to every gang in Hong Kong and the New Territories."

"What kind of message?"

"*Don't try to fuck with us. We won't take it.*"

"I agree with that message," Wang said. "But why would you talk to every gang when our problem is with Tai Po?"

"The Hong Kong and Kowloon gangs don't want trouble out here. The cops don't care about gang boundaries; if there's trouble, they'll starting hammering everyone. It's in everyone's best interest to keep things calm. Since that's the case, we should be pressuring the other gangs to lean on Tai Po, and anyone else we think could be a threat. But they'll only apply pressure if they take us seriously and really believe we're ready to fight to the bloody end."

"You've been thinking about this," Yu said.

"Nothing I've said is terribly original. Gao was a good strategist, and so is my old mentor Tian. I simply took the time to listen to them."

Yu sipped from his fresh beer and looked at Wang. "I don't listen so badly myself, and I like what I've been hearing. Now, what can we do about it?"

"Do about what?" Wang asked.

"We have twenty-four hours to make Uncle our new Mountain Master," Yu said. "I can bring my men along with me. Can you bring yours?"

THE VOTING STARTED AT TEN IN THE MORNING AND
Pang had scheduled it to end at eight in the evening. Chow
arrived at the gang offices at nine-thirty, after breakfast with
Xu and Fong. Pang was there with his assistant, but there
was no sign of Ren or any of the other executive committee
members.

The desks in the outer office had been pushed to the right,
leaving a single desk on the left. Two cardboard boxes sat
on top. Behind the desk was a screen with a partially drawn
curtain that revealed a small table.

"How is this going to work?" Chow asked.

"There are 161 numbered slips in that box," Pang said,
pointing to one. "We have a list of all our initiated members.
When someone comes in to vote, we check their ID, mark
their name off the list, and allow them to take a slip from
the box. They mark their slip behind the curtain and then
put it in the other box. At eight o'clock we'll tally the votes.
If all the slips taken from the first box are in the second and
no number is duplicated, we'll have a clean vote."

"That sounds simple enough."

"It's been a long time since we've done this, but it will work."

"Can I leave Fong or Xu here to keep an eye on things?"

"You can leave them both, for all I care."

Chow turned to them. "Sort it out between the two of you. Just make sure someone is here at all times."

"We'll take turns. When we're not here, we'll be out rounding up votes," Xu said.

"You seem particularly interested in how we're conducting this election," Pang said. "Does it have anything to do with the rumour I heard this morning?"

"I haven't heard any rumours."

"I was told that Yu is trying to get his men to oppose Ren."

"I wouldn't know what Yu is doing."

"It isn't smart, you know. Especially for someone who should be thinking long-term."

"The last thing I'd say about Yu is that he isn't smart."

"I wasn't referring to Yu when I mentioned thinking long-term."

"I know, but I don't have anything more to say."

Pang shrugged. "You're too young, Uncle. Our men know they need experience at the top. They know the other Mountain Masters would run all over you."

Chow turned away. "I'm going to Dong's Kitchen," he said to Xu. "If you need me, you know where to find me."

He left the office and took a taxi to Dong's. He had thought of calling Tian the night before but knew that he and his wife went to bed early; he saw no reason to disturb them. When Chow had called earlier that morning, his wife told him that Tian had already left the house. Chow assumed that he'd gone to the restaurant, but when he arrived, it seemed to be closed. He tried the door. It opened, and he saw a couple of servers setting tables and Tian sitting at his usual spot in the back.

"Where is everyone?" Chow asked.

"It's early. There won't be many customers until around eleven."

"Then why are you here?"

"I need to get organized."

"I would have thought you could do that in your sleep."

"Do what?"

"Run the business."

"That's not why I'm here."

"I don't understand," Chow said.

"Wang called me last night."

"I was going to, but I didn't want to disturb you."

"There are some things important enough to warrant a late-night call."

"So Wang told you that I've agreed to let my name stand for Mountain Master?"

"He did, and I have to say I was surprised. Not by your decision, you understand, but by his attitude. Wang isn't a man who shows emotion, and he was so enthusiastic it shocked me," Tian said. "I don't know what happened between you two, but he's totally committed, and with him on your side, you can count on many of his men supporting you."

"How about you? Do I have your support?"

"You don't have to ask. I told you before that I think you're ready for the job."

"I didn't want to take your support for granted," Chow said. "And I'm still trying to get used to the idea that I've agreed to this contest."

"And I'm here in the restaurant because I told all my men that I want to see them," Tian said. "When they arrive, I'll tell them that you're running, that I'm going to vote for you, and that I expect them to do the same. Then I'm going to the office to make sure they fulfill their obligations."

"You can't tell people who to vote for."

"Yes, I can. I can't force them to vote for you, but I sure as hell can tell them they should."

"What if they say no?"

"Not many will."

"I don't know how to respond to that."

"You don't have to say anything," Tian said. "What you need to do is go and round up more votes. You're wasting your time hanging around here."

Chow left the restaurant and stood on the sidewalk, unsure about what to do or where to go. He hadn't thought past talking to Tian, and as he considered Tian's suggestion, he felt distinctly uncomfortable. It was one thing to ask people to support Ren; it was quite another to request their support for himself. Besides, he had Tian, Wang, Yu, Fong, and Xu collecting votes. Who could he approach without duplicating their efforts? No one came to mind, so he decided the best thing to do was keep a low profile and stay out of the way.

He bought a racing form for the coming Wednesday and made his way back to the congee restaurant. Jia raised an eyebrow when she saw him. "Twice in one day?"

"I need a place to hang out for the afternoon."

"Take any table in the back, and let me know if you need anything. Otherwise, I'll leave you alone," she said.

Fortified by several pots of tea and half a pack of

cigarettes, he worked his way through the form and then started over. It wasn't as distracting as he'd hoped it would be. His mind kept returning to the reality of what was going on in the office. Part of him didn't quite believe that he could become Mountain Master, or that he was in the contest at all. Yet when pressed by Wang and Yu the afternoon before, he hadn't put up any resistance. Given the circumstances, it had seemed like a reasonable request; the doubts he'd expressed to Tian several days before, when he'd made the same suggestion, no longer seemed relevant. So he had agreed to run. The relief that Yu displayed justified his decision instantly, and Wang's enthusiasm confirmed it.

Chow tried not to think about the following day. Win or lose, his life was going to be different. He swore to himself that he wasn't going to change who he was. He had thrived within the gang by putting his own needs second. That didn't mean he was reluctant to give his opinion, but it was always in the context of what was best for the gang. Now, if he won, his opinions would be taken as directions. But somehow the idea of being responsible for the lives of 160 men and their families didn't faze him. If he was true to himself, he reflected, things would work out. As he contemplated these thoughts, he started writing across the top of the racing form the names of the people he wanted for his executive committee. It would be a good group, he thought when he'd finished, and was taken with the realization that he might actually be able to make it happen.

The time dragged, and even the racing form couldn't hold his attention. Several times he left the restaurant and went for a short walk. When he returned, Jia had a fresh pot of tea waiting for him. Eventually the day turned into evening, and at six o'clock he made his way back to the office.

There were two men at the entrance whom Chow recognized as forty-niners. He figured Wang had placed them there for security. He nodded as he walked past them. As he started up the stairs he thought he heard one of them say "Uncle" and then the word *boss*. Chow stopped and looked back. The men were talking to each other, paying him no attention.

He was halfway up the stairs when he heard voices above engaged in excited conversation. He entered the outer office to find it crammed full of brothers. He stood in the doorway and then saw Fong hurrying towards him.

"Where have you been?"

"I was at a restaurant."

"We've been trying to contact you."

"What's going on?"

"It's been an incredible day. The men were eager to vote, and now everyone has, except for you, Ren, and Pang." Fong said. "Yu brought twenty men, Tian almost the same number, and Wang came with at least forty. Xu and I didn't do so badly either. None of the men want to leave until the votes are counted."

"This is remarkable," Chow said, noticing that every eye in the place was fixed on him. Then he saw Pang standing by the ballot box. "I guess I should vote now."

As he approached Pang, the older man lowered his head ever so slightly. As subtle as it was, that show of deference, of respect, caught Chow off guard. "I'll vote now," he repeated.

Pang moved to one side and motioned at the box. "Only three slips of paper left."

"When is Ren coming?" Chow asked.

"He's not."

"Why?"

"He heard about the way things are going today. He doesn't see any need to embarrass himself."

"What did he hear?"

"I phoned him a few hours ago after Wang showed up with his crew. Tian and Yu were already here with theirs. I told him you were going to win by a very large margin," Pang said, and then looked around the room. "You know I supported Ren, but I have to tell you, if he loses, I'm pleased it's going to be a clear-cut result. There won't be any doubt hanging over your head and you'll have the strongest possible mandate to lead."

Chow nodded. "Thank you. Now I'd like to vote." He reached into the box and took a slip of paper.

Pang did the same. "Ren isn't going to vote," he said, loudly enough for the room to hear. "So when Uncle and I have cast our ballots, the counting can begin. Does anyone object to that?"

"No! Vote!" Tian shouted.

"Vote!" Wang yelled.

Pang walked behind the curtain, wrote on his slip of paper, and then dropped it into the box. "Now it's your turn," he said to Uncle.

Chow stepped towards the table. As he did, the room became very quiet, and for the first time he was aware of the tension in the room. He opened the slip and saw the number twenty-four. It was his birthdate — a good omen? He put the paper on the table, picked up a pen, and carefully wrote his name. When he put down the pen, he noticed that his fingers were trembling. He held up the slip of paper. "There's no secret here. I voted for myself," he said.

There was a wave of laughter and cheers as he joined Pang at the ballot box.

"Will you count with me?" Pang asked.

"Gladly."

"We don't have to count them all. We can stop when you have eighty-one, if you want."

"These men took the time to vote, so I think we should take the time to count all their ballots," Chow said.

Pang nodded and reached into the box to take out the first slip. He read out the name "Uncle" and then hesitated.

"Can we agree that some men may have voted for Chow as Uncle and others may have used his proper name?" Yu asked, moving to Pang's side. "As long as their intent is clear, I don't think it matters, do you?"

"No, I don't think it matters," Pang said, and took out another slip.

Chow watched as either "Uncle" or "Chow" appeared on slip after slip. Pang read aloud each name and then slowly and precisely placed the ballot in the pile for either Chow or Ren. While he did that, his assistant kept a running tally. Chow's pile soon dwarfed Ren's and a second had to be started. As the count proceeded, the men began to crowd closer to the table. When the last slip was read, it was completely encircled.

"What is the count?" Wang asked.

"We have a new Mountain Master," Pang said.

"What is the count?"

"One hundred and thirty-six votes for Uncle Chow Tung. Twenty-four votes for Ren Tengfei."

Tian stepped forward, wrapped his right hand over his left fist, lowered his head, and moved his hands up and down three times. Around him, the other men followed his example. Chow began to protest and then stopped. The men were simply showing their respect for the new Mountain Master. And, as unlikely as it seemed, that new Mountain Master was him.

IT WAS ABOUT TWENTY KILOMETRES FROM CHOW'S
apartment in Fanling to the Ancestor Worship Hall in Yuen
Long. It was a trip he normally made only four times a year —
on their birthdays, at the Chinese New Year, and during the
Qingming Festival — but this was a special morning, and
he shared everything special in his life at the Worship Hall.

He was up early, as usual, and by seven had shaved, showered, and dressed in a crisp white shirt and black suit. He
never ate before going to Yuen Long. Normally he would
have headed directly downstairs to get a taxi, but he had
extra responsibilities now. With everyone still on edge, he
didn't want people panicking if they tried to contact him
and couldn't reach him. He phoned Xu.

"This is Chow," he said when Xu answered.

"Good morning, boss. How was the rest of your night?
Did you manage to talk to any more Mountain Masters?"

"I reached Kang and Chin, and it went much the same
as with the others. There were lots of congratulations and
promises of support, some of which might even be genu-
ine. I told all of them that I still have concerns about Tso's

intentions, and that we will react swiftly and violently if he makes another move. They promised me they'll talk to him."

"Did you manage to talk to him yourself?"

"I did. We had a brief but pointed conversation. He tried to tell me that what happened on Sunday was the result of a misunderstanding, and he tried to pin the blame on Ren for not communicating properly with us. I decided to be blunt. I told him there's no chance of us ever becoming partners, so he can forget whatever secret arrangements he made with Ren. Then I told him that if he wants war, we're up for it; we're prepared to fight to the last man to preserve our independence. I also told him that I'm giving Wang the money to buy as many new weapons as he thinks necessary — that while we might be outmanned, we'll never be outgunned."

"You really said all that? Did he take offence?"

"I wouldn't have cared if he did, but the truth is he didn't. In fact, he told me to calm down, that I was blowing things out of proportion," Chow said. "But he got the message. And after I finished with him, I phoned Ren and told him what I'd said to Tso."

"How did he react?"

"He was smooth. He congratulated me on my win and said he'll fully support any decision I make about Tai Po."

"Did he ask to stay on as Vanguard?"

"No, he has too much pride for that. And I didn't raise the subject either. It wasn't the time."

"So, all in all, it was a good evening?"

"I think so. If everyone is to be believed, things should stay calm."

"Great."

"We'll see how great it is in a few days. But that isn't why

I'm calling," Chow said. "I'm going to be out of touch for the morning, but I should be back in circulation by noon. I don't want anyone to worry about where I am or what I'm doing. I just have some personal business I need to attend to."

"I'll let everyone know."

"Tell Wang to stay alert. When we meet this afternoon, we'll put together a longer-term strategy for dealing with Tso."

"Okay, boss."

"I wish you wouldn't call me that."

"What would you prefer?"

"Uncle is fine."

"Things have changed," Xu said. "But I'll do as you ask."

Chow ended the call and walked into his bedroom. He reached into the closet and took out a small folding stool and a paper bag. Carrying the stool and bag, he left the apartment to look for a taxi. Thirty minutes later he had the cab stop at a grocery store on the outskirts of Yuen Long. Ten minutes after that, it dropped him off at a path that led uphill to the worship hall perched on top.

The path was about a hundred metres long and flanked by hillsides covered in shrubs, gorse, and wildflowers. He was the only person on the path, and as he neared the hill's summit he saw that the hall was also empty of people. He preferred to be alone in the hall, so he always came early enough for that to be a possibility. It was often empty on their birthdays and sometimes at the Chinese New Year, but during Qingming the place was packed from sunrise to well past sunset.

The building faced northeast so that it overlooked the sea and caught the morning sunlight. It was about thirty metres across and fifteen metres deep, with a red tile roof and curved, sweeping overhangs. The front was completely open to the environs. Chow had visited several cemeteries and worship halls before he found this one at Fo Look Hill, and he was immediately drawn to its feng shui. It had a great position at the top of the hill, and its openness and sightlines were wonderful. There was a small stream running by one side and a fountain gurgling near the entrance steps. All of them were welcoming to *qi*, promising peace and tranquility for the spirits of the people being memorialized there.

Chow reached the hall and climbed the five steps that led inside. He walked past a statue of seated Buddha and another of a Taoist god. He approached the hall's back wall, which was a mass of small alcoves or niches, every one devoted to a loved one who had died. The niches could accommodate an urn, some small mementos, and not much more. Nearly all of them displayed a photo of the deceased.

Gui-San's niche was on the left end of the wall at about chest height. Chow stopped just short of it, unfolded the stool, and extracted a small whisk broom from the paper bag. He reached into the niche, removed the urn, and placed it gently on the ground. He picked up the two oranges and the small bowl of dry tea leaves that he had left on his previous visit. The oranges were dry and shrivelled and the leaves had turned to dust. He emptied the bowl and put the oranges into the bag. The niche was now empty except for a photo of Gui-San — taken in Wuhan on her twenty-first birthday — that had been enlarged and laminated. Under the photo in gold lettering it read:

LIN GUI-SAN

BORN IN CHANGZHAI, HUBEI PROVINCE, 28 OCTOBER 1934

DIED NEAR HONG KONG, 28 JUNE 1959

FOREVER LOVED

FOREVER MISSED

Chow took a cloth from the bag and wet it in the fountain. Back at the niche, he carefully wiped away the dust and grime that had collected on the photo. Then he took the whisk and swept the niche's floor. When that was done, he ran the cloth over the urn and returned it to the niche. He then removed two new oranges and fresh tea from a second bag, refilled the bowl, and placed it and the oranges next to the urn.

He lit six incense sticks with his Zippo lighter, the one with the faded black crackle. He placed three of them in a slot cut into the front of Gui-San's niche, then put the others between his palms. He raised his hands to his chest and lowered his head. He prayed until the sticks were close to burning his skin. When he stopped, he turned and put what was left of them into a receptacle, then sat down on his stool facing the niche.

When he first settled in Fanling, Chow had made monthly trips to Yuen Long, where he would go to the beach and relive the horrors of June 28. They didn't find the bodies of Gui-San and Mai that morning, but they had certainly tried. Jin Hai had talked a local fisherman into taking them into the bay, and for hours they went back and forth, searching every inch of the water. When they returned to shore, Chow stayed on the beach until dark, hoping Gui-San would somehow emerge. He returned the next day, and the day after that, until Tam convinced him it was pointless and that they had to move on to Fanling.

For the next two years, a day didn't go by when he didn't think of her and blame himself for her death. He had talked her into the swim, he reasoned, then he had allowed her to swim in open water. And when she and Mai were in distress, he had been lying on the door, no help to them — no help to anyone. A burden to all.

The following year, he went to the beach again before making his first visit to the hall on Fo Look Hill. As he stood on the sand, looking over the choppy water in the grey light of an overcast morning, it struck him that Gui-San had become part of the bay, part of the water, part of the beach. Her body might not be there, but his memory of her was etched into everything he was seeing. Later that day, he bought an urn and filled it with sand from the beach. He took the urn to the hall and placed it in her niche. The next day he returned with the only thing of value he had brought with him from China, his mother's jade bracelet. He buried the bracelet in the sand in the urn and then stood back. "I would have given this bracelet to you when we arrived in Hong Kong, when we were married," he said. "Now you have it, and you will have it forever." And thus began his conversations with Gui-San.

"Our life has been so crazy this past week," he said. "Gao was killed. He was hit by a van as he was leaving his girl-friend's apartment early in the morning. Everyone wants to believe it was an accident. I don't think it was, but there's nothing to be gained by revisiting it now. He's buried, and his wife and son would only experience more grief if the story changed. So it's best to leave it alone, don't you think?

"I reacted badly to his death. I immediately began to think about the implications of Ma's assuming his position. He was always opposed to my night-market idea, and just about any change I proposed. So, rather selfishly, I began to promote Ren for the job. That was a lapse in judgement. That's what I meant when I said I was rash, because despite the issues I had with Ma, he was loyal to the gang. Ren's loyalties lie elsewhere. I didn't see it at first, but gradually I started to understand, and I felt foolish when I did.

"I believe that right from the moment I spoke to him about becoming Mountain Master, Ren started negotiating with his friend Tso in Tai Po about a merger. I'm not sure why he didn't want the job. Maybe he didn't want the pressure or the responsibility, but it's obvious to me now that he just wanted to hand it off. My problem was that I'd encouraged him to run and had committed my support, so no matter what I was beginning to sense, I couldn't walk away from him.

"But when I spoke to Ren on the morning of Gao's funeral, his reluctance was too obvious to ignore. He pushed me to tell him what I really thought of his chances, and I wasn't dishonest. He used my reservations to justify his decision to step down. It turned out he was playing me for a fool, and that became even clearer when Ma was gunned down later that day and his body dumped in the courtyard of the funeral home . . . "

"Gui-San, it's so hard sometimes pretending to be in control of my emotions," he said, dropping his head to his knees. Chow remained in that position for several minutes as various thoughts bounced around in his head. When they began to settle, he said, "I now believe that Ren conspired with Tso to have Ma killed, and he might have had a hand in Gao's death too. Tai Po wants control of Fanling and they thought they could get it through Ren. We aren't as large as they are, but we generate more income. Our success has created jealousy, spiked greed, and earned us unwanted attention. Two days ago, even before Ren was supposed to be named Mountain Master, Tai Po tried to set the stage for taking us over by moving in on some of our betting shops. We fought them off. I organized the resistance, Gui-San, and I have to say I did it well. There was no fear, no doubt — it came very naturally to me. Maybe that certainty I felt is what takes hold of someone when they've already lost everything in their lives and there's nothing more that can be taken from them.

"Anyway, Yu and Wang were impressed by my behaviour and urged me to oppose Ren for the position of Mountain Master. You and I have never discussed that possibility, but why would we? Until a few days ago it would have been far-fetched, if not unthinkable. You do know that I have ambition, but perhaps not the extent of it. I hope it doesn't disappoint you that I want to do more, to be more than I am. This is my roundabout way of telling you that I agreed to run against Ren.

"And Gui-San, I won. I won in a rout. Yu, Tian, Fong, Xu, and Wang brought nearly the entire gang over to my side. It was gratifying, and maybe a little humbling. But truthfully, when I found out I'd won, I felt a sense of rightness. I thought, *I'm ready for this and I can handle it.* I hope you don't think my ego is out of control, but I've discovered that when I know what I want and I understand why I want it, I have confidence in my ability to make the decisions needed for it to happen. And when I'm confident, people take me seriously — everyone, except possibly Tso.

"When I talked to Tso last night, he was still pretending that he has nothing but our best interests at heart. He tried to spin the story that he and Ma, and then he and Ren had verbally agreed that Tai Po would provide us with protection in exchange for a share of our gambling revenue. He even asked me to honour that agreement. He must think I'm stupid or weak. I was very abrupt with him. I told him that Tai Po has no claim on Fanling. We want nothing from them and we have nothing that we're willing to give.

"After talking to him, I began to call the other Mountain Masters to tell them about the election. Most of them knew about the results already, but I thought it was important for me to tell them personally that Fanling isn't in play for Tai Po or anyone else. I said we're prepared to defend our turf at any cost and we'll go against anyone who thinks it can be taken from us. They all assured me that the last thing they want is a war of any size, and several of them said they'd call Tso and tell him I have their support.

"After a few calls like that, I was starting to feel comfortable. And then one of them asked me what I'm going to do about Ren. The question caught me off guard. I still don't know what to do. There's no place for him in the gang anymore. I can't trust him, and I can't have someone I don't trust so close to me. I've already decided he'll have to leave the executive. I'm going to make Yu my deputy. Tian has agreed, for a while anyway, to be Vanguard. Xu will replace me as White Paper Fan. I've made Fong the Straw Sandal, Pang will remain as Incense Master, and Wang will stay on as Red Pole. I actually wanted Wang to be my deputy, but he's such a good Red Pole that while things are still up in the air, I thought it wisest to leave him in the position. But what to do with Ren?

"I have to believe he still has supporters in the gang. He still has economic interests in Fanling. He is undoubtedly still in touch with Tso. Do you understand where I'm going with this?" he said, and reached for a cigarette. He lit it with the Zippo and then held the lighter up towards the niche. "I know that your father's lighter looks like it's near the end of its useful life, but it still works beautifully. Xu and Fong bought me a gold Dunhill as a New Year's gift last year, and I know they're disappointed that I'm not using it. But how do I explain the emotional attachment I have to this one?"

He stood and turned towards the entrance of the Ancestor Worship Hall. The sun shone in a cloudless sky, and in the clear morning light even the murky waters of Shenzhen Bay looked inviting. "I have to decide what to do about Ren," he said, leaving the hall and stubbing out his cigarette on a rock.

When he returned, he sat on the stool with his legs straight out in front of him, his ankles crossed and his arms folded across his chest. "The easiest thing would be to do nothing, but I think that would be irresponsible, for all the reasons I mentioned earlier. This is not to say that Ren poses any imminent danger, but if he has free rein he might be tempted to meddle and interfere, and if he did and there were no consequences, who knows where it could lead? So at the very least, I need to tell him what my expectations are for his behaviour. I need to make sure he understands that there will be consequences if he does anything that runs contrary to my direction and the gang's well-being," he said. Then he sighed. "But Gui-San, I don't think that's enough. As much as I want to believe it is, I can't.

"The problem is that he's taken the Thirty-Six Oaths. He's been a triad since he was a teenager, and he will stay one until he dies. But when he conspired with Tso to have Ma — and maybe Gao — killed, he broke our most sacred oath: to protect our brothers above all, even at the cost of our own lives. That's why the question from the Mountain Master caught me off guard. He wasn't really asking me what I'm going to do with Ren in the context of our gang structure; he was asking me how I'm going to deal with a man who has broken his oath in the vilest way imaginable. And believe me, Gui-San, the prevailing opinion among those Mountain Masters, even if they won't say so directly, is that Ren had a hand in at least Ma's death. So this is an early test for me. They'll be watching to see what kind of Mountain Master has joined their ranks. Is it one who takes the easy route? Is it someone who sits back and hopes for the best? Or is it one who is decisive, who can be depended on to do the right thing, regardless of difficulty?

"I'm sorry to go on like this, but I'm struggling to make the right decision, and it helps to talk it through," he said, and paused to light another cigarette. He took a deep drag, then turned his head so the exhaled smoke didn't go towards the niche. "Actually, I know what the right decision is; I'm just reluctant to say it. Ren must die.

"There, it's said. He broke his oath when he conspired to kill Ma, a brother and a man who was supposed to be his friend. Ma deserves some measure of revenge. Ren also has to die because it would be careless of me to let him live, to be constantly looking over my shoulder to see what he's up to. Still, I've been undecided about what to do until now. After all we went through, you and I, the idea of taking any person's life is repulsive. But now I have 160 men, and all the lives attached to them, depending on me. So, as sad as it is for me to say it, Ren must go."

He rose from the stool and walked over to the niche. He gently pushed the urn to one side so he had a clearer view of Gui-San's photo. He put his right hand to his mouth, kissed his middle finger, and then pressed it against her lips. "I'm sorry for going on so long about Ren, but I wanted you to know how much it has been troubling me. Now I have to go back to Fanling and take care of our business," he said. "I'll see you next month for sure. Actually, Gui-San, I expect I'll be coming here more frequently. This new job of mine brings with it many complications; some I know of already, but I'm certain there are others that I haven't even imagined. I'll need someone to talk to, and I'm so grateful you're here to listen. I love you."

Chow replaced the urn and folded the stool. He took one long last look at her photo. Then he turned away from the niche and began to walk back into a life that in many ways still seemed less real to him than the time he had just spent with Gui-San.

COMING SOON
From House of Anansi Press
in January 2020

Read on for a preview of the next thrilling
Uncle Chow Tung novel, *Foresight*.

May 1982
Fanling, New Territories, Hong Kong

CHOW TUNG HATED THE CHINESE COMMUNISTS. HE HAD good reason. Born in the village of Changzhai, near the city of Wuhan in Hubei province, he had left there more than twenty years before, in June 1959. His entire family had died of starvation, brought on by a famine that was a direct result of the economic policies of Mao Zedong's Great Leap Forward. Between 1958 and 1960, more than twenty million others had died during what the Chinese referred to as the "Years of Slow Death" or the "Bitter Years." Chow had left his village along with a group of other young people. Each of them had decided to risk death trying to escape China rather than wait for the famine to take them the way it had taken their families.

They had journeyed almost one thousand kilometres to Shenzhen, a Chinese farming and fishing town on the northern border of Hong Kong's New Territories. From there, in the middle of the night, they swam four kilometres across the dirty and dangerous waters of Shenzhen Bay to Hong

Kong. The water wasn't the only threat that night. They also had to avoid patrol vessels of the People's Liberation Army, vessels filled with soldiers with orders to shoot swimmers on sight. No one from their group was shot, but, tragically, three had drowned during the swim. Among them was Lin Gui-San, the love of Chow Tung's life. He held the Communists accountable for her death.

Since arriving in Hong Kong, Chow had flourished and prospered. He'd settled in Fanling, a town in the northern part of the New Territories, and joined the local triad gang. After apprenticing as a Blue Lantern, he took the Thirty-Six Oaths and became a full gang member. He had worked as a forty-niner — a foot soldier — for several years, until his intelligence, self-control, and reliability caught the attention of his superiors. He was promoted to assistant White Paper Fan, an administrative and financial management position. When the incumbent retired, Chow had replaced him. As White Paper Fan, he fostered development of the gang's involvement in less exploitive — although still criminal — businesses such as gambling, trying to move it away from activities that attracted more active police attention, such as drugs and the protection racket.

During his tenth year with the Fanling triads, the gang had come under attack from a neighbouring gang in Tai Po. The Fanling gang had been going through an upheaval at the time. Its Mountain Master had been murdered, and then a few days later his likely successor was killed as well. The deaths left a vacuum that the Tai Po gang tried to take advantage of. Chow stepped into the breach, organized the resistance against Tai Po, and, in the aftermath, was elected Mountain Master. It was a position he still held, and in the years since he ascended to it, he had continued to build the strength of the Fanling triads. The gang wasn't by any means the largest in Hong Kong, Kowloon, or the New Territories, but it was among the wealthiest and considered to be particularly well run.

There were multiple reasons for this success. Chow kept the gang's activities as far as possible under the police radar and he made it clear to other gangs that any interference in Fanling business would be met with maximum resistance. His business decisions balanced risk against return, and he hated any risk he couldn't accurately assess. And finally, everything he did was with an eye to the future.

It was the future that had his attention as Chow sat in a congee restaurant not far from his apartment in Fanling. He was reading the morning edition of the *Oriental Daily News*. The front page announced that Deng Xiaoping, China's leader, was pleased with Shenzhen's progress as a special economic zone. *What does the fact that he's pleased actually mean? And how much progress has really been made?* he thought. Three years before, Shenzhen had been given status as a city. At the time, Chow had thought it odd that a farming and fishing community — a cluster of four villages with a total of no more than thirty thousand people —should be given that designation. One year later it made more sense, when Shenzhen was named one of the first of five special economic zones in China. In the two years since, the article stated, its population had tripled to nearly a hundred thousand.

Chow hadn't set foot in China since he'd left, even though the Shenzhen border wasn't much more than a thirty-minute drive from Fanling. Now he was starting to contemplate making the trip. As much he hated the Communists, he was fascinated by Deng Xiaoping and the changes he seemed to be spearheading in China. Chow had been tracking Deng's recent career and had made a hobby of learning about his colourful past. Now, he wondered, what was this little man — the ultimate survivor — up to with these special economic zones? Was he really an agent of change? Were the zones as successful as the newspaper seemed to believe?

Chow's notion of Deng as a little man was a statement of fact rather than a derogatory term. Deng was only four feet eleven inches tall; even the diminutive Chow, at five foot five inches, would have towered over him. And thinking of him as a survivor was both a statement of fact and a compliment. Deng had been born in 1904, and his life spanned the entire history of the Chinese Communist Party. It was a life filled with ups and downs that Chow, despite his antipathy towards Communists, could only admire on a personal level.

Born into a middle-class landowning family, Deng was sent to Paris for his education while he was in his teens. There he met Zhou Enlai and other Chinese students and became a Leninist. He joined the Chinese Communists in 1923, and from then on he devoted his life to the Party. He served it in Shanghai, Wuhan, and Chongqing. He was on the Long March. When Mao ascended to power, Deng eventually became vice-premier and minister of finance. However, his financial policies favoured economics over ideological dogma; he ran afoul of Mao and his Great Leap Forward and was demoted.

A few years later, during the Cultural Revolution, Deng and his family were targeted by the Red Guards. His eldest son by his third wife was tortured and thrown out of a window on the top floor of a four-storey building. This wasn't the first child he'd lost — his first wife and child had both died while he was on the Long March. And his son's death wasn't the only torment the Cultural Revolution and the Red Guards would impose on Deng. In 1969, at the age of sixty-five, he was sent to the Xinjian County Tractor Factory, where he was employed as a regular labourer. He stayed there for four years.

On Deng's return to Beijing, Zhou Enlai talked Mao into letting him back into the government. He was appointed first vice-premier and given the responsibility of reconstructing the country's economy and raising production. This time around he was careful to avoid contradicting Maoist ideology, but even that couldn't stop him from getting into trouble. The Cultural Revolution wasn't over yet. A radical political group called the Gang of Four, led by Jiang Qing, Mao's wife, was competing for power in the Party, in essence positioning themselves to take over when Mao died. Zhou was ill with cancer, and the Gang saw Deng as their greatest threat. They went after him in a campaign called "Criticize Deng and Oppose the Rehabilitation of Right-Leaning Elements." Mao sided with the Gang, and Deng was forced to write a series of self-criticisms. They didn't satisfy Mao, however. When Zhou died early in 1976, Deng was once again stripped of his positions.

The death of Mao late in 1976 brought his chosen successor, Hua Guofeng, into power. Hua immediately purged the Gang of Four, pardoned Deng, and restored him to his senior positions. That was a mistake on Hua's part. In December 1978 Deng grabbed the reins of power, and soon he had mobilized enough supporters within the Party to outmanoeuvre Hua and have him ousted from all his leadership positions. He did allow Hua to retire quietly, though; that was a departure from the physical harm that had come to previous senior leaders who had lost power struggles.

What interested Chow was what Deng had done with his power. Beginning in 1979, he introduced economic reforms that accelerated the open-market model. While many of the leaders in Beijing were still mouthing old-style Communist rhetoric, Deng was dismantling the commune system that had taken Chow's father's farm from him and contributed to the Bitter Years. Deng also gave peasants more freedom to manage their land and allowed them to sell their products on the market. At the same time, there was talk of opening up China's economy to foreign trade.

Has China really opened up? Chow thought as his bowl of congee arrived and he put down his newspaper. What was going on in Shenzhen? If things were changing because of the city's new status, he needed to understand what a special economic zone was and how it really operated.

Congee, a boiled rice porridge, is by itself a bland dish, but Chow never ate it by itself. He had been coming to this same restaurant virtually every morning for fifteen years and Jia, co-owner of the business with her husband and its only waitress, didn't ask what accompaniments he wanted; she simply brought them to the table. That morning he added white pepper, a touch of soy sauce, scallions, sausage, and a duck egg. On a side plate were two sticks of youtiao, or fried bread. He ate quickly, a habit he blamed on the hungry times in Wuhan. No matter how much money he had now, he couldn't shake the irrational fear that it and the food it bought could be taken away from him again. He finished the bowl and it was quickly replaced by another. As he was working his way through it, he saw the familiar face of Xu, his White Paper Fan, coming towards him.

The gang's headquarters were in the centre of town, about a twenty-minute walk from the restaurant. Chow assumed that Xu had already been in his office for several hours, squaring the accounts from the previous day's business. Like Chow, Xu was originally from the Chinese mainland and had been a triad there, but he had left and eventually found his way to Hong Kong. His departure from Shanghai hadn't been voluntary; after seizing power in 1949, Mao had ordered that the mainland triads be destroyed. Xu had got out before he could be caught. Unlike Chow, his former assistant was married and had a son.

"Good morning, Uncle," Xu said as he slid into the booth across from his Mountain Master.

"Uncle" was what Chow was called by virtually everyone who knew him. It had started when he was appointed assistant White Paper Fan and had begun wearing a black suit and buttoned-up white shirt to work every day. He thought the sombre, conservative look fitted his personality and reflected his responsibilities. The younger triads who had given him the nickname at first joked that he dressed and acted like an old man. The older men who adopted the term did so as sign of respect for his demeanour and the careful way he carried himself and did business. Now no one thought twice about where the name had come from. He was simply Uncle or, sometimes, Boss.

"How was business yesterday?" Uncle asked.

"Not bad. About the same as we did last Thursday and, in fact, about the same as we did a year ago on the same date," Xu said. "No one's complaining. That won't start until mid-July, when the Happy Valley racing season ends and our income nosedives for the rest of the summer. I don't know why the Hong Kong Jockey Club doesn't operate the track year-round, and why they have only two race days a week."

"They've been doing it that way for more than a hundred years, and they're the most successful horse-racing organization in the world. Why should they change?" Uncle was a rabid horse player who rarely missed a race day. "Besides, their reluctance to change anything has made us millions. If they ever opened off-track betting operations we'd lose our biggest source of income. What percentage of our money comes from our betting shops?"

"If you include the mah-jong parlours and the mini casinos, the total is a bit more than seventy percent."

"That's dangerous. We shouldn't be so dependent on one part of our business."

"I know you think we should be more diversified. Believe me, we're looking for ways to extend business, but there are some realities we have to deal with," Xu said. "Fanling isn't one of those densely populated Hong Kong or Kowloon districts, and there are only so many things we can do without attracting police attention."

"Maybe it's time we looked outside Fanling."

"What do you mean?" Xu asked, a look of alarm on his face.

"Relax. I'm not talking about moving in on another gang's turf or business," Uncle said, reaching for his newspaper. "It

says here that the special economic zone the Chinese government created in Shenzhen is already a success."

"That's what I've heard as well, but I don't know anything
about how it operates."

"Me neither, but I want us to find out as quickly as possible.
Deng seems to be opening doors to China. It's logical, given
its proximity to Hong Kong and Hong Kong's relationship
with the rest of the world, that Shenzhen is now one of those
doors. And the thing about doors, Xu, is that they let you in
and they let you out. There are no triads in Shenzhen. We
could be the first."

"There are no triad gangs anywhere in China that I know
of. Mao drove us all out of the country," Xu said.

"Maybe Deng will be more accommodating and let us
back in."

"I can't tell you how much I'd love to be living in Shanghai
again," Xu said. "I still own a house in the French Concession.
For years my wife has wanted me to sell it, but I couldn't
bring myself to do it."

"It's too soon to be talking about something as ambitious
as Shanghai, but there are things in motion in China that
we need to understand," Uncle said. "I sense that the times
are changing, and I want us to be out in front of whatever
is coming. There aren't many rewards for being second to
recognize what the future will look like, and Shenzhen could
be at the forefront of that future."

"We do have some connections there."

"Official ones?"

"No. We're doing business with a small factory that makes
knock-off shirts we're selling in our night market."

"I didn't know that."

"We just started up with them a few months ago. The amount of business we do is so small that I didn't think it worth mentioning."

"How did we find them?" asked Uncle.

"They found us. The factory owner knew someone who knew Fong. He was looking for a market on this side of the border and contacted him. Fong met with him and brokered a deal." Fong was the gang's Straw Sandal, the man in charge of communications within the gang and maintaining connections with other gangs.

"Then I need to talk to Fong. Call his apartment and ask him to meet us at the office."

"He's already there."

"Really? It's unusual for him to be so early."

"He was in Macau last night. I don't think he's gone to bed yet."

"Whatever. Let's go and talk to him," Uncle said. "I need contact names."

"What are you thinking of doing?" Xu asked.

"If we're going to understand how a special economic zone operates, we have to start somewhere. This factory owner has set up a business, so he must know a thing or two about how things are run on that side of the border."

"You're serious about Shenzhen, aren't you."

"I'm serious about growing and expanding our business, and unless you know something I don't, I think we've maximized our opportunities here. Where else can we go? What else can we get into that will add that much value?" Uncle said. "There may be nothing for us in Shenzhen and this special economic zone thing may amount to absolutely nothing, but we won't know unless we investigate it."

"Do you want us to ask the factory owner to come here for a meeting?"

"No, let's you and I go there. I want to see what Shenzhen looks like now. I haven't seen it in more than twenty years."

"Even though I'd like to be living in Shanghai again, it's hard to forget or forgive what the Communists did to us."

"I feel the same, but maybe we should stop thinking about them as Communists. Maybe we should start thinking of those people who did so much damage as Maoists," Uncle said. "This man Deng suffered in his own way under Mao, but he persevered and managed to survive. There has to be a reason for that kind of persistence. It could be that he has a vision for the country that's quite different from Mao's crazy schemes. If he can forgive and forget the shit they did to him and look to the future at his age, then the least we can do is try to understand what he's attempting to accomplish."

"I care more about what you think than what Deng thinks. If you believe we should go, then I'm all for it."

Uncle put money on the table to settle his bill and slid from the booth. "Let's go and see Fong."

Uncle and Xu walked from the restaurant to the office, which was above a women's clothing store. They entered the building through a door that was to one side of the shop and climbed a long flight of stairs. The office layout was basic. A large expanse of floor dotted with desks was surrounded by seven offices, one for each of the gang's executive members. As Xu had said, Fong was sitting at his desk.

An incorrigible gambler and night owl, Fong was seldom in the office before midafternoon. Uncle walked over to the open door and poked his head inside. "Hey, did you really stop in here on your way home from Macau?" he asked.

"That's not funny."

"So it was from Macau. And from your sour tone, I'm guessing it was either baccarat or roulette that did you in," Uncle said.

"Roulette," Fong said with a groan. "I read about this system that's supposedly foolproof. You bet on the first twelve, second twelve, or third twelve numbers where you get odds of two to one if you hit. But you don't bet on any of them until one of them doesn't hit twice in a row. That's when you keep doubling up until it pays off. When it does, you start all over again."

"What went wrong?" Uncle asked.

"I was betting on the last twelve numbers. Somehow not one of them was hit ten times in a row. Mathematically that's almost impossible."

"You should have learned by now that there's no such thing as impossible when it comes to gambling."

"You don't have to tell me," Fong said. "I feel stupid enough as it is."

"I'm only expressing a brother's concern," Uncle said.

"I know."

"And regardless of the circumstances, I'm glad you're here, because I need your help with something."

"What?"

"I understand that you put together a deal to buy some knock-off clothing from a factory in Shenzhen," Uncle said.

"I did. Is there a problem with that?"

"Not unless you know of one."

Fong shrugged. "The last I heard, everything was going well."

"I'm glad to hear that. I'd like you to call your contact there and arrange a meeting for us."

"A meeting with whom?"

"The guy who owns the factory."

"Uncle, this is really just small potatoes," Fong said. "Both the deal and the guy, I mean."

"I understand that, but I want you to set up a meeting anyway."

"For when?"

"As soon as you can."

"The owner won't be a problem, but we need visas to get across the border. I use an agent in Hong Kong, but it could take a day or two. The agent will need your HK ID numbers and passport information."

Uncle took his Hong Kong identification card from his wallet, collected his passport from his top desk drawer, and passed them to Fong. "Get started right away,"

"Who else would be going from our side?"

"Me, Xu, and you, if you want to join us."

"What reason should I give for us wanting a meeting?"

"Tell them we want to talk to them about ways of expanding our business."

Fong looked at Uncle and then at Xu. "They make knock-off shirts of so-so quality in a small old factory."

"I don't care what they make or where they make them," Uncle said. "This is about the future. I've been reading about Shenzhen and its growth as a special economic zone. I want to understand what's going on there and see if it's a place where we can expand."

"I know it's a special zone; that's why the factory is allowed to sell to us," Fong said. "But that doesn't mean the government will permit triad gangs to operate in China."

"Start the visa process and make the call to the owner. We'll worry about what the government will permit if and when the time comes," Uncle said. He turned away and headed for his office.

Xu had left the account summaries of the business activity of the previous day on Uncle's desk. Uncle leafed through them, doing calculations in his head. The gang's operations were profitable but stagnant. There was virtually no growth on a year-to-year basis, and with overheads constantly rising, their cash flow was getting squeezed. When Happy Valley shut down for its summer break, that cash flow would get much tighter; no other activity came close to generating as much money as their betting shops. So far it hadn't gotten so tight as to be an emergency or a reason for panic, but if the trend continued for another year or two, the gang could find itself substantially weakened.

"The factory owner says he'll meet with us whenever we can get there," Fong said from the doorway.

"That didn't take long."

"We're a valued customer," Fong said. "In fact, we're his main — maybe even only —source of foreign currency."

"That's a good thing to know," Uncle said. "How about the visas?"

"Our man is working on them. He thinks he might be able to get them sent to me by tonight."

"If he does, we can go tomorrow. How would we get there?"

"We should take the train to the Luohu railway station in Shenzhen. The factory owner will meet us there with his car."

"We could drive ourselves," Uncle said.

"The border crossing is small, understaffed, and usually

---

jammed with trucks. It's a pain in the ass getting through," Fong said. "The train is easier. At the station we can get through Hong Kong Immigration and clear Chinese Customs and Immigration within about half an hour. With a visa and your Hong Kong ID card and passport, it isn't a big problem."

"Tell Xu that we're likely on for tomorrow," Uncle said. "If you do get the visas, call me at home and let me know. You and Xu can meet me at the congee restaurant at eight tomorrow morning. We'll leave for the train station from there."

ACKNOWLEDGEMENTS

This is a book I did not plan to write, although in retrospect it makes perfect sense. But then, you can't depend on a writer to make the best decisions about what or what not to write.

The idea came from my publisher, Sarah MacLachlan, and my editor at the time, Janie Yoon. They waylaid me in Janie's office and said, why don't you write a series about Uncle's early life? I immediately liked the idea, and the next day I sent an outline for a trilogy to Janie. *Fate* is the first book in that trilogy. So a big thanks to both of them for their ongoing support and creative juices.

As is often the case with my work, finding the right structure and form for the book was a struggle. I don't do much planning or pre-plotting, so while this eliminates the tedium of working from a template, it can lead me down various dead ends and leave me with a first draft that needs to be restructured. Such was the case with *Fate*. I don't share work in progress with anyone, so after I sent out the first draft to my first readers — my wife, Lorraine; my editor, Kristine Wookey; and Robin Spano — I waited anxiously. Two drafts later, I got it right. My thanks to all of them. And a big thanks to my agents Bruce Westwood and Carolyn Forde for their continuing support.

I actually worked with two editors on this book. Initially, I was working with Janie Yoon — as I had for all the Ava Lee novels — but then was transitioned to Doug Richmond. Doug and I finished the book together, and I have to say he was a pleasure to work with. We've just finished the next Ava Lee together, and there are three or four more books in our pipeline. My only hope is that I end up doing as many books with him as I did with Janie.

Lastly, I want to thank all of the Ava Lee readers who stuck with me when Uncle passed away in book six of the series. The Ava Lee story arc is fluid and comes to me in strange ways. I was writing book three when I realized Uncle was going to die. I knew when and how it was going to happen, but what I couldn't tell you was why the certainty of it came to me in the first place. I was advised by more than one of my first-draft readers not to let him die. But it wasn't my choice. The story was already written in my mind. The great thing about *Fate* is that Uncle lives again. I can only hope that my readers enjoy the young Uncle as much as they enjoyed him in his later years.

IAN HAMILTON is the author of twelve novels in the Ava Lee series. His books have been shortlisted for numerous prizes, including the Arthur Ellis Award, the Barry Award, and the Lambda Literary Prize, and are national bestsellers. BBC Culture named Hamilton one of the ten mystery/crime writers from the last thirty years that should be on your bookshelf. The Ava Lee series is being adapted for television.

 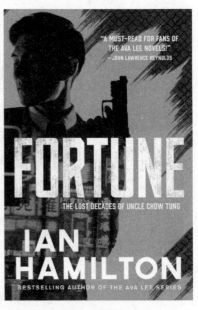

NOW AVAILABLE
From House of Anansi Press
The Ava Lee series.

Prequel and Book 1

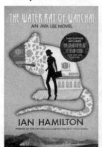

Book 2

Book 3

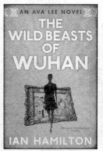

Book 4

Book 5

Book 6

Book 7

Book 8

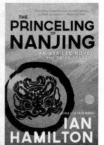

Book 9

Book 10

Book 11

www.houseofanansi.com • www.facebook.com/avaleenovels
www.ianhamiltonbooks.com • www.twitter.com/avaleebooks